NEW MILFORD PUBLIC LIBRARY
3 4021 13044 6699
W9-BOB-493

SEP -- 2018

DYING ECHO
The Fourth Grim Reaper Mystery

"Those willing to accept the fantastical premise will find themselves caught up in Casey's quest to come to terms with her past and move on."

—Barbara Bibel, *Booklist*

"Having Death as her tipster makes sleuthing easier for Casey, whose latest adventure provides mystery, romance and the hope that she'll get her life back together."

—*Kirkus Reviews*

FLOWERS FOR HER GRAVE
The Third Grim Reaper Mystery

"...you have to hand it to Judy Clemens for providing her amateur sleuth with a genuinely offbeat gimmick: she travels with Death. *Flowers for Her Grave* catches Clemens in the amateurish effort of explaining in detail how Casey Maldonado comes to be running from the law in the company of a specter who is addicted to reality TV shows and loves to dress up in outlandish costumes...we're free to appreciate her companion's wit and dress code: skintight Spandex for a Zumba class; a flowered bathing suit and shades for the pool; and an all-white ensemble with brass-handled walking stick to make a fashion statement ("I am the epitome of cool"). Not even Cosmo Topper, who was advised by two charming ghosts, can beat that one."

—Marilyn Stasio, *The New York Times*

"... the outlandish premise somehow works, and most readers will find themselves thoroughly entertained by this oddly appealing mix of the jaunty and the macabre."

—*Booklist*

"The book offers plenty of suspense as well as humor..."

—*Publishers Weekly*

THE GRIM REAPER'S DANCE
The Second Grim Reaper Mystery

"A must for those who like their mystery spiced with danger, dark humor, and a fascinating heroine whose toughness is tempered by compassion."

—Charles Todd, *New York Times* bestselling author of the Inspector Ian Rutledge and the Bess Crawford Mysteries

EMBRACE THE GRIM REAPER

The First Grim Reaper Mystery

"An interesting premise (shades, almost, of *The Fugitive*) and a vulnerable but strong protagonist are the highlights here, though the character of Death adds an unexpected dimension. Clemens, author of the Stella Crown series, could have another winner."

—Sue O'Brien, *Booklist*

"Clemens is adept at creating an appealing cast of characters while keeping the plot moving at a fast clip. Casey and Death make an oddly entertaining pair, and readers will hope to see their relationship fleshed out in future titles."

—*Publishers Weekly*

Clemens features a new leading lady with the promise of depth..."

—*Kirkus Reviews*

"Clemens, author of the well-received Stella Crown series, explores intriguing new territory in this series debut, and adventurous mystery buffs may want to hitch a ride."

—*Library Journal*

Beyond the Grave

Books by Judy Clemens

The Grim Reaper Series
Embrace the Grim Reaper
The Grim Reaper's Dance
Flowers for her Grave
Dying Echo
Beyond the Grave

The Stella Crown Series
Till the Cows Come Home
Three Can Keep a Secret
To Thine Own Self Be True
The Day Will Come
Different Paths
Leave Tomorrow Behind

Writing as J.C. Lane
Tag, You're Dead

Beyond the Grave

A Grim Reaper Mystery

Judy Clemens

Poisoned Pen Press

First Edition 2018

10 9 8 7 6 5 4 3 2 1

Library of Congress Control Number: 2018932407

ISBN: 9781464209888 Trade Paperback
ISBN: 9781464209895 Ebook

Poisoned Pen Press
4014 N. Goldwater Blvd., #201
Scottsdale, AZ 85251
www.poisonedpenpress.com
info@poisonedpenpress.com

Printed in the United States of America

Chapter One

"I think it's broken." Death studied Casey's wrist.

Casey didn't have to think about it. Her right arm might have been numb, but the angle at which it lay on the hard, tiled floor of the general store gave it away. Her head spun as the blackness subsided. She had no idea how much time had passed.

"What's lying on my legs?" She couldn't twist far enough to see, and the nighttime security lights provided minimal visibility.

"Expired baked beans, mostly. Still in the cans. Although I see some creamed corn, too. And tomato soup. Plus, of course, the shelving."

No wonder she couldn't move. Casey closed her eyes and listened. Was her attacker still in the store?

Something thumped. Casey started, her heart racing. Death glanced up, then swooped away.

Casey scooted forward inch by inch, bearing her weight on her elbows and good hand. Her right ankle sent sharp pains all the way up her spine to her head, and she took a slow, deep breath. It couldn't be broken, too. Please, God.

Death returned, accompanied by a rush of cold air. "Still in the store. In the bread aisle."

"Coming this way?"

"Staring at the ceiling."

"*Dead*?"

"I'm still here, aren't I? But badly injured. Not moving. Lots of blood. The scissors you used did a thorough job."

Not what she had wanted, but… "Did you see the gun?"

Death made another quick fly-around. "Several feet from the body, by the day-old donuts."

Casey clenched her teeth and pulled herself further from the shelving wreckage. She wrenched herself into a sitting position and rolled cans off her legs. Once free, her ankle still hurt, but she could move it. Not broken. Thank goodness.

She gasped, remembering. "Where's Nell?" She tried to get up, but her head went fuzzy and she dropped back down, hard.

"Do not stand up," Death said. "You know I can't catch you."

"*Where is she*?"

"In the freezer, I suppose. That's where I put her at the start of all this."

"How long has it been?" Casey lurched to her knees and waited for the room to stop turning.

"Not long enough for her to freeze. Again, here I am. With you. Not carrying nine-year-olds to the Other Side."

Casey took a deep breath and rose to her feet, leaning on fallen cans and boxes of Kleenex, incongruously placed together in a catch-all row. She stumbled to the end of the aisle and glanced toward the freezer, then the opposite way, in the direction of the bread and donuts and possible dead person. First, the gun. No point in letting Nell out of the freezer just to have her get shot.

Casey limped forward, watching for movement. She arrived at the end of the "carb aisle," as the townies called it, and peered around the shelves. Too dark for her, a mere human, to see something as slender and dark as a gun.

She stretched her left arm toward her back right pocket and used her index and middle finger to slide out her phone. The flashlight app sent a ray of bright light down the aisle.

There was the gun, half hidden under the shelves of flour, which had exploded in clouds of powder during the destruction.

Casey crouched and peered through the stack of packaged cookies at chest level. Death was right about the body. Lots of blood, seeping into the tile, sprayed all over the bagged bread. She must have hit an artery. With that amount of blood loss, at least Casey didn't anticipate being attacked again. No matter how much she regretted the violence.

She scooted to the gun, scooped it up with her good hand, and disappeared back behind the Oreos. She needed to call an ambulance to attend to the body on the floor. But not until Nell was safe.

It was probably too late for the paramedics, anyway.

Another thump sounded, and Casey realized it was coming from the freezer. She hobbled to the door and yanked the handle. The large panel swept open, releasing a cloud of frigid air almost as cold as Death.

"Casey!" A whirlwind of a girl dove out of the freezer and slammed into Casey, wrapping her arms around her waist. Casey grunted with pain, but encircled the girl with her left arm. Nell shivered and ground her face into Casey's chest.

"Come on." Casey moved forward. "Let's get you away from the cold."

Without letting go of each other they lurched their way to the storefront. The door was unlocked from when Casey and Nell—and their attacker—entered earlier. The security light over the front door spilled into the tiny parking lot. No vehicles in sight except the rusty gold Chevy that had been for sale since Casey came to town.

Casey grabbed a blanket off the shelf of camping supplies and threw it around Nell's shoulders. The girl's teeth chattered, and her skin had taken on a blue hue. Or maybe that was the poor lighting. Casey also grabbed an elastic athletic wrap from the first aid shelf, hoping it might ease the pain in her wrist until she could get taken care of by people who actually knew what they were doing.

Casey tucked the ends of the blanket against her own body so it wouldn't fall, and led Nell outside. She slid onto the picnic table bench and dialed 911 with her thumb, her arm still around Nell's shoulders, her broken wrist resting on her thigh.

"Who are you c-calling?" Nell stammered.

"The ambulance." She had called from the store, but no one had arrived. It felt like forever since she'd spoken to the dispatcher, but most likely it had been a few minutes.

However long it had been, for sure it was too late now. Death was gone.

Casey attempted to wrap the athletic band around her arm, but couldn't do it by herself. Nell took the end of the fabric and wrapped it around Casey's wrist and torso, strapping her arm to her side. Casey grimaced and bit her lips so she wouldn't cry out and scare her young friend.

The 911 operator answered with a professional tone. "What is your emergency?"

"You need to come to Vern's. In Armstrong. There's been… an accident."

"What kind of accident?"

Gravel crunched at the far side of the parking lot, feet rather than a car. Casey pushed Nell below the tabletop. "Who's there?"

A shadow separated from the darkness, a faceless shape in the night.

"Hello?" The 911 operator's voice sounded tinny coming from the phone.

"Don't come any closer." Casey gently lay Nell all the way onto the bench and pressed on her shoulder to tell her to stay down. She eased her leg over the boards and stood, finding her balance. Her wrist throbbed, but at least it was out of the way. Her other arm could strike, and her feet find a mark. "Who's there?" she asked again.

"No need to worry, Casey," a smooth voice said. "It's only me."

Oh, God, no.

Casey set her phone, still connected to the 911 operator, on the bench where Nell could reach it. Then Casey took a deep breath and stepped away from the table.

The night was about to get worse.

Chapter Two

FIVE DAYS EARLIER

The clacking of the train on the tracks was numbing. And exhilarating. Casey Maldonado woke with a start in the early morning hours. After a quick check of the car, which confirmed all other passengers asleep and harmless, she leaned back to watch the scenery as it also awoke from a night's slumber. The Rocky Mountains loomed dark and beautiful to the east as the train curved north through Utah, past the austere and mysterious terrain surrounding the Great Salt Lake.

"Might I interest you in a hot beverage?" Death stood in the aisle wearing a periwinkle suit with yellow trim, gold buttons, white gloves, and a top hat. "Moist towelette? Something to eat?"

Casey took a long look. "Okay, I'll bite. What—or who—are you supposed to be?"

"Really?" Death pouted. "You don't recognize the conductor from *Murder on the Orient Express*?"

Casey rubbed her eyes. "I just woke up. Not a good time to test my knowledge of obscure movies."

"Obscure? This is Dame Christie we're discussing. Anyway, I thought I'd wake you up before they did." Death indicated a couple sitting across the aisle with an infant. The father leaned against the window, lips parted in sleep, while the mother drooped on his shoulder. The blond baby girl, almost a toddler, squirmed in her father's arms.

"The kid is going to let loose howling," Death said, "and I know how you are about crying babies."

The child opened her eyes and squinted up at her dad. Her dark pink lips pinched and she whimpered, her chest heaving in preparation for what Casey was sure would be a piercing scream. Casey shot out of her seat and through Death, making her shiver.

"Hey." Death brushed off the tasseled jacket.

"Which way is the dining car? Which way?"

"No need to get snippy. I told you she was going to wake up."

The mom of the little blond girl blinked up at Casey and pointed her thumb toward the back of the train. "I think the dining car is that way. But I'm not sure if they're open yet."

"Oh." Casey averted her eyes from the baby. "Thank you." She grabbed her duffel bag from the shelf above her seat and strode down the aisle, banging a woman in the shoulder as she passed. The woman jerked awake, her bright blue eyes scorching Casey from beneath hair so white Casey wondered if it could possibly be natural.

Casey held up her hands. "Sorry."

The woman frowned, but that was life. It wasn't like Casey hit her on purpose.

Casey stopped off in the minuscule restroom before finding a seat in the dining car. It was empty except for her, since, as the young mother had predicted, breakfast hours had yet to begin. Casey slouched, looking up only when Death took the place across from her.

"No," she said.

"Oh, was someone sitting here?"

"I meant no to your outfit. What is that?"

Death had changed into a black evening gown, accented by pearl and diamond jewelry, complete with a small tiara. "That's twice you've disappointed me, dear heart, and the day has just begun. This is Audrey Hepburn's dress from *Breakfast at Tiffany's*. Have you no class?"

"You're the one wearing a dinner gown to breakfast."

"Darling, the movie was about breakfast."

Casey shook her head and watched the scenery fly by. The rising sun touched the desert with gold as it rose above the mountains. Before long other passengers straggled into the car and a server, more chipper than necessary, came by with coffee.

Casey waved off the menu the server presented. "I'll take a bowl of oatmeal and some of that fresh-squeezed orange juice, please."

"Are you serious?" Death frowned. "They're bound to have Eggs Benedict. Or crepes with strawberries and whipped cream. Or even a Western omelette. Live a little. And allow me to live vicariously through you."

"Oatmeal and orange juice," the server echoed. "Coming right up!"

Casey stared dully at Death, who vanished in a dark cloud of maple syrup-scented disapproval.

Casey pulled out her new iPhone, a gift from Eric VanDiepenbos, her—dare she name it?—boyfriend. Lover. Friend. She was still getting the hang of it—the phone and the man—even after a couple months of trial and error. She mostly used the iPhone for listening to music and texting, which in itself was its own trial. She wasn't used to someone being able to contact her whenever he wanted. Or look up her location. At least that was something she could control. Eric helped her turn off anything that could physically track her down, and she trusted him, because he was a good person. Plus, he showed her his own phone, which he set so she could always see where he was. Her phone's settings were the opposite, so she figured that was good.

Her breakfast came and she ate it as the train wound its way across the Utah-Idaho border. The ground turned to farmed fields, even as the mountains kept their watch from a distance, and Casey tried to identify the crops, unlike anything she saw in the Midwest.

She was re-entering the passenger car to sit in her assigned seat when Death stopped her. "You're not going to like it."

"What?"

The woman with the bright blond hair glanced up at her, and Casey forced a smile so the woman wouldn't think she was crazy. The woman's eyes widened, and she shifted in her seat to show Casey her back.

Death aimed a long finger toward Casey's previous seat, now occupied by another young mother with a baby. Only this time it wasn't a light-haired little girl. This time the child, a boy, bore the dark hair and eyes of Casey's son, Omar, dead now for over two years. The mother of the blond girl playfully pinched the boy's fat legs, and his gurgled laugh sent an arrow through Casey's heart.

"How close are we to the next stop?"

The woman at Casey's hip glanced over her shoulder. "Are you asking me? Because I don't know."

Death sighed. "Alas, I don't either."

"Never mind." Casey pushed through the door to find a conductor.

She had no luck in the next car, or the one after that, and didn't bother trying to find a different seat because it seemed the children were multiplying. Everywhere she looked, babies, toddlers, children the age Omar would have been in a year, two years, five…

Finally, she came across a conductor who assured her a stop was coming up in less than twenty minutes, if she really wanted to get off. Casey made her way to the caboose, where she clung to a rail and stared at the track as miles clacked away. Death sat on top of the railing, leaning against the caboose with feet propped on the iron, oblivious to the dangers that applied to an actual person. The black evening gown flapped in the wind.

"Why are there so many children on this train?" Casey said. "And so many mothers?"

"I'm sorry, but you know what Tiffany said."

Casey huffed. "I have no idea what Tiffany said. And I really don't care."

"She said," Death continued, "'No matter where you run, you just end up running into yourself.'"

"Oh, shut up." Casey shoved her earbuds into her ears.

Chapter Three

As soon as the train stopped, Casey got off. The tiny station—Merrimore—was only a pause along the way to somewhere else, a desolate track on the crest of a weed-strewn hill.

The conductor hovered in the train car door, halting Casey halfway across the warped wooden platform. "You sure you want to get off here?"

"No. But this is where it has to be." Casey couldn't take any more of the Children's Express. Not when her own child lay moldering in a grave on a Colorado mountainside.

The conductor checked up and down the empty deck, gave her one last inquiring glance, and shook his head. "All aboard," he cried flatly, to no one. He stepped back into the stairwell of the train car, the door slapped shut, and the locomotive ground away.

Casey didn't stay to watch.

The road at the bottom of the hill lay littered with old buildings. A gas station long since boarded up, a grocery store with graffiti-covered windows and CAUTION signs, and what had probably been a video store, back when those existed.

Not much civilization to hang out with.

Casey pulled out her phone and brought up a map of the area. The road she stood on led north and south, meeting up with a bigger perpendicular road eventually, but not for miles. She had landed herself in the middle of nowhere—no doubt causing the conductor's confusion. So what was she going to do?

She smiled.

She would start walking.

The air was chilly, so she dug her sweatshirt out of her bag and headed north. She breathed in the freshness, happy to be off the train, pleased to be on the move, away from home, away from people, away from everything.

The past two months had been…fun? Interesting? Suffocating? She was glad to spend time with her mom and her brother, Ricky, but seeing her mother in her aging condition was difficult, and Ricky had just been through the death of a close friend and wasn't himself. Casey was glad to support them, but she needed space. Time to herself. For a little while.

And then there was Eric…

The train tracks ran parallel to Casey for a few miles before curving across the road and heading west. Casey played with the idea of following them, but kept with her original plan, remaining northern bound. She passed fields of knee-high plants, nothing that looked familiar from her recent travels. Onions and red beets, she thought, as well as what looked—and smelled—like mint. Farmhouses and barns punctuated the landscape, and mountains lay in the distance like bookends to either side. Casey didn't know exactly which mountains they were, but they were beautiful and reminded her of home, which wasn't altogether welcome.

Home meant thoughts of Reuben and Omar, her family killed in the car accident two years previously. Perhaps she had made her way toward peace. Maybe the first glimmers of joy. Her travels in the past year—even the past several months—had taken her through Ohio. Kansas. Florida. Texas. In each place she learned something new about herself. At each place she met people who changed her and helped her see that life could go on. Must go on.

At least she no longer wanted to die.

But returning home wasn't what she thought it would be. She had gone back to help Ricky, not meaning to stay. Not planning to rediscover the roots she'd planted there when she was a child, roots that deepened after she met Reuben and gave birth to Omar. But Eric, with his kindness, his intelligence, his persistence, found her and joined her there, threatening to expand those roots—to help her branch off in new directions. She thought she was ready. She thought she could love him. Death had even disappeared, at least she had thought so, and while she felt empty with her sidekick absent, she also welcomed a new lease on life.

But being back there, in the home she shared with her family, chipped away at her readiness. It turned out Death remained there all along, lurking in the shadows. Calling to her. Until she had to get away.

The road she traveled now wasn't desolate, but nearly. She counted four trucks, a tractor, and one packed minivan as they passed. The trucks slowed as they approached, but she waved them on. The van didn't stop, or even slow down much, but Casey saw faces at every window, so she didn't blame the driver for passing her by.

Death left her alone, proclaiming her "too boring to live." Casey was glad for the time to herself. The emptiness of the fields and road allowed her to relax her senses. Anything coming would be seen long before it arrived.

As evening fell she reached the outskirts of a small town whose faded and chipped sign proclaimed its name as BELTMORE. She passed several run-down house trailers, tiny single-family homes, and a school which had not been built during the present generation. Or even the one before that. Finally, she reached a park she could barely see in the dusk. Two light poles held broken fixtures, leaving the playground nearly invisible. After listening for any human sounds and hearing only cicadas and crickets, she took out her phone and shone the flashlight, risking the neighbors seeing her. But she wouldn't stay somewhere she hadn't vetted.

She walked the area, memorizing the layout. Rusting slides and jungle gym, an overflowing trash can, one scraggly tree, and a pavilion with several splintering picnic tables. The park, like the town surrounding it, was a place that time—and Idaho—had forgotten. A notice declared it open dawn to dusk, but she saw no sign of security cameras, or any life in the closest houses. She should be safe to spend the night.

The pavilion was too exposed for her liking, but a stone fireplace sat at the far end, which would protect her back. She covered up with a weightless blanket she had crumpled in her bag, and, after a few minutes of deep breathing, she fell asleep, the night sounds washing over her.

A different sound woke her a few hours later. Senses tingling, Casey sat up.

Death, dressed all in black, leaned close and whispered, "Someone's coming."

Chapter Four

Headlights swept across the playground, briefly illuminating Casey on her stone ledge. Had someone called the cops? But no, the lights were too high for a police car, even a government SUV, and the rumble of the exhaust sounded louder than any law enforcement vehicle she'd ever come across. Families wouldn't be bringing children at that time of night, although it could be a couple looking for a place to park.

"Ew." Death's nose wrinkled. "Don't even think that. Although that would be more interesting than a lone woman walking desolate country roads for an entire day."

The headlights flicked off, along with the engine, and Casey blinked away the images left in her eyes, hindering her night vision. The darkness returned, as did the silence, even quieter than before, since the loud truck had scared the late hour's insect chorus. Casey slid her legs free of her blanket, watching and waiting. Should she make a run for it? Definitely preferable to a confrontation. But her bag and blanket lay ready to betray her, and any movement was bound to give her away. Besides, without her phone's flashlight she could trip over a piece of a broken swing set, or twist her ankle in a hole. Staying put was the best option for the moment, especially since she didn't know if the truck's passengers were even a threat.

As her vision cleared she could make out the shape of a four-door pick up truck, its tires larger than standard, the chassis lifted so high a good bit of the undercarriage was exposed.

"Rednecks," Death muttered.

Casey shook her head at Death's name-calling.

"What? There's a confederate flag in the window. We're in Idaho. Even if there were any legitimacy to the whole 'Heritage not Hate' posse, tell me how these guys could possibly be part of it. We're two thousand miles from the South side of the Civil War."

Casey took a deep, steadying breath to keep her heart rate down, trying to ignore Death and consider her options. She hadn't seen the occupants of the truck, but Death's assessment of the owner's flag wasn't reassuring. She hoped it really was a couple looking for a make-out spot. Their sex life wouldn't cause her injury. Unless she thought about it too much.

One truck door opened, then another, illuminating two men as they climbed down from the cab. Boots hit the ground.

"Get your ass out of my truck." The driver leaned back into the cab. "I swear, Crash, if you barf in there I will kill you dead."

"As if there's any other way," Death growled.

Another door opened and a large figure spilled out of the backseat. "I'm not gonna barf."

So. Not a couple searching for Lover's Lane. Casey was not relieved.

The three doors slammed shut. Casey heard the clink of bottles in the returning darkness, and could see the shapes of the men as they moved. If she hadn't known they were there, it would have been hard to make them out, so she hoped her presence remained a mystery. Without any illumination from the busted light poles, she sat in complete shadow. Unless they came too close, she would be okay.

The front seat passenger set an opened case of beer on the first picnic table and dropped onto the bench. "So Marly's not answering her phone?" He swigged the last drops of his bottle before flinging it into the darkness, where it hit the ground with a thunk.

"Nice," Death growled.

"I don't know what her problem is," the driver said. "I texted her like five times in the last hour and she won't text me back. I don't even know where she is."

"Sleeping?" the passenger said.

"Better be. Better not be with that asshole she was talking up at the races last weekend."

The guy from the backseat—Crash, the driver had called him—wandered toward the next table, too close for Casey's liking. Slowly, silently, she stood, shifting balance between her feet. Focusing. She berated herself. She should have snuck away when she had the chance. Although at the time she didn't think running was a viable option, or even necessary.

The shotgun passenger unscrewed the top of another beer and flicked the cap into the grass. "Don't you have that thing on your phone? The one where you can see where she is?"

"I don't know. Maybe."

"Let me see."

The driver tossed his phone to him and grabbed a bottle, obviously not his first, the way his hand overshot the case. He'd been behind the wheel moments before.

"These are the people who keep me up at night," Death grumbled. "Literally."

Casey kept her eyes on Crash, who continued making his unsteady way toward the fire pit.

"See," the passenger said, "there she is. She's...where is that?"

The driver's face glowed blue as he leaned over the phone. "Hell, I don't know. Not her house. Not her mom's."

"Guess that answers it."

The driver slammed his hand on the table. "She's mine, dammit. She should know that."

Crash bumped a picnic table and staggered toward Casey's hiding place.

"Here he comes," Death said, and then the man was standing over Casey. Close up, he was even bigger than Casey had calculated. Easily over six feet, with enough extra weight on him to be both clumsy and strong.

Death gestured toward the playground. "Maybe you could still go and he wouldn't remember."

Crash frowned. "Guys?"

"Too late."

Casey swiveled so she wasn't trapped with the fireplace ledge behind her, and gauged the distance to the road. She could beat three drunk guys in a foot race, right?

"Guys!" Crash said again. "There's a girl over here."

"Well," Death muttered, "'girl' is pushing it a little, don't you think?"

Casey turned to run, but Crash shot out a meaty hand and grabbed her arm. "Don't go away."

The driver and the other guy shambled over and took their turns staring. Alcohol fumes, now tripled, floated through the air. Casey thought maybe they were strong enough she could be affected just by breathing them in.

"What are you doing here?" the passenger said.

Death indicated Casey's makeshift bed. "Not too bright, are they?"

"Told you it was a girl." Crash's expression was one of toddler pride, like he wanted a pat on the head. Or a cookie.

Casey surveyed her options. Crash's hand completely encircled her arm. No way would she be able to pry it off. She was outnumbered three to one. Crash's size alone was enough to give him the advantage in a fight, and he had backup. But she had one huge plus over each of these three idiots.

She was sober.

Crash used his free hand to poke Casey's shoulder, as if testing to make sure she was actually there.

The passenger laughed. "She's real, Crash."

"Real pretty." The driver leered and took a step closer. "I think we got handed a present tonight, boys."

Death hissed.

Crash smiled, making Casey's insides turn. What had she gotten herself into this time?

"She is real pretty," Crash said. "I like pretty girls. I think she'll like me, too."

"She'll like all of us." The driver took another step toward Casey, and her nerves went on high alert.

"Calm," Death said.

Casey took a deep breath and let her arm go slack, loosening Crash's fingers just enough she could take half a step back. She peered up at the driver. "What about Marly? If she's yours, doesn't that mean you're hers, too?"

He blinked. "Huh?"

The passenger narrowed his eyes. "You eavesdropping? Or bein' a smart ass?"

Casey smiled. "Both." She swiveled on her heel and kicked Crash in the balls.

He released her arm with a howl. Casey dodged around him as he clutched his groin. He stumbled and banged into Casey, knocking her onto all fours.

"Up!" Death shouted.

Casey jumped forward, spinning to face the drunks, whose reaction time was delayed enough they didn't get her while she was down. But a picnic table was at her back, and the driver was running toward her. The passenger headed around the far side so she couldn't escape.

Casey hopped onto the table. As the driver approached she steadied herself on her left foot and lashed out with her right, smashing him in the face. His head jerked, tipping him backward. He screamed, hands covering his nose.

The passenger grabbed Casey's left ankle from behind and

pulled. She fell forward, bashing her ribs on the edge of the table. Her face slammed into the bench, and she rolled, landing on top of the driver. No time to catch her breath, or feel for the blood on her face. The passenger was still coming. She closed her eyes briefly, focusing, then clawed her way off the driver. She swept her right foot at the passenger's ankles, getting him the way he'd gotten her. He keeled over sideways and Casey shoved him onto his back with her foot.

She got up to run, but the passenger recovered and tackled her from behind. She toppled forward, breaking her fall with her hands, protecting her head. He had her around the knees, and even in his inebriated state, his grip was strong. Casey couldn't break free. She felt around the dirty concrete and her hand landed on a bottle one of them had dropped, wet and sticky, lying in a puddle of beer. She grabbed the neck and used the passenger's own weight to leverage a swing. The glass cracked him on the head and he reared back, letting go of her knees.

She jumped to her feet, using her momentum to swing around and chop his neck with the side of her hand. She followed up her slice with a forward kick to his chin. His head whipped sideways, and he fell against a picnic table. He groaned, but struggled to his knees, swaying. "Bitch."

"Get him," Death said.

Casey glanced to check on Crash, but he was gone, staggering toward the truck, still holding his balls.

The passenger lurched up and threw a punch at Casey. She ducked, easily avoiding his amateur attempt. His swing spun him halfway around, and Casey side-kicked him in the back. He fell forward, cracking his head on the fireplace ledge.

"Whoops," Death said.

Casey felt the guy's pulse. Still going strong. Was that good?

The driver held his nose and moaned, no longer a threat. So now it was only Crash.

A click sounded behind Casey and, very carefully, she turned.

Crash pointed a rifle at her. The truck door hung open, and light from the cab spilled over Crash's back and shoulders, turning him into an even larger, silhouetted monster.

Death froze. "No sudden moves. He may be a drunk moron, but his finger's on the trigger."

Casey slowly raised her hands. "I just want to leave."

Crash swallowed, and the rifle rose a couple of inches. "Who are you?"

"I'm nobody. Simply passing through."

He shuffled forward a few steps. "Why'd you do that?" He frowned toward his friends, lying on the ground at Casey's feet. "Why did you threaten me?"

"I didn't."

"You grabbed me, said I was going to like you. We both know what you meant."

"I didn't mean nothing."

"Okay. I believe you. I'm sorry."

"I was surprised to find you here, that's all."

"Okay."

"And I thought you were pretty."

Oh, boy.

"And I did think you might like me, too."

Because all women being manhandled fell in love with their inebriated attackers.

"Can I put my hands down now?"

"How did you do that?" He was back to sounding like a toddler.

"Do what?"

"Hurt my friends."

She kept her eyes on his face. "I didn't want to. But they scared me. They were trying to hurt me."

He shook his head. "No. No, they wouldn't hurt you."

"Okay." Gradually, she let her arms lower until they were at her sides. She took a step toward Crash, around the table. "And you wouldn't either, right?"

He shuffled his feet. "Wouldn't what?"

"Hurt me."

"No. But why did you do that?" He looked at the driver, who still groaned quietly. The rifle lowered, since Crash was too impaired to multi-task.

As his face was turned, Casey slipped to the side into the darkness, and then behind him. She quietly slid the half-filled case of beer from the picnic table and fit her fingers into the carrying slot.

Crash turned back toward where she'd been. "Hey. Where are you?" He raised the gun.

Casey swung the box at Crash's stomach and hit him square on. He doubled over. Casey swung the beer back around and clocked him in the face. He dropped like a brick.

"I'm right behind you." She swayed and dropped to the ground, letting her head droop onto the patchy grass.

Death swirled around her head. "Let's go. Before one of them realizes you're still here."

Casey rolled onto her knees, her head ringing from slamming the picnic table bench. Pain shot through her side.

Death nodded. "You can do it."

Casey got to her feet and picked her way around the men to the fireplace ledge, where she gathered her things. "I can't leave these guys here."

"Why not?"

"Because they're a menace."

"I wish I could take care of them for you."

Casey glanced at Death. "Seriously?"

"Sometimes it would be nice."

"I don't want to let these guys get away with this. But I'm not exactly innocent in this carnage."

Death let out a sharp laugh. "They were asking for it. Plus, you were defending yourself."

"Sure. But what if one of them is the local chief's son or cousin or something? I really don't want to get stuck in this forgotten town because of them."

They stood quietly, once again considering options. As she surveyed the scene, Casey's eye caught on something glinting in the light from the truck. It was the driver's phone, which had fallen during the fight. Painfully, she scooped it up and dialed 911.

"What is your emergency?" the dispatcher said.

"I'm at a playground in Beltmore. There are three men here who have been driving drunk, and they assaulted a woman. Me."

"What is your name, please?"

"If someone comes soon, they'll find them. I can give you the license plate on the truck." She shone the phone's light and called off the number.

"Can you give me any more idea of where you are?" the woman asked.

"Sure. You can track the GPS on this phone."

Casey wiped her fingerprints from the case—because her info was definitely in the system—and set the phone on the picnic table.

"Ready to go?" Death asked.

Leaving the door of the truck ajar, they set off down the road.

Chapter Five

The night was cool and dark, and the rest of the town slept as Casey limped away, side aching, face on fire.

"You've got to take care of that." Death indicated her cheek. "It looks nasty."

"I don't see an Urgent Care Center, do you?"

"No. Or even what could be a doctor's office during the day. No matter how primitive it might be. The school might have a nurse, but I'm not going to guarantee it."

"A school nurse would be home in bed right now."

"Right. Human hours."

Casey hobbled on, gently prodding her cheek, which had puffed out to an alarming size.

"Car," Death said.

Casey ducked behind a tree as a cop cruiser raced past, headed in the direction of the playground.

Death watched it go. "You don't want to stay and be a witness? Make sure those idiots don't bother any more women?"

Casey waited until the cops were out of sight and continued down the road, glad they couldn't see her uneven gait. The police might mistake her as the drunk one, the way she weaved down the street. "They won't be harassing anyone else tonight. Except maybe the cops, who are better equipped than most people to deal with idiots. Maybe once I'm settled I can call the station and give them more details."

"Why would they believe you, seeing how you took off from the scene?"

"What woman would hang around with her attackers? I would think any woman without my—"

"—talents? Night vision? Rock-hard abs?"

"—knowledge of self-defense would run as far as she could get."

"Not every woman would think as clearly as you in that situation."

"Which means she would run."

Death nodded. "You could have locked yourself in the truck."

True. But then she would have been stuck in town indefinitely, and have to explain why she took on and defeated three men. It would be her story against a bunch of locals. "I'll take some selfies once I find a place. Document my injuries."

"Or…"

"Or what?"

"You make a return visit and track them down. You do know the license plate number."

"I'll never remember that."

"I will. And I don't want to see it at an accident some future night when they kill someone."

Casey held up her hands. "Okay. We'll take care of them. I promise."

"Good."

"Good."

They walked through what would have been the village's downtown, had any of the stores not been boarded up. No motels, city buildings, or even a convenience store with a restroom. Houses crouched dark and dingy with overgrown lawns, cars on blocks, and cracked plastic toys cluttering the broken sidewalks. The roofs held peeling shingles, and the homes were covered either with flaking paint or siding that had seen better days. Casey shuddered at the thought of living in one of the derelict houses, but within a few minutes she and Death were on the other side of the occupied lots, headed into open land once again, where she could breathe.

"Ghost town," Casey said.

Death grunted.

Casey dug in her bag for some ibuprofen and swallowed two of them dry. She heaved her pack onto her back, wincing at the pain in her side. "I can't go much longer. It might have to be a field this time. Only for a few hours. At least it's corn, rather than the short crops we were seeing earlier today."

"You're in no condition to be lying on damp ground."

"I might not have a choice."

"Give it a few more minutes. I have a feeling…"

Casey pounded out another mile before a light rain began to fall. "Great. I'm stopping." Corn, especially at this time of year when it was ready for harvest, offered minimal shelter, but if she made her way far enough in, she could drape her waterproof blanket over some stalks and make herself a little lean-to.

"Hang on." Death pointed. "What's that? Think it's open?"

A small white church loomed out of the darkness, smack on the corner of an intersection of two township roads. Its sign lit up the night, declaring the building the home of the Harvest Church of Saints.

"Sounds kinda creepy," Death said. "Like they're kidnapping people for their kidneys."

Casey laughed, then stopped, holding her side. "Let's check the doors. Sometimes churches take the idea of hospitality literally."

But the double doors in the front were locked. Casey peered through the glass, hands on either side of her face. She yearned to be inside, out of the mist, with a pack of ice on her face and a something soft underneath her.

Death left, then swooped back immediately. "Back door."

"It's open?"

"Don't know. But at least there is one."

Casey trudged around the building, across the gravel parking lot. She tried not to get her hopes up when she spied the small brown door. "Well, here goes nothing."

The door opened.

Casey's eyes watered as she stepped inside, and she swiped away tears of relief. She reached for a light switch.

"I wouldn't," Death said.

"Oh. Right." Who knew what other drunks were cruising the roads that night? Or even those cops.

The church was tiny. Using the glow from her phone, Casey found two rooms on the main floor, both locked, most likely the pastor's office and a library, and two classrooms in the basement. She finally located a restroom, where she could close the door and turn on the light. Not such a good idea. The mirror told her more than she wanted to know, and she palpated her swollen cheek.

"Anything broken?" Death asked.

"Don't think so." She pushed on her side with the flat of her hand, wincing at the sharp pain. She'd bruised ribs before, but this felt like more than that. God, please don't let them be broken. "I'm going to have a pretty rainbow on my face by morning."

"But for posterity's sake, you need to document how it looks tonight."

Casey stood against the plain white of the far wall to take some pictures of her swollen face. It took a few tries, as selfies weren't something she'd had much practice doing, but eventually she figured out how to get the camera pointed toward herself and angled correctly. It took a little more effort to get shots of her ribs and still have her face in the photo for identification, but she did the best she could.

"Probably want to do that again in the morning, once the colors start to show," Death said.

Casey agreed.

After the photo session, Casey cleaned up as well as paper

towels and hand soap would allow, while Death took a tour of the church.

"Found a kitchen." Death now wore ministers' garb, black shirt with white collar, gray pants, and shiny black shoes. "Hopefully, there's ice."

There was. Casey crushed some of it in two Ziplocs she found in a drawer, and lay on a cushioned pew in the sanctuary, one bag on her ribs, one on her face. She'd taken off her wet sweatshirt and hung it on the pew in front of her, along with her jeans, socks, and underthings. Her sneakers sat with their laces loosened and their tongues sticking out. Casey hoped everything would dry out before morning, because she didn't want to resume her journey in her T-shirt and pajama shorts.

Her phone chirped.

Death read the screen. "Eric."

Casey didn't open her eyes. What would she say to him? She didn't want to admit that on her first night she'd incapacitated three men and gotten herself bruised and battered. She wasn't a good enough liar to get away with saying everything was fine.

"He's worried."

Casey didn't move.

"You should at least answer him. Let him know you're all right."

"Am I?"

"You're talking to me, aren't you?"

Casey sighed and felt blindly for her phone, which she'd set on the floor. She located it and held it above her face as she thumbed a response, squinting with the one eye not covered by the ice pack.

Doing fine. Sleeping in a church. Hope all is well with you.

She set the phone back down.

Death's eyes rolled. "You sound like you're talking to someone you hardly know."

Casey didn't respond. Did she know him? They'd met half a year earlier, and spent only a couple of months in each other's company. She liked him, sure, but how well had she actually gotten to know him? Or let him get to know her? He was sweet, kind, funny, smart, good-looking…everything one would want. But then, Reuben had been all of those things, too, plus exotic and a little bit dangerous. He'd also been the father of her son. Her partner. Her everything. How could she throw that away for a guy she'd accidentally found in some small Ohio town?

"You're doing it again, aren't you?" Death said. "Comparing him to your dead husband."

Casey stayed quiet.

"I understand it, honey, I do. But it's been two and a half years. It's time to move on. And don't get all on your high horse. I'm not saying forget Reuben, and certainly not Omar. I'm saying… Reuben loved you. He would want you to find it again."

"Find what? I can't find him again."

"Exactly." Death patted her shoulder, leaving it chilled. She could have just used Death as an ice pack. "You aren't supposed to find him again. He was special. Unique."

"I know that!" Casey jerked, sending her face's ice pack to the floor. "That's the whole problem! I can't replace him."

"You're not supposed to replace him. No one will fill the place he had in your life. That will always be his. But you can fill a different place, with a different person. Reuben would be okay with it. I promise. He'd want you to find—"

"Will you shut up?" Casey snatched the ice pack off the floor, sending shards of pain through her side. She smacked it back onto her face and dropped her arm over her eyes. What did Death know? Had Death lost a spouse? A child? She thought not.

The quiet in the church grew, until Casey felt the emptiness.

When the guilt of her outburst got the best of her she opened her eye, ready to apologize.

But Death was gone.

Chapter Six

Casey woke with a start. A woman stood over her, her expression unreadable.

Casey shot to her feet, gasping at the pain in her side. The now melted bags of ice slid to the floor with wet splats, and Casey quickly took in the rest of the sanctuary. No other people. Exit free and clear at the back of the room. The woman held no weapon, unless you counted two cups of takeout coffee, and a plastic bag draped over her arm. The woman's noncommittal expression changed to a smile, and Casey let out the breath she'd been holding. She yanked her sweatshirt from where it hung on the pew and painstakingly pulled it on. She wished she could put on all of her clothes, but it felt a little weird to be getting dressed with some strange woman watching.

"I didn't wake you," Death said from the next bench, "because she doesn't look like much of a threat. Besides, I think she's the minister." Death had apparently joined another branch of the Church this morning, and now wore Catholic robes. Probably from some horror movie where the priest killed everyone. "From what I see in their pamphlets and such, the Harvest Church of Saints leans toward the pacifistic variety of Christian organizations, and does not, as its name suggests, participate in the black market of human organs."

Casey returned her attention to the woman, who, as opposed

to Death, wore normal, everyday clothes. Jeans and Nikes and a sweatshirt declaring, "I don't know how it happened. God just made me this way." She was in her forties, probably, with dark hair streaked gray, a cushiony build, and something active and lively behind her eyes. A woman to be watched.

"She can't see me," Death said, "which is interesting, seeing how a woman of the cloth should believe in the afterlife and all. But I guess pastors are human too. I mean, they are, right?"

"Hey, there," the woman said. "I brought you this." She handed Casey a steaming cup of coffee, Styrofoam with a Shell insignia.

Casey hesitated, then took it, wrapping her hands around its warmth.

"May I sit?" the woman asked.

Casey used a foot to scoot her bag and blanket closer, making room for the pastor, if that was what she was.

The woman sat. "I'm Sheila. The pastor here."

Casey ignored Death, who was giving her an "I told you so" look, and took a sip of coffee. "My name's Casey. Casey Brown."

"That's a new one," Death said. "Common. Hard to argue with."

The pastor met Casey's eyes with a knowing look, then sat back and took a drink from her own cup. "Ahh. Nothing like a fresh cup of java after a bad night's sleep."

Light filtered through stained-glass windows which Casey hadn't noticed the night before. Scenes of Jesus and lambs and what Casey assumed were prophets and disciples and Jesus' mother, Mary. The colors lit up the western side of the room.

The small sanctuary itself wasn't fancy, other than the windows. A dozen rows of wooden pews on each side, the first few with padded benches and hearing aids. A pulpit stood at the front on a raised platform. A simple wooden cross adorned the wall. A piano and drum set occupied half of the stage, and Casey assumed the instruments accompanied hymns sung from the green and purple songbooks in the back of the pew.

After a few minutes of not entirely uncomfortable silence the pastor set down her coffee and held out the bag. "Have one." Casey reached in and grabbed an egg and cheese croissant with bacon.

"See?" Death said. "I told you she was all right."

Casey warily regarded the pastor and her offerings. Had she already been into the church, seen Casey, and gone back out to get food? Casey didn't like that she hadn't heard her. Perhaps an effect of too many painkillers the night before.

"Thank you." Casey belatedly remembered her manners.

"You looked like you could use some nourishment. The gas station down the road has these and they're good if you can get them before they've been sitting under the heat lamp all morning."

Casey finished her sandwich before Sheila was halfway through hers, but that could have been because the pastor spent her time studying Casey instead of eating. Casey could tell Sheila thought she was being surreptitious, watching Casey from the corner of her eye, but it was fairly obvious.

Casey wiped her mouth. "Thank you for letting me sleep here. I was really happy the back door was open."

"I'm glad you found us. We leave the door unlocked for just such emergencies." She waited again, perhaps hoping Casey would fill the silence with an explanation. But Casey had no intention of telling this stranger her story, no matter how much she appreciated the coffee and sandwich.

"Does he know where you are?" Sheila finally said.

Casey paused in the middle of crinkling up her sandwich wrapper. "Who?"

Sheila waved her hand at Casey's face. "Whoever did this to you."

"Oh." Casey touched her cheek. The swelling had gone down, but she assumed the colors had come out in all their glory. "It wasn't one guy."

Death chuckled. "It was three."

"Then who? Or, should I say, how?"

"No one you need to be concerned about."

The pastor sucked at her teeth. "You're not from around here. I mean, I haven't seen you before."

"That's right."

If the pastor desired information, she was going to be disappointed. Casey wanted nothing more than to pack up her bag and be on her way.

"Someone should take a look at your face. One of my congregants is a retired doctor. I'm sure he'd be glad to come over."

"I'll be fine. It's just a bruise." As was the injury to her ribs, she hoped. But she wasn't about to check her mid-section's morning colors with the pastor looking on.

Sheila leaned forward. "Was it someone from our town? Or are you running from somewhere else?"

"I'll be fine," Casey said again.

A phone rang, the sound coming from the hallway. A shrill jangle from a rare landline, impossible to miss. Sheila didn't move. The phone rang again.

"You can get that," Casey said. "I'm okay."

Sheila looked around the sanctuary as if one of the characters from the windows might save her the trouble of answering the call. "I'll be right back."

Casey drank her coffee and watched the woman hustle down the aisle and out the doors at the back. She entered one of the locked rooms Casey had seen the night before. Her office, Casey suspected.

Casey set her cup down and pulled on her jeans, mostly dry, and a different pair of socks with her shoes, which were still cold and damp. She rolled up yesterday's socks and shoved them in her bag's side pocket.

"She's too curious." Casey glanced toward the hallway to make sure the pastor wasn't returning. If she heard Casey talking to no one, it would make her call to that retired doctor seem all the more necessary.

"She wants to help."

"More than I'd like."

Death indicated the sandwich wrapper. "You ate the food she gave you."

Casey dug in her bag for a few dollars. "I'll pay her for it. That way she won't feel I owe her my life story."

"Oh, she'll still feel that way."

That's what Casey was afraid of.

"Look alive," Death said. "She's back."

The pastor leaned against the end of the pew. "So. What can I do for you?"

Casey held up her coffee cup. "You already did it."

"I don't mean that. I mean about..." She jerked her chin toward Casey's face.

"You don't need to do anything. In fact, I'm leaving." Casey held out a five. "Here. For the food and coffee."

The pastor backed away, hands up. "It was a gift."

Casey set the bill on the pew. "For the offering, then."

The pastor began to say something, then stopped. She chewed her lip. "They were talking at the gas station this morning."

The back of Casey's neck prickled.

"It seems a few locals ended up at the police station last night."

"Uh-oh," Death said.

Sheila absently tapped the bench. "They claimed a woman beat them up for no reason." *taptaptap taptaptap*. "But with those three guys, there's always a reason. Ten reasons."

Casey gave a small smile. "That's odd, isn't it? That one woman could beat up three guys?"

"Yes. That is odd."

Casey painfully picked up the two sloshing Ziploc bags. "Where shall I get rid of these?"

"I didn't tell them about you. The people at the gas station.

Although if that woman from last night would happen to be you—I'm not saying it is, but on the off chance—it would be great to have a police report detailing why you would attack those men and flee. Because these guys…nothing's going to happen to them. It never does."

Death hummed with displeasure. "I told you we needed to get those idiots. You didn't listen."

"They've done this before?" Casey asked. "Given women reasons to beat them up?"

"Or shoot them," Death growled.

The pastor nodded. "Oh, sure. But no one's had the nerve to go to the cops, since one of the guys is the brother of an officer."

"You guessed cousin," Death muttered. "This is worse."

"What about the chief?" Casey said. "Is she in on it?"

"He. And he's new, came from some other precinct. Had to be a demotion, don't you think? Coming to a place like this?" Her lips pinched. "He wants to give his officers the benefit of the doubt. Says he can't start off his tenure by accusing them of playing favorites, or believing every bad thing people say. It's not like their offenses got documented." She shook her head. "I can't blame him for making sure he knows the truth before cleaning house. When I came to this church, I couldn't believe everything the members told me—and there was a lot of it—because it contradicted itself. One person's truth is completely unbelievable to someone else. Churches, unfortunately, work that way. I guess it's the same with police departments."

Casey wasn't sure how to respond to the pastor's monologue.

"What all this means is that those other women, the ones who have plenty of reasons to report these guys but never do it? They're the ones who end up paying."

"Why doesn't anyone do something? Why don't you?"

"You think I haven't tried?" The pastor's jaw bunched. "Maybe you have to be here longer than a night to see it, but this isn't a quaint little village. This is a down-on-its-luck, bitter, underprivileged armpit of a place, and there's a lot of darkness here. Some might say Evil itself hangs around."

"The place time forgot," Death said, as before.

"I came here to make a difference." Sheila's eyes shone with tears. "So don't accuse me of not trying. It just hasn't worked so far."

Casey gazed at the scuff marks on the brown tile floor. "What would happen if the woman from last night went to the cops? Would any of them listen?"

Something in Sheila's eyes sparked, and she gripped the back of the bench. "They would, if she got the right one."

Casey looked at Death. Death nodded. "We've got the time, and nowhere else we have to be."

Casey tossed the Ziploc bags onto the bench, grimacing as the water leaked onto the cushion. She snatched them up and pinched the tops together as she considered her next words. "Would you be able to get the right one to come down to the church?"

Sheila's lips twitched, then stretched into a Grinch-like smile. "Oh, I can get the right one."

Casey thought of Crash and his friends who had been terrorizing the women of the area for far too long. When Casey imagined she'd be fighting the cops on her own, the decision had felt murky. Now she had this determined pastor by her side.

"Make the call. Let's give the cops something they can't cover up."

Chapter Seven

The pastor punched the air, letting go with a *whoop*.

Death laughed. "I like this one."

Casey smiled. She did, too.

Sheila raced to her office, and fifteen minutes later a young cop named Maddy Justus was at the church, driving a cruiser bearing the crest of Beltmore, Idaho, and looking like she'd retrieved her uniform from the box on her very first day. She was taller than Casey, and a little thicker, but the look in her eyes was more reminiscent of Bambi than the hunter.

"Sorry it's only me," she said to Pastor Sheila. "I wish the chief was along, but he and Connor are at the school teaching the kids gun safety."

Sheila smiled warmly. "We're glad you came. Let's get this documented."

Officer Justus dug a pen and notebook from her pocket.

"Think she'll get a Girl Scout badge for this?" Death wore a police uniform also. That badge read, Detective Cagney.

Casey finally got a reference.

Casey hoped Officer Justus could stand up to what would be coming her way once she went against the majority of the force and the cop brother. Casey trusted she could, since there wasn't another option, and told the young cop everything that happened the night before, right up to when she and Death found the church door unlocked. Of course she didn't mention Death's role in it all.

"And why were you sleeping in the park?" Justus asked.

"Nowhere else was open."

"But why were you there in the first place?"

Casey regarded the cop and her notebook for a few moments before saying, "I'm doing some cross-country hiking."

Pastor Sheila raised her eyebrows, but didn't comment.

"Is there anything else you need?"

"Your info, I guess. Driver's license. But I think I asked everything." Justus took Casey's ID and copied the necessary information. Casey noticed the pastor peering over the cop's shoulder, and realized she now knew Casey's name. Maldonado was a whole lot different from Brown.

Oh, well.

Justus handed Casey's ID back to her. "Thanks for talking to me. I hope this is enough to get those assholes in trouble for once." She winced and glanced at the pastor, who graciously acted like she hadn't heard the uncouth word Justus used.

Casey had finished packing her things while waiting for Officer Justus to arrive, and now she stood, sliding her arms into her bag's straps. Her ribs sent pain through her body, and she clenched her teeth to keep from using her own un-church-like words. "You have my phone number. Feel free to call."

"Wait." Justus looked up. "You're leaving?"

"If you don't need anything else, I don't need to stay, right?"

"But..." She looked beseechingly at the pastor.

"I promise I'll answer my phone," Casey told her.

The officer's radio crackled, and a man asked her location. She paled.

"Justus?" the voice barked again.

Justus took a deep breath and let it out, meeting the pastor's steady gaze. "I'll do what I can."

The pastor nodded. "Be careful."

Justus walked out to the foyer. Casey could see her through the windows in the back wall, and heard her say, "I'm at the church."

"The chief?" Casey asked.

"I don't think so. It sounded like Officer Willis." The pastor's nostrils flared. "The brother."

Great.

"You should go now. If he figures out Justus talked to you, he'll be down in a shot, and he won't be alone."

Casey held out her hand. "Thank you for everything."

"Don't say good-bye yet." She hustled toward the front of the church, where she disappeared around a corner. After a moment she reappeared, gesturing. "Come on."

Sheila led her behind the pulpit, where a door opened to the outside. She pointed to an old silver Honda Civic. "Get in. I'll take you wherever you want to go."

Casey eased her bag into the backseat. When they were buckled in, Casey pointed north. "Can you take me up the road a few miles?"

Sheila glanced into the rearview mirror as they left, seeing right through Death in the middle of the backseat, who wore a sweatshirt like hers, proclaiming ignorance of God's process. Casey had to think Death actually did know how it happened.

Pastor Sheila drove stiffly, not relaxing until the village was out of sight. "I don't think I should drop you off on this road. It would be too easy for them to come after and find you."

"What do you suggest?"

"You're determined to go north?"

"I guess it doesn't matter. I don't really have a destination."

Sheila glanced at her with curiosity, but didn't say anything.

"It's killing her not to ask," Death said.

Casey knew it was.

Sheila's purse began ringing, and she and Casey both looked at it.

"Can you see who it is?" Sheila asked.

Casey fished in the cavernous bag until she found it. "Says it's Maddy."

Sheila puffed out her cheeks. "Can you put it on speaker?"

Casey did.

"Hello, this is Pastor Sheila."

"This is Officer Justus." Her voice came through formal and stiff. "I came by the church to see you and you're not here. Any chance you're coming into work soon?"

Casey held her breath.

"I'm running a few errands for the church. I'll be back in, oh, a half hour or so. Anything I can do for you before then?"

"No, that's fine. Give me a call at the station when you're here."

"Sure thing." Sheila hesitated. "Everything all right?"

"Yes. Officer Willis wanted me to ask you a few questions."

Willis, who may have been standing right beside her.

Sheila's face went stony. "About what? Did something happen?"

"We can talk when you get back. Thank you. Drive safely."

Sheila nodded, and Casey ended the call.

"That was fast," Sheila said.

Casey felt a little guilty that the pastor might have to lie for her. A little. Not a lot.

Fifteen minutes later Sheila turned left, drove a few more miles, and turned right again, stopping at a Dollar General on the edge of another small town. Small, but nothing like Beltmore.

"Will this do? You can take this road as far north as you like."

"It's perfect. Thanks."

Sheila's forehead creased. "I hope the creeps don't look too hard for you."

"I'll be fine." Casey smiled. "You did your job. Showed hospitality. Stood up for the vulnerable."

Sheila blinked. "I think that was your part."

"We both did it, then. Thank you."

The pastor watched as Casey climbed slowly, painfully, from

the car. Finally the pastor pulled away, and Casey made her way into the store, where she bought food and water for the day's journey. And another bottle of ibuprofen.

She downed some painkillers and headed out of town, glad to be away from people and questions. The open fields gave her the freedom to breathe, although every time she inhaled too deeply she felt a stabbing pain, and every time she heard a car coming she tensed, afraid the cops—or the men from the night before—had found her. She hoped those idiots would be prosecuted. She also hoped the cops—or at least Officer Justus—could take care of them without calling her.

After a while Casey grew warm and shed her sweatshirt. Her stomach was growling by the time she spied another town in the distance. She checked her phone's maps again—she was getting all too used to that convenience—and saw she was approaching the village of Armstrong, Idaho. Population twelve hundred forty-two. Looked like it had all the basics—an elementary school, two churches, a general store, and several other small businesses. Maybe she could find something to eat that would be more substantial than a granola bar and peanut butter crackers.

But no matter how long she walked, the town seemed just as far away. Was she hallucinating? Was this a desert trek story? She grew thirsty, and wished she'd bought more water. The last bottle had been empty several miles back. Where was Death and that stupid conductor outfit now, when she actually needed a beverage?

The sound of a vehicle began as a hum and grew into a full-throated rumble. Casey's heart raced, then calmed when she saw it was a tractor and not a familiar four-wheel-drive truck. The tractor, pulling a wagon of baled hay, drew up beside her.

The farmer yelled down to her. "Need a lift?"

"Would love one!"

He jerked his thumb toward the wagon. "Hop on."

Casey set her bag on the back and climbed up, settling against the hay, her feet swinging freely. She gave the farmer a thumbs-up, and the tractor jerked to a start. She sucked in a breath as the movement jolted her ribs, but at least the ibuprofen was muffling the worst of the pain.

"Now this is more like it." Death reclined next to her on a bale, wearing dusty brown pants and shirt, leather boots with holes, and a tattered hat.

Casey squinted. "Who are you this time?"

"Not even an attempt?"

"No."

"A tiny, little smidgeon of a guess? Okay, how about a hint. Traveling across the country."

Death waited.

"Accompanied by loved ones."

Still nothing from Casey.

"Granted, we're not in the Dust Bowl."

"Oh, for heaven's sake, fine. Are you Tom Joad? From *Grapes of Wrath*?"

"Ding, ding, ding! Toss the woman a tomato!"

"I thought the Joads traveled in an old truck."

"Close enough. An old truck with a grandma who kicked the bucket halfway there."

"Nice." Casey leaned forward, hands on the back edge of the trailer, and watched the road roll slowly past. "Don't you have a dead person somewhere to be taking care of?"

"Nah."

"There's got to be one. More than one. Isn't the global death rate something like one hundred a minute?"

"A hundred and five. Two every second."

"So why are you here?"

"Because I like you. And I can be in more than one place at once. You know that. The whole timeline thing is very complicated. Now, if there's something huge, like when the Titanic went down, or that horrible tsunami, I might need to focus more. But on a normal day, my helpers gather souls. I don't have to do it all myself."

"Helpers?"

"Sure. What boss, or immortal Horseman of the Apocalypse, doesn't have a few helpers?"

"You trust them to gather souls?"

"Of course."

"But you are aware of everyone who dies?"

"Only if I need to be." Death flicked a piece of fake straw off the wagon and it dissolved into thin air. "They are very well trained, my *yamadutas*. Very gentle. Very kind. They know how to do their job—my job—and I leave them to it. I don't want to be one of those hovering bosses. If they come across something they can't handle, they let me know and I take care of it. It's only death, after all."

"Only death?" Casey stared at her companion with a mixture of disbelief and horror.

"Oh, come now. Don't act all holier than thou. Death is a part of everything, not something only a special few get to experience. People are born, people live, people die. It's hard for you humans to understand until it happens, but there is a plan that spans all time. It's beautiful, really."

"It wasn't beautiful when Reuben and Omar died in that car."

"Of course it wasn't. Tragic death is never beautiful. It is excruciating and surprising and debilitating and haunting. But what comes after all this…" Death waved a hand. "That, my child, is where you find beauty."

Death's feet swung like Casey's, the boots' shoestrings flapping, and Death's face tipped toward the sky. "Today, nothing unusual is happening, no grand scale soul-gathering, no universal mystery, so I can hang out. Isn't that great?"

"You know, Azrael, it kind of is."

Death blinked. "You mean it?"

"Sometimes you're good company."

Death's mouth opened slightly before spreading into a smile. "I never thought I'd hear you say that."

Casey averted her eyes, gazing at the horizon. "I couldn't see you there for a few weeks when Eric and I were…happy. And the past couple of months you've hardly been around." She blinked the dust out of her eyes, because surely that was why they were watering. "I've missed you."

Death leaned back on the hay and tipped the hat to shield the sun.

Ten minutes later Death slipped away, most likely to some interesting death, or a call from a *yamaduta*. The tractor approached an intersection close to the town. Close enough Casey knew for certain the buildings weren't a mirage. When the tractor halted at the crossroads, Casey eased herself down and walked forward to thank the farmer. He gave her a little salute and turned west.

Casey made her way into town, which could have been a copy of most towns she'd visited. Modest homes, streets named Jefferson and Washington and High, and a small "business district," consisting of several old brick buildings housing a post office, a hair salon, the police, and a tiny branch library. A bank. Several oddly placed doors with addresses reading "1/2" that led to apartments.

Casey meandered past one of the two churches she'd seen on her phone, crossed the street at the single blinking traffic light, and followed the smell of grilling meat to the far side of Main Street, where she found the general store.

The parking lot was filled with a variety of amenities. A locked ice chest, a hose for putting air in tires, two vending machines with pop and Gatorade, and a battered picnic table beside a large grill. The lot was also filled with men in work clothes who milled around buying burgers, eating, and hanging out in clumps of twos or threes. Casey saw lots of white faces, but also a healthy number of darker ones, which surprised her. Perhaps it was her recent travels to Midwestern towns that had her expecting a more homogenous population, but whatever the reason, it was a bit disconcerting, as everywhere she looked she saw a man who reminded her of Reuben, with his dark shiny hair and copper skin.

But she couldn't think about that.

An older man, taller and rounder than the others, with a complexion more like Casey's own pale pink, wore an apron and flipped burgers on the grill. He watched her for a few moments, nodded a greeting, then returned his attention to the meat laid out in lines in front of him.

The men at the table glanced up at Casey, noted her black eye, then went back to their conversation. So either they were used to seeing bruises or they appreciated what it meant to leave other people to their own stories. Either way, she was glad they didn't make her injury into a thing.

On the far side of the lot two gas pumps sat under a protective awning, with a large sign proclaiming the day's prices. A big red F250 crouched at the pumps, but Casey couldn't see the driver, except for the boots on the other side. For a split second she worried the truck was from the night before, but realized quickly that besides the fact there were a multitude of pickups in the world, she couldn't see everything beneath the cab because the tires were normal size. She let out the breath she hadn't realized she was holding and allowed her shoulders to relax.

The vending machine lured Casey with its promise of a cold drink, and her assessment of the scene gave her no worries for her safety, so she started across the pavement. As she grew near, the cook smiled at her, again making no obvious sign that he noticed her eye.

A flash of movement at the pumps caught Casey's attention. The driver of the red truck stalked around the bed and stopped beside the driver's door to look at Casey. Dressed in jeans, boots, and a flannel shirt, she was the only other woman in the lot.

Casey raised a hand in greeting and took a few steps toward her. The woman frowned, looking from the man at the grill to Casey, then jumped into her truck and drove away.

Well, Casey thought. So much for female bonding.

Chapter Eight

"Don't worry about her," said the old man at the grill. "The rest of us are a whole lot friendlier."

The surrounding men, however, didn't seem so much friendly as hungry, concentrating on their burgers and conversations. Their earlier notice had apparently been enough to satisfy whatever curiosity they might have felt. Which was fine with Casey. The less curious the townspeople, the more she liked a town.

Casey gave a carefree wave, wincing at the sharp pain it caused in her side, and watched as the red truck pulled away. "No problem. She doesn't have to be the Welcome Wagon." She dug some change out of her bag to buy a drink from the vending machine. The water bottle clunked down to the receptacle and Casey drank half of it at one go, surreptitiously downing some painkillers with it. As she finished the second half, she leaned against a rusting gold Chevy Impala with a *For Sale* sign in the window, parked in a shady corner of the lot. The men's voices drifted on the air as they ate and talked about work, hunting, and trucks.

Vehicles shuttled in and out, dispensing passengers who either went into the store and came out with purchases, or queued up for a burger, hungry for red meat. Some stood around and ate, some joined the guys at the table, and still others bought their food and drove away. It seemed like the place to be, a hub of activity in the quiet town.

By the time Casey finished a second bottle of water, the lunch traffic had slowed and the man at the grill was packing up his leftover buns and condiments. "Got one more burger that needs a home." He held it up with a metal spatula.

It did smell good.

Casey accepted the sandwich and enjoyed it at the table while the man cleaned up.

"I'm Vern." He gestured at a peeling sign above the store's front door. *Vern's Market.*

"Casey." She licked ketchup from her thumb after her last bite. "I don't have my own sign."

He snorted a laugh and heaved up the box of supplies. "Come on in. I'll show you around, and you can take a load off in the AC. You look like you wouldn't mind a few minutes out of the sun. And maybe an ice pack." His eyes flicked to her face, then away.

The plate-glass windows by the front door were plastered with signs for lottery tickets, photos of high school athletes, and the price of a six-pack of Bud Light. A small, faded black-and-orange sign in the bottom corner read, *Help Wanted.*

Casey followed Vern into the store, where she saw the usual gas station fare—candy bars, a cappuccino maker, beef jerky. One wall was filled with DVDs, another with newspapers and magazines. The counter itself felt like a box office, with a small window for the cashier, fronting a small, paper-strewn office. Surrounding the cashier's window, tacked to the plywood wall, were more photos of sports teams, people receiving awards, and hunting triumphs. If Casey were to go by hairstyles, the pictures dated from the present back several decades.

Vern pointed through the cashier's window at another elderly man who sat on a stool behind the counter. Vern raised his voice to ear-splitting decibels. "This is Roger. He helps out when I need him."

The man nodded, his jowls jiggling with the effort.

"Hi, Roger." Casey spoke loudly. "I'm Casey."

Roger blinked hard several times, but other than that didn't respond. Casey wasn't sure if he hadn't heard her, didn't understand, or didn't speak, so she smiled awkwardly and hoped for the best.

"Looks like I might be getting to know him sometime soon."

Casey jumped at the sound of Death's voice in her ear. Death was dressed as a farmer this time, most likely from a movie Casey had never seen. Or maybe Death was going local. Jeans, flannel shirt, boots, like the woman at the gas pump. The old man Roger looked right through Death, as did Vern, who was preoccupied with his box of mustard and relish.

Death waved a hand in front of Roger's face. Apparently the old guy was still clinging onto life. Casey had met a few people in the past couple of years who saw her companion, but they were the exceptions—people who for one reason or another were not afraid of dying, or, in more extreme cases, yearned for it. Casey herself had been in the latter category for most of the two years, only recently recognizing a desire to stick around a little while longer.

Eric had something to do with that.

Vern jerked his head for Casey to follow, and carried the box through the store. The farther they walked, the more different the store felt from a generic traffic stop. The space became a grocery store with shelves of off-brand vegetables and dusty cans of fruit, sweatshirts sporting the local high school's logo, and a sparse supply of first aid remedies. From the faded and retro labels, Casey guessed some of the products had been there since she was a kid. Vern took her past a small produce section of wilted lettuce and spotted pears, a bread aisle with both prepackaged buns and homemade loaves and rolls, and a freezer aisle holding everything from meat to huge, frost-covered tubs of vanilla ice cream.

Things weren't exactly flying off the shelves.

They crossed through a double-sized open doorway into an

area with tables and chairs and red-and-white checked tablecloths. A door at the front led to the outside, and an exit in the back opened into a hallway, but Casey couldn't see far enough back to know what was there.

Two old women sat at one of the small round tables, finishing up something that didn't look like the hamburgers Vern had been grilling. Tuna, maybe?

"Hello, Ethel. Wilma," Vern said. "How's the chicken salad?"

One of them frowned. "All right, although there are too many grapes. And it could use more almonds."

"Oh, stop," the other one said. "You're so picky. I think the chicken salad is delicious." She blinked so rapidly at Vern Casey thought she had something in her eye.

Death snorted with laughter. "I believe that's what you call 'batting your eyelashes.'"

The woman's expression supported Death's claim, her eyes bright, her cheeks a blotchy pink. She looked like a teenage girl whose crush walked by in the cafeteria. Casey wasn't sure if it was cute or creepy, and wondered what Vern thought. He didn't seem to reciprocate her feelings, seeing how he kept on walking and didn't blink or blush or even give her a second glance.

Once he was out of range, the women eyed Casey, who wasn't sure whether their gazes were malevolent or curious. She would go for curious.

Both woman had obviously dyed hair that didn't match their aging skin, bright lipstick smudged by their lunches, and dressier clothes than Casey would have imagined for a lunch at the local gas station. The idea that this was the epitome of Armstrong's culture—or, at least, their lunchtime possibilities—made her sad, and a little eager to keep walking to the next town.

Casey stared right back at the women until they broke eye contact and leaned toward each other, whispering. Weird.

"Wouldn't mind being a fly on the wall for that conversation," Death said. "Or, maybe not a fly, since this is an eating establishment. Sort of."

"You don't have to be a fly," Casey muttered. "They can't see you."

Casey caught up with Vern at the far end of the little cafe, where he stepped around a glass-fronted deli counter displaying raw meats, potato salad, and already made-up sub sandwiches. He opened the door of a battered white refrigerator and transferred the condiments from the box.

"So, you're new in town." It wasn't a question. He spoke what he knew to be true, his back to her.

Death swooped through the glass of the counter to check out the food, then settled back at Casey's side with a neutral expression. "Seems fresh enough, if you like that sort of thing."

"Just got in," Casey answered Vern. "I'm…sightseeing."

Vern barked a laugh and shut the refrigerator door. "In Armstrong?"

"It's sort of a cross-country trip, stopping wherever I end up."

"And you ended up here, of all places?"

"I don't know. It seemed as good a place as any." Although she was having second thoughts after the weird-old-ladies-at-the-gas-station-deli thing, as well as the unwelcoming woman at the gas pump, even though she'd told Vern that didn't really matter. Maybe only the women were odd in this town. Vern seemed friendly enough.

"If you say so." He tossed the empty box in the corner and wiped his hands on a towel. "Hang on a sec."

Behind the deli counter was another door leading to the grocery side of the store, and he disappeared through it. A minute later he was back, holding an ice pack, maybe from that paltry first aid shelf. He gestured toward her face. "That looks pretty fresh. Use this."

She accepted it, glancing at the old women, who practically got whiplash pretending they weren't watching. The ice pack was the kind you break open to make it cold. She didn't think they expired, but she couldn't see a date right off. "Thanks. I'll use it as soon as I have a chance to sit down."

He waved toward the closest table. "Sit down now."

Casey checked out the chair and tablecloth. They didn't look too sticky. "Okay. Thanks." She sat and bashed the ice pack on the edge of the table, feeling the cold rush to the surface. She placed it against her cheek, wishing she had another one for her ribs. But that would be...awkward.

Vern went back behind the deli, messing with some boxes and wiping down the glass. "So, you planning on sticking around here for a while? Or continuing on?"

"Haven't really thought about it."

"But you should." Death perched on the counter's sneeze shield, bootlaces dragging through the macaroni salad. "Think about it, I mean. You're in no condition to be sleeping in a field tonight. Or a playground. And where are you headed, anyway? Canada? Alaska?"

Death was right. Her ribs ached, her face throbbed, and she was more than ready for a soft bed. She was ashamed. One night on the road and she was ready to give up. If only her Hapkido master could see her now. He would wonder, quite rightly, where his star black belt's backbone had gone.

"If there's a spot for me, I guess it might be nice to stay. Unless you think Armstrong's not worth getting to know."

Vern came around the counter, striding through Death. He shivered and glanced at the refrigerator, making sure he'd shut the door. He sat across from Casey, his back to the ladies. "It's home, I suppose. I've been here all my life, except for one summer in Portland, when I went up for a business class. Met my wife, Dottie, there."

So, no wonder he hadn't reciprocated the behavior of the flirty old woman. He already had someone. This was a small town—did the other woman not know he was married? Or did she just not care?

Vern grimaced. "Not sure Dottie would say this place was as good as any, but she came here when we were first together.

We planned to go somewhere else when we were financially stable, but then my dad died and I had to take over the store." His eyes got a faraway look, but snapped back into focus after a few seconds. "So, this is where we stayed. She grew up as a city girl, which forced her to make adjustments. Lots of them. People here haven't been exactly…receptive." He half-glanced over his shoulder, as if remembering the old ladies behind him. "Want to meet her?"

"Uh…" Casey glanced at Death, who was now sitting with the two old women, listening to their conversation as if an active participant. Death wore a black tailored suit with a white blouse, black heels, and a red sash. Casey was sure she could recognize yet another character from a movie if she cared enough. In fact, Death had conjured up a good resemblance to Meryl Streep.

The women swiveled toward Casey at the exact same time, saw her looking at them, and immediately turned back toward each other. Death gave Casey a wide-eyed, "Did you see that?" look.

"We live next door," Vern said.

"What?"

"You can meet my wife. We live beside the store."

"Oh. Right. Of course." Why he was so determined she meet his wife, she had no idea, but it didn't matter. It wasn't like she had anyplace else to go, and if it made him happy for some reason, and maybe led her toward a place to sleep…

"Give me one minute." He untied his apron and hung it on a hook. "I'll see if Roger can stay a little longer."

Vern hustled toward the front of the store and Casey meandered to the nearest wall, where shelves of local homemade products filled the country-style wooden shelves. She picked up a carved cow to look at the price and immediately put it back, not wanting to pay more than seemed wise for something she really didn't want.

"So this is interesting," Death said.

"These knickknacks?" Casey winced, realizing she'd spoken out loud. She coughed to cover it.

"Of course not. Don't be daft. The lunchers over there. Seems they're no fans of Vern's wife."

Casey checked out the women, who were getting up to leave.

"The one in the flowered…whatever that is," Death said, "she doesn't understand how Vern can still believe it's okay that he ever brought her to this town. His wife, she means. Apparently something is making her angry all over again. Not Vern's wife, the old woman."

Casey looked a question, since she couldn't actually ask it.

"No, I don't know what Vern's wife ever did to old Flower Pants, except you saw how she behaved when Vern entered the room. She's obviously harboring a crush on the old guy. Who knows how long that's been going on? The other woman, the one in the shade of orange no person with her chalky complexion should ever wear, agrees that Dottie, or even Vern, never showed any remorse, but that it has been a long time since 'Dottie drove poor Edmund to his death,' as well as 'that whole thing with Marianne.' Although 'that whole thing'—whatever it is—seems like yesterday, and the whole town still feels it."

Casey frowned.

"Right. You're wondering, as am I, why, if it's been such a long time, they're still obsessing over it."

The women looped their purses over their arms, glanced once more at Casey, and slowly made their way out the door. They left their dirty plates, napkins, and empty coffee mugs on the table, even though a trash can and a dish tub sat by the front door.

"Nice," Death said.

Casey waited until they'd gone, then stacked the dishes. She was setting them in the dish tub when Vern returned.

"All right." He glanced at the now-empty table. A flash of annoyance crossed his face, but it was gone in a moment. "Thank you. You didn't have to do that."

"I didn't mind."

He studied her before heading toward the door. "Roger says he's got a couple more minutes. Enough for you to meet Dottie."

Casey wasn't sure she really wanted to meet Dottie, but she was kind of stuck in the town for the time being, and she didn't want to antagonize the first person she'd met in Armstrong who'd actually been nice to her.

She followed Vern out into the sunshine.

Chapter Nine

Stepping into Vern's ranch-style home reminded Casey of visiting her grandmother's house, but not in a good way. Rather than the comforting smells of Snickerdoodles and her grandma's lilac hand cream, it was like stepping back into a time that had stalled during an especially ugly, dark, unfashionable period.

Worn gold carpeting, grayed upholstery with large orange and yellow flowers, and heavy curtains filled the front room with gloom and such a sense of despair that Casey turned to walk right back out. She stopped when the room flooded with light as Vern swept aside one of the drapes. He skirted the room opening them all, revealing the drab but clean interior. Not as haunting as Casey had first imagined, but still depressing. And the smell... What was that?

"Dottie?" Vern indicated for Casey to hang on a second, and disappeared into the next room.

As she waited, Casey took a closer look at her surroundings. Vern and his wife had obviously cared about decoration at one time, but now the artwork was faded, the lampshades outdated, and the only knickknacks were those often associated with the elderly. Hummel figurines, China plates featuring U.S. presidents, and those abridged Readers Digest books with the gold lettering. The furniture, while aged, had at one time been stylish. Now it just seemed tired.

Strangest of all, Casey saw no photographs. So either Vern and his wife had no family, or they didn't like them enough to display their pictures. The whole atmosphere felt…sad. It was like Sorrow itself hung over the house, suffocating. Dampening.

Mumbled voices drifted into the room, then the shuffle of feet. Vern reappeared with a woman. Other than her age, she was the opposite of the two women from the store. Her narrow, makeup free face was framed by thin gray hair, and her clothes were what Casey expected from what she'd seen of the house. Black slacks, a fitted white blouse, and pearl earrings. Classy at one time, now left behind. Her shoulders were hunched, and the gray under her skin a tad alarming.

So that's what Casey had smelled. Sickness.

"Yikes. Looks like she's going to need me before too long. Like that Roger guy. Although seeing her puts him farther down the list." Death hovered beside Casey, dressed in a starched white nurse's uniform, complete with cap and hair swooped up like devil's horns.

"Nurse Ratched," Casey whispered. "Really?"

"Oh, is *Cuckoo's Nest* too dark? How about this?" The outfit changed to a brown vest and wide-brimmed hat. Death gave a "What do you think?" gesture, arms spread. "Dr. Quinn, Medicine Woman? Dottie definitely could use someone with internal medicine knowledge."

Casey shook her head.

Vern led his wife to the sofa, where she perched on the edge of the cushion, her age-spotted hands clasped on her knees. Vern gestured for Casey to take a chair catty-corner to them. Casey eased onto the puffy cushion, doing her best to both breathe through her rib pain and act like it wasn't happening.

This is Casey," Vern said, "a young woman traveling around the country. She came to get a hamburger today."

Not quite how it happened, but that was okay.

Dottie turned watery eyes toward Casey. Her gaze caught on

Casey's damaged face, and something shifted in her expression. "Where did you come from?"

Casey assumed she meant literally, rather than philosophically, but with someone as sick as she it could easily be the other way around.

"Colorado."

"Denver?"

"No, a small ski town. Well, bigger than this one."

"And what do you think of Armstrong?"

Casey spoke carefully. "The scenery is very beautiful." From what Vern had implied, Dottie wasn't crazy about the place. Even so, Casey shouldn't diss Dottie's acquired home. Besides, Armstrong wasn't the worst place Casey had ever been.

"The mountains." Dottie nodded. "Some people think having them around forgives anything we throw at life. Or what life throws at us."

"You don't?"

Dottie kneaded enlarged knuckles. "I don't think mountains, or those contained within their view, have the ability to forgive anything at all."

"Speaking of dark..." Death muttered.

Vern spoke too cheerfully. "So, do you think you'll stick around for a while? Or a few days?"

Something in his voice spoke of desperation, and Casey's stomach twisted. She'd gotten off the train for a reason the morning before, although she couldn't remember what it was—

"Crying baby," Death reminded her.

—and she didn't feel like hopping onto another hay wagon, not when her phone's map gave her no hope of finding anything other than another small town in the near vicinity.

"I suppose I'll stay the night," she finally said. "Is there a motel or bed and breakfast in town?"

"Not really," Vern said. "Closest thing would be two towns over, where there's a drive-in motel. Only B and B is twenty miles away and sits upwind from a hog farm, so they have trouble keeping business." He grunted, not unlike one of those pigs, and Death let out a high giggle. "Other than that, you'd have to go to Boise, and that's a good twenty miles."

Casey didn't feel like traveling twenty miles, even if Vern offered to drive her. "Do you think one of the town's churches would mind if I borrowed a pew?"

Vern and Dottie shared a long look before Vern offered Casey a small—secretive?—smile. "We have an empty apartment, actually. Well, more of a room. Shall I show you?"

Casey felt apprehensive about the way the invitation unfolded so easily. But Vern had been kind, and Dottie friendly, even if the two old ladies didn't like her. Casey glanced at Death to get a reaction, but Death had gone. Stupid Death. Never around when she needed help.

She forced a smile. "Sure. That would be nice."

Vern patted Dottie's leg and led Casey to a door through the kitchen. "I'm sorry, but there's no outside entrance to the basement. There's a fire escape window in case of emergency, but you'll have to come in through one of our doors."

Casey shuddered. Her flight from Colorado hadn't happened because she couldn't spend another hour alone. Quite the opposite, in fact. She yearned to be on her own, out in the open with only nature to keep her company. But with her injuries, and her worry that the idiot guys from Beltmore might catch up to her, she couldn't help but think this opportunity to lie low in an actual house might be a gift from the universe. She didn't want to turn it down just because she felt a tad claustrophobic.

Casey gritted her teeth and held her arm against her side as she followed Vern down the steep staircase. Fortunately, he took his time, as if he were afraid of losing his balance. At least if Casey stayed she wouldn't have to worry about him surprising her. Once she heard him coming she could be out the fire escape window and halfway down the street before he hit the bottom of the steps—even with her ribs restricting her movement.

They ended up in the basement, which was finished with drywall on one half, and simple gray concrete blocks on the other. On the far side, past shelves of dusty canned goods, a pile of sleeping bags, and an old exercise bike doubling as a storage rack, Vern opened a door into a brightly painted bedroom. Casey could see a square of it over Vern's shoulder as he hesitated in the doorway. His back went stiff, and he gripped the doorway like he was having trouble standing. Casey was about to ask if he was okay when he gestured her forward.

A queen-sized bed covered with a handmade quilt filled a good portion of the room accompanied by a dresser, which matched the headboard. A soft chair sat in a rectangular "L" offshoot at the corner straight ahead, with an oversized pink stuffed puppy resting on the seat cushion. A large, three-sided window acted as a fire escape and let in a good amount of light. Two more small windows sat along the top of the outside wall, so the room didn't feel as much like an underground cell as Casey had been expecting.

In the far corner, close to the chair in the "L," a mobile hung from a metal arm. It was the kind of thing usually suspended above a crib. Omar's had airplanes. This was Noah's Ark. Two lions, two parrots, two monkeys…

The L with the chair and mobile was accented with a wallpaper border of calliope horses, all beautiful and soft and feminine. The border stopped before the main part of the room. The front wall of the L held a full-length mirror, a Homecoming ribbon draped diagonally over the top. On a shelf above the chair sat a diploma from Boise State University, a dried bouquet of flowers with a white ribbon, and a photo of a young mother and baby boy. What was this place? They didn't have any pictures upstairs, but here they had a shrine?

She looked away before Vern felt he had to explain. The whole thing was a little bit creepy.

The bedroom door, she was quick to note, had a slide lock on the inside, as well as a doorknob push button. One checkmark in the I-guess-I-could-sleep-here column. Another was that the room was as far opposite of the upstairs living space as possible, which made her wonder again why they had this beautiful unused room while they lived in drabness.

"It's simple," Vern said, "but comfortable. There's a small closet over here."

"I don't have much."

"True." He glanced at her backpack, then looked away quickly, as if not wanting to show too much interest. Sort of like her and the weird corner of stuff. "There's a bathroom outside here that would be all yours."

He showed her a pleasant space painted light blue, with a shower and a head-height window. This door had only the kind of lock where you twist the doorknob, but that was better than nothing.

"The whole basement would be yours. We never come down here except to clean, and if you're here, you could take care of that. It's too much trouble getting down the stairs." He paused. "So. What do you say?"

"How much would you charge?"

"How long are you staying?" It was said as a challenge.

"I don't know. I was thinking a night or two—to let my face heal."

It looked like he wanted to ask about that, since she'd brought it up, but he refrained and glanced toward the stairs. "Would you like a job?"

The smell of Dottie's illness stuck to the inside of Casey's nose. "Part of the reason I left home was the stress from seeing my mother aging. I'm not really cut out for caregiving."

In fact, if it weren't for feeling a little desperate about a place to stay, she would never have let herself get dragged into a home with another sickly elderly woman.

"Oh no. I'm not asking for help with Dottie. Whatever I

can't do for her she can do herself. I was thinking of the store. You looked like a natural cleaning up that table today, and you did it without asking."

Casey remembered the faded *Help Wanted* sign in the store window. "Anybody can clean up a table."

"Maybe. But they don't." A flash of something—sorrow? Anger?—lit his eyes, and Casey felt a fresh wave of uncertainty. Did the town's resentment of his wife cut so deeply no one even wanted to work at the store? Or was it the idea of people's general laziness that seemed to annoy him?

"Anyway, there are lots of things to do other than clean tables. You could run the cash register, stock shelves..." He grinned. "Grill burgers."

Did Casey want to stay in Armstrong, Idaho? If she didn't, where would she go? The town itself seemed as good a place as any, although she couldn't quite rid herself of niggling doubt.

Or growing curiosity about this man and his story.

"If you take the job you can have the room for free. Plus, I'll pay you an hourly wage."

It seemed a little too good to be true. Casey could envision unwelcome things in her future—running errands for Dottie, doing chores around the house, being bored out of her mind. But again, what would she be doing if she continued down the road? She could leave whenever she was ready. And that niggling doubt? It was probably an aversion to staying in one place too long. She would stick it out a day or two, and if the feeling remained, keep heading west.

"All right. We can try it."

Vern's shoulders slumped, and the worry lines on his forehead relaxed. "You can start tomorrow, bright and early. Unless you're a late night person?"

"I can do either. And I may as well begin today."

He smiled. "Great. Why don't you get settled, then come on over?"

Casey tossed her bag onto her new bed. The painkillers were finally kicking in. "I'm settled. Why don't we see how fast I can learn?"

Chapter Ten

As soon as they arrived in the store, Roger, the old guy behind the counter, ran off, darting suspicious glances at Casey, like she was going to beat him up and drag him out behind the Dumpster. If by "ran off" you meant shuffling slowly around the counter, across the room, and out the door, where he sat at the picnic table and waited for his grandson to come pick him up.

Between serving customers Vern gave her a tour of the walk-in freezer, the employee bathroom, and the supply room. Casey was glad he didn't want her to do actual work, because her painkillers were wearing off, and her ribs were sending reminders about the picnic table incident.

Casey noticed a photo of Vern and his father hanging in the office. "So you took over for your dad?"

"Sooner than I would have liked." He messed with some papers on his desk. "I took that business course right out of high school, but mostly because it was free through a grant for family operations. I wasn't expecting to actually use it to run the whole thing myself, at least not the very next year. Dad had a heart attack one day, just boom. He was gone. Dottie and I had been hoping…"

"What?"

"We wanted to get out of this town. Live somewhere else, at least for a while. But Dad left me the business."

"You couldn't sell it?"

"Not if I wanted to take care of my mother or have any kind of inheritance. He made it a provision in his will. If I sold the business, the money went to the church. If I ran it, I kept the money. We were nineteen, newly married. It wasn't like we could afford to pass it up."

So his dad was a controlling jerk. "Had you known that before?"

"About his will? No. He changed it after I got married to make sure I stayed. It worked. Now, let's show you how to run the cash register."

Close to five-thirty Vern was getting ready to run fried chicken home for Dottie when a police cruiser pulled into the parking lot. Casey went hot, then cold when she recognized the Beltmore insignia. The officer in the driver's seat was definitely not Maddy Justus, and Casey wondered if he was the drunk moron's brother. He took off his sunglasses, set them on the dash, and opened his door.

"I'm not here," Casey told Vern. "I never was."

"What?"

She pointed to her face. "This? It has to do with that cop."

Vern's jaw dropped. "A cop did that?"

"No, I—I'll explain later. Please. Tell me you're a good liar."

He gave a wry smile. "Oh, I'm a good liar, all right."

Casey speed-walked to the back room, considering whether or not to run to Vern's house. But she didn't want to scare Dottie or involve her in the lie. Plus, the cop might see her crossing the yard. If she heard him coming toward the deli area, she would lock herself in the bathroom.

Several minutes later she heard footsteps and made a bee-line toward the women's room.

"Just me," Vern called. "He's gone."

Casey breathed a sigh of relief and met him in the cafe.

Vern waited. "Spill."

The front door dinged, saving Casey from answering. For the moment. She grabbed the packed-up fried chicken. "I'll take this to Dottie. Be back in a minute."

He frowned, but Casey didn't wait.

Dottie was in her bedroom with the door closed when Casey arrived. She left the food on the table and hesitated, not wanting to return to the store.

"Vern?" Dottie's voice drifted into the kitchen.

"It's me, Mrs…Dottie. Bringing some supper."

"Oh, thank you." She appeared in the doorway. "Are you staying to eat with me?"

The smell of the house had taken away Casey's appetite. Did one ever get used to that? The smell of age and disease and forthcoming death? "I have to get back. I'm sorry. Do you need anything else?"

Dottie's face fell. "No. Thank you. I'll just…be here."

Oh, God, what had Casey gotten herself into? If she wanted to deal with this kind of thing, she would have stayed home and taken care of her mother, who she actually knew and loved.

"Yeah, I'll…see you later."

Casey escaped back to her new job, where Vern was waiting. "Are you wanted by the cops? Because I can't deal with trouble right now."

"I'm not." Casey had lived as a fugitive, and it certainly wasn't fun. Being on the right side of the law was a good thing, and while beating up those Beltmore idiots wasn't the best choice she'd ever made, it had been necessary. She gave Vern an abbreviated version of the previous night's events, leaving out details of how she'd gotten there, why she'd left home in the first place, and who her traveling companion had been.

He frowned. "I'm still not clear why you were sleeping in a playground."

"Yeah. I'm a little unclear about that, too."

"But—"

The bell on the door clanged with a loud staccato, as if blown open, and a woman charged inside, digging in her purse. Her hair was as white blond as it could get. Casey groaned. She had seen that hair before.

The woman smiled at Vern before her eyes caught on Casey. Her smile faded. "You?"

Casey shrugged. "Me."

Vern looked back and forth between them. "You know each other?"

Casey made a face. "Not exactly. We were on the same train yesterday." Where the woman had thought Casey had a screw loose. Or a few of them.

The woman scrutinized Casey's black eye for a few moments, then held out some cash. "Thirty dollars of gas, please."

Vern punched some buttons on his computer while the woman and Casey worked very hard not to look at each other. Finally, the woman went back out to her car.

"What was that about?" Vern asked.

"She was on the train. That's all I know." Casey leaned against the doorway of the cashier area.

"You're tired," Vern said.

"I am." Her face had also started to hurt, which was spreading to her head, and her side felt like someone was aiming flat-handed strikes at her ribs. Repeatedly. It was time for more painkiller.

"You can head out. I can manage here until closing."

"You sure?"

"I do it every night."

Casey wasn't going to say no.

"Grab something to eat on your way out. Chicken, or a sub."

"Thanks. I will." She took off before the white-haired woman came back in. That way the woman could ask Vern about Casey, and he could tell her whatever he wanted without Casey having to listen.

Casey snuck into the house through the kitchen door, avoiding

Dottie. She took some painkillers along with her supper, then lay on the bed to let the meds kick in.

She woke several hours later. It was dark. She fumbled for her phone to check the time, then texted Eric:

Found a place to settle for a bit. Will let you know when I move on.

Her brain spun with everything Vern had shown her that afternoon, but mostly she couldn't believe he would be trusting her with money. Granted, the cash register didn't hold all that much, and she didn't know the combination to the safe, but still.

Eric responded within seconds:

Glad you're safe. I'm heading home to Ohio. Ricky will look after your place and your mother.

A stab of guilt shot through Casey. Not about her house so much, but her mom…

Thanks. Hope things are okay in Clyde.

Casey felt a little sick at the thought of Eric's hometown. Earlier that summer she had worked at Home Sweet Home, Eric's soup kitchen, acted in a play…and killed a thug from Louisville. She then spent several weeks avoiding the police until she had to go home to get Ricky out of jail for killing his girlfriend. Which of course he hadn't done. Casey had been exonerated for the thug, but the stress had taken its toll.

Life was so complicated.

Eric texted:

Stay safe.

You too.

She lay in bed, relieved the painkillers had taken effect, and gazed out the fire escape. It was dark on her side of the house, and she could see stars and the glow of the moon, just out of sight. She'd been glad to get a shower, washing away the itchiness of the hay wagon, and the bed was really comfortable. She couldn't imagine the mattress had been used much, since there was no perceptible canoeing effect.

She knew it was hard on Eric, not knowing where she was, not even asking. Without sharing her location on her phone it would be impossible for Eric to track her down. Well, not impossible, but unlikely. She couldn't believe she'd found the one guy in the world willing to live this way.

"So this is nice."

Casey jumped. Death lay next to her on the bed—or hovered, if one was to be precise—wearing plaid flannel pajamas.

"Would you stop doing that? And who are you supposed to be now? Or are those regular pjs? Which, by the way, you are not using to sleep in this bed with me. Not unless you also come equipped with an electric blanket."

Death held up a finger. "First, if you have a suggestion as to how you would not be terrified each time I show up—"

"I'm not terrified. I'm startled. There's a difference."

"—I am all ears. You realize I don't make actual sound in your world, so I can't knock, although some psychics seem to think beings from my realm have that ability. Anyway, how can we keep you from being such a scaredy-cat—?"

"I'm not—"

"—Should I say, 'hey there,' or 'ding-dong,' or 'Here's Johnny?' Didn't your grandmother have a signature call when you came to visit?" Death's voice rose to a falsetto. "*Yoo-hoo! Who's come to visit me*?"

Casey glared at Death. "How about appearing in front of me instead of behind?"

"Technically, I was beside you this time. Okay, okay, don't get all huffy. I'll try harder not to freak you out, okay?"

"Freak me out? Since when do you say that?" Casey hated it when Death used current lingo.

"Since now. So, back to questions number two slash three,

about who I'm supposed to be and what's the deal with these pajamas. Don't they look familiar?"

"I've never owned men's flannel pjs. And neither did Reuben." Her late husband preferred to sleep without anything on, but she couldn't dwell on that.

"Hmm." Death looked at the clothes. "Picture them several sizes smaller."

"Smaller? For a little person?"

"In a sense. A person who is little, but will get bigger."

Casey sighed, weary of the game. "So you're supposed to be a kid."

"A boy."

"A boy in plaid pajamas. I thought they were striped."

"Oh, my Lord, not that depressing movie. Think Christmas, being abandoned by your parents…"

"*Home Alone*?"

Death jumped up, raised fists disappearing into the ceiling. "She's a winner!"

"I'm not so sure."

Death dropped back to the mattress, but it didn't bounce an inch. "What's wrong?"

Casey scooted up to sit against the headboard and hug a pillow. "Don't you feel it? Something is weird here."

"Seems like a normal room. Except for that corner over there." Death indicated the "L," with the odd collection of memorabilia.

"Not the room." Casey threw the pillow at Death, but it went right through and banked off the wall onto the floor. "This whole…situation. From the moment I showed up it's like…I don't know…like Vern was waiting for me."

"You, specifically? Or you, as in somebody he'd never seen?"

"Either, I guess. It's strange, how he latched onto me. He's giving me all this responsibility, and letting me handle money. Does he really not have any other employees?"

"The old guy—"

"Roger hardly counts."

Death's head tilted back and forth in agreement. "That *Help Wanted* sign has obviously been there a while, and he and Dottie do have this room ready for an occupant."

"Which is also weird."

"Plus, those women at lunch were no fans of Dottie."

"Then why eat lunch at her husband's place?"

Death chuckled. "Flower Pants obviously likes seeing Vern. Also, did you see any other place to eat in this town? Unless you want to make your own lunch, Vern's is the place to be."

Death had a point.

"So back to the whole people-not-liking-Dottie thing, and the waiting-for-you-to-come-along thing. Maybe Vern was just happy to see a friendly face, although I wouldn't describe you that way, the way you scold me all the time. You're more like a judgmental face."

Casey rolled her eyes. "Another oddity. Did you notice there are no photographs upstairs? No family reunions, or vacations, or anything. Do they even know anybody outside this town?"

"Dottie came from somewhere else."

"Didn't we all?"

"But most people end up going back, at least to visit. Do you think she's ever gone back to Portland?"

"Who knows? I don't have the first clue about these people, and here I am in their basement. You've got to admit it's a little creepy."

"But necessary. You couldn't keep going today, not after what happened last night."

Casey sank into the pillows. Death was right. "It still feels weird."

"You know you have a tool to do a little research on them."

"I do? Oh, my phone. Hadn't even thought about that."

"You'll get used to it. Once I got the MyPhone, I couldn't think how I'd done without it." Death smirked, then went on point, as if an alarm had sounded. “I have to go, but listen, get a good night’s sleep. You can always leave in the morning if you want. There’s nothing keeping you here.”

“I promised to work for my stay.”

“You also have money. You’re under no obligation further than that. Besides…” Death began to fade. “…there’s no way they can hunt you down. They don’t even know your last name.”

Death vanished in a puff of peppermint-scented mist.

Casey plugged in her phone, which was teetering on five percent, and went to type in the names of her new landlords. She stopped short, and felt less guilty about withholding information from them. She didn’t know their last name, either.

Chapter Eleven

It didn't matter that Death had wished her a good night, or that she'd spent time surfing the web until her eyelids drooped. After her post-supper nap, Casey couldn't sleep. She sat in the well of her fire escape with the cool air drifting through the screen, and held an ice pack to her side. Her face she didn't mind so much, but the ribs...

She hadn't found much online concerning Vern and Dottie, except for a few small articles about the store. Their last name was Daily, but that didn't help. Casey still didn't know Dottie's birth name, and without that, there was no telling which Dorothy from Portland, Oregon, she was looking for.

Casey wondered if Eric was sleeping, or if he lay awake also, eager to get home. She wondered who was running his soup kitchen while he was gone, but figured the staff was taking care of it, the group she'd met when she'd been there.

She missed him.

She missed Reuben.

She missed the smell of Omar after his bath, snuggled in her lap as they read *Goodnight Moon*, and *Are You My Mother?*

When would the pain end? Ever? Never? If it didn't, could she also feel something else? Find her own new spiritual and emotional painkiller?

Something clanked, and Casey went on alert. Not even Vern,

as energetic and busy as he seemed, should be moving around at three in the morning. Casey listened, hardly daring to breathe. The sounds weren't coming from inside the house. They were outside.

Casey closed her eyes and focused. The night became still again, until she heard rattling, and then a long hiss.

Spray paint.

Casey popped the screen from its frame and climbed into the outside portion of the fire escape. She stuck her head above ground level but could see no movement in the backyard. Climbing painfully out of the well, she padded softly toward the store in her bare feet, following the sound of the paint.

The vandal found a shadowy corner toward the back of the store, one dark circle beyond the range of the security lights. Casey saw a person-shaped silhouette there, its arm moving up and down. Casey eased toward the offender until she stood a few feet behind. Careful not to cast a shadow, she angled toward him—for it was a him, she could see that now.

With a quick step, Casey grabbed his wrist, knocking the can from his hand, and twisted his arm behind his back. A tiny nudge sent him to his knees.

"Stop! Please! Aaaaah!"

He fought, jabbing her in the ribs with his elbow. She bit back a cry and wrenched his arm higher against his back. After waiting for his screams to drop into a low moan, she reached for her phone.

But she didn't have it. She was in her T-shirt and pajama shorts. She wasn't even wearing a bra. Or underwear.

Keeping a firm grip on his arm, she patted his pockets—to his accompanying howls of displeasure—until she found the telltale shape of a phone.

"What are you—aaaah!"

Casey slid it from his pocket and dialed 911. When she'd given the dispatcher the necessary information, she punched on the flashlight app and lit his face.

To no one's surprise, she'd never seen him before.

He was in his upper teens. Dark hair, mild case of acne. Standing, he would be taller than Casey by several inches, and his body was thick in a farm boy kind of way. He would undoubtedly be stronger than she, which would counter-balance her martial arts skills, making it anybody's guess who would win a battle. The main reason she had him on the ground in an arm lock was that she'd caught him off-guard.

"Who are you?" She twisted so she could look in his eyes.

He groaned and shook his head.

Casey pulled his elbow a little higher.

"Lance! My name's Lance. Lance Victor."

She relaxed his arm. "Why are you vandalizing Vern's store?"

His eyes flicked all around, but Casey stared unwaveringly at his face.

"Tell me." She lifted his elbow.

"Ow—It was a dare, okay? A dare. That's all."

Casey spun around, still holding the boy's arm, so that her back was to the store. If Lance was acting out a dare, it was possible his friends were watching. She held him still and listened. She couldn't hear anything except the usual night sounds.

"Are you alone?"

He didn't answer.

"I said, Are? You? Alone?"

"Yes. Ouch, I said yes!"

"How were your buddies going to know you did it?"

"I was going to take a picture." His tone betrayed how stupid the question was.

But she kept going. "You don't personally have anything against the Dailys?"

"No. I mean, nothing more than anybody else."

"And what would that be, exactly?"

He shrugged, then thought better of it when she yanked his arm. "It's not him. The old guy, I mean. He's fine. But she thinks she's better than everybody else."

"And she's treated you badly?"

"No. But I've heard stuff all my life."

"Yeah, well, you can't believe everything you hear."

Casey shoved the guy's phone back into his pocket and jerked him toward the parking lot, where the cops—or, more likely, a singular cop—would find them. She plunked him onto the end of the picnic table bench, not releasing his arm. A couple of times he wrenched around, like he was trying to escape, but a not-so-gentle tug kept him seated.

Within two minutes a cruiser pulled in. Casey hadn't realized how tense she was until saw the insignia—definitely Armstrong. Not Beltmore. An officer stepped out, staying behind the car as she took in Casey, the kid, and their awkward predicament. Hand on her belt, she walked toward them, stopping a few feet away to glare at the kid.

"Lance, what the hell?"

He hung his head.

She jerked her chin, and Casey let go of Lance's arm. He whipped it around and held it against his chest. The officer didn't remark on how Casey had been holding a teenage boy on her own. In her pajamas.

"Officer Whistler," the cop said.

Would Casey have to give her personal information at the station? She took a chance on the answer being No. "Casey Brown. I'm staying with the Dailys."

Whistler nodded. "Heard about you." Rather than expanding on that, she returned her attention to the kid. "Okay, let's see what you did." She grabbed Lance's good arm and hauled him to his feet. "Which way?"

Lance didn't answer, so Casey led her—Lance in tow—toward the side of the store.

Whistler shone her flashlight at the wall. Casey had obviously interrupted Lance mid-graffiti, for it said only, "DIE BIT."

"Was that going to say what I think?" Whistler shook Lance.

"She is one," he mumbled. "And she's about dead anyway. I mean, look at her."

He was lucky the officer was there or Casey would've done more than put him in an elbow lock. She hardly knew Dottie, but you don't disrespect a dying woman.

"Why would you do this?" Whistler demanded.

Lance looked away.

"He told me it was a dare," Casey said. "Because Dottie Daily isn't a nice person."

Lance glared at her.

"Seriously, Lance?" Whistler yanked his arm. "Come on, let's go."

Casey followed them to the cruiser, where Whistler could have been gentler getting Lance into the car. She slammed the door.

"Thanks for calling. How'd you even catch him?"

"My window was open. He tripped over something, then I heard the paint."

"Good ears."

"Quiet night."

Whistler gave Casey a slight smile and rounded the hood to the driver's door.

"What will happen to him?" Casey asked.

Whistler leaned on the top of the car. "I'll call his folks. They'll come get him. They'll pay a fine. If we're lucky, he'll have to fix what he did."

"You mean paint over it?"

"I guess."

"So that means I can't do it tonight?"

She watched Casey while she thought, then pushed off the car. "Wait here a sec. Make sure he doesn't escape."

She headed back to the graffiti, and Casey saw flashes.

Whistler returned. "I got pictures. Give me a few minutes to obtain his confession, which he'll give me because he's dumb, and then you can paint over it. In fact, I'll text you, okay? His parents won't fight the charges. They realize he's a tool. Not a terrible kid, just a jerk who follows whatever his friends do."

"Thank you. Vern and Dottie shouldn't have to see this."

Whistler nodded once. Twice. "Have a good night."

"You too. Thanks."

Whistler got in the car and pulled slowly away.

Lance Victor's white face glowed eerily in the back window. He snarled, and gave Casey the finger.

Chapter Twelve

The quiet streets and unpopulated country roads would have made for easy running if Casey's ribs had cooperated. As it was, she downed another dose of painkillers, wrapped her torso with tape, and gritted her teeth. It still hurt. But she couldn't spend another day in Armstrong if she didn't get out of town for a few minutes.

Casey strapped her phone to her arm—since when had she needed that reassurance?—but chose not to listen to anything while she ran. Like most women, and every martial artist, she wanted to be able to hear what was going on in her immediate vicinity. Footsteps, cars, any threat.

Security concerns aside, she wanted to become familiar with her surroundings, including the rumble of farm machinery, farmers' voices carrying across fields, and the blare of music as a truck sped past. She felt almost a part of the place. Almost.

She returned to the house, refreshed and sweating, glad she made it through the run. Her next aim was to clear out space in the basement to perform one of the more subdued katas which her ribs could handle, before joining Vern at the store. She stopped in the kitchen for water and was surprised to hear voices coming from the living room.

"But how did it get here?"

"I don't know, Vern. I'm sorry." Dottie sounded close to tears.

Not wanting to eavesdrop, Casey headed toward the basement.

"Did you see who left this?" Vern appeared in the doorway between rooms, holding out a plain white envelope. His face was pale, and his hand shook, rattling the paper.

She looked at it. No name, no return address. "No. Where was it?"

"On the front step."

"What is it?" It wasn't Casey's business, technically, but Vern was the one bringing it to her attention.

"You're sure you don't know?" He sounded angry, and scared, and disbelieving.

"I really don't. I'm sorry."

Dottie's voice drifted in from the living room. "What did she say?"

"She doesn't know, Dot." He frowned at Casey. "You didn't put it there, did you? Someone didn't ask you to? I need to know."

Casey took a step back. "Nothing like that happened. I don't have any idea what it even is."

He tapped the envelope against his leg, watching her face, as if she would give away a secret penchant for leaving anonymous notes on doorsteps. "Never mind," he finally said. "It's... nothing."

Didn't seem like nothing, but what could Casey do? Beat it out of him?

"I was going to take a shower then head to the store. Do you need me to go over now, since you're here?"

Vern glanced at the clock. "I've only been gone a few minutes. Dottie called when she found this." He looked at the envelope again, as if seeing it fresh.

"I'll hurry," Casey said.

He went back to the living room.

Casey limped downstairs and got into the shower.

"The plot thickens."

Casey didn't jump this time as Death appeared in the misty

shower stall. She also didn't attempt to cover herself. She'd finally gotten over that impulse, realizing Death didn't care if she was naked or layered up like an Eskimo.

She wiped suds from her eyes. "Were you there? How come I didn't see you?"

"I was with Dottie. I've been getting weird vibes from her. You know she's not well, but I think the anonymous note set off warning signs. Turns out she's not dying today. But I'm telling you, this couple has something going on."

A towel surrounded Death's body while another curled on top, like a turban. If Casey were to guess, Death was dressed like the woman in *Fletch*, a movie she and Reuben had watched numerous times, laughing at each and every viewing. Casey refrained from saying she'd hit a water buffalo and needed a towel.

"They seem really spooked." Casey rinsed her hair. "And they don't even know what happened last night."

Death perked up. "What did I miss?"

Casey told the story of the teenage vandal and how she'd painted over the aborted message.

Death groaned. "I can't believe I wasn't around for that. I hate when I get left out of the good stuff..."

"It wasn't good."

"You know what I mean. Good for me. Interesting." Death ran a finger through a trail of suds on the shower stall. They crackled and froze.

Casey spit soap from her lips. "I wonder what the anonymous letter said."

"I couldn't get a look. By the time I knew something was happening other than her imminent demise, the letter was re-folded and back in the envelope." Death gave Casey a look. "You'll have to sneak a peek."

Casey turned off the shower. "It's none of my business."

"It is if they're going to accuse you of sending them hate mail. And you live here now. If something's going on, you have a right to know."

"I don't live here."

"You do. Till that goes away." Death gestured at the purplish blotch on Casey's side. "And that." Her face. When she looked in the mirror she was greeted by quite the color wheel.

Casey wrapped herself in a fluffy blue towel and went to her bedroom, where she pulled on jeans and a T-shirt. The dress code at the store was fairly lax, which was good, since she had a limited wardrobe.

Death followed, giving her what teenagers would describe as a "Mom look."

"Okay," Casey said. "If the opportunity comes up I'll find the letter, all right?"

"I think you should."

"Fine."

"Fine."

The kitchen was empty when Casey got upstairs, and everything was quiet. Casey poked her head around the corner to see that Vern had gone and Dottie's bedroom door was closed.

"So…" Death said.

Casey shook her head.

"Vern's gone, and Dottie's—"

"Would you like some breakfast?" Dottie came into the room from down the hall. "I could make you something." Dottie looked, if possible, grayer than the day before. Casey wondered if it was her health or the shock of the anonymous letter, as Death had suggested.

"I was going to grab a banana, if that's okay."

"You're sure that's enough? There's cereal. Or eggs."

"Cereal might be nice. Thank you. I told Vern I'd get to the store as soon as I could."

Dottie opened a cabinet door to reveal several cereal boxes. She grasped the door as if needing it for stability, and Casey shot over to keep her from falling. Dottie waved her away and tottered to the refrigerator. "Vern's used to working on his own.

He'll be fine while you eat something. He wouldn't want you going hungry."

Once Casey had her food Dottie settled at the table across from her with a cup of tea. Casey waited for conversation to start, but when she looked up from her bowl Dottie was staring over Casey's shoulder into the living room.

"Go on," Death said. "Grill her."

Death was now dressed like one of the characters from M*A*S*H. Colonel Potter, maybe.

Casey swallowed her bite of Shredded Wheat. "So, I understand you're not from around here?"

"Not what I meant." Death's eyes rolled.

Dottie picked at the tablecloth. "I grew up in Oregon. Portland. Right downtown. Vern came there for a business course right out of high school. We met, and...I soon moved here with him."

"Do you get back much? To Portland?"

Dottie shook her head. "I don't have anyone there. My parents are gone, and my sister lives in California. We don't really...talk much." She took a slow breath and let it out.

"Ask her about the note," Death urged.

Before she could, Dottie had taken up the questioning. "You said you're from Colorado?"

"Right."

"Do you have family?"

"My mom and brother are still there."

Dottie glanced at Casey's hand. "Not married?"

"No." There was no reason to get into the tragedy that was her life. She would soon be gone.

Casey finished her cereal and stacked her dishes in the dishwasher. "Can I get you anything before I go?"

Dottie wrapped her hand around her teacup. "No, thank you."

"You're sure?"

Dottie smiled. "You and Vern are right next door if something comes up."

True.

Casey brushed her teeth, Death nattering nonstop about how she missed her chance to find out the letter's contents. Casey fled the house and Death's scolding barrage, making it to the store in record time. The door's bell jingled, and she bumped into the woman she'd seen at the gas pumps the day before.

"Watch it!" The woman held out a cappuccino so she wouldn't spill it on herself.

"Sorry."

The woman studied her, and Casey studied her right back. Up close the woman looked older than Casey had imagined. Forties, maybe. But a fit forties.

"Aren't you the one who showed up yesterday at lunch?" the woman asked.

"That's me."

"So you sticking around, or what?"

"Thought I might for a little while. Vern gave me a job."

The woman glanced at Vern, who was obviously "not watching" Casey and the woman as he sold a customer a two-liter bottle of Mountain Lightning and a donut.

"Yeah, well," the woman said. "Good luck with that."

And she breezed out the door.

Chapter Thirteen

"Don't ask." Vern handed the cash register over to Casey.

She didn't ask. If it was important for her to know why the woman treated Vern—and Casey—with such open disdain, she'd find out sometime. If not, she would soon leave Armstrong anyway, forgetting about Vern and the woman within a day or two.

The morning crept by as she sold coffee and donuts, put together sub sandwiches, and switched out the previous day's newspapers with current issues. Casey gritted her teeth and hefted the day-olds out to the recycling bin. She gently stretched her back, hands on her hips, and looked up at the clear, blue sky.

"Who're you?"

Casey turned to see a girl, maybe eight or nine, staring up at her from the picnic table. She had bright white hair, huge brown eyes, and a smattering of freckles. Over her spidery body she wore an oversized Beck's Seed sweatshirt and jeans tucked into pink cowgirl boots. A book lay in the crook of her arm, and she ate from a pack of peanut butter crackers. Casey couldn't help but notice the hair. The girl had to be related to the woman from the train, because that glowing hair wasn't an everyday sight. Great. Would the girl think Casey was a nutcase, too?

"My name's Casey." She smiled, hoping for the best. "What's yours?"

"Nell." The girl cocked her head. "You working here now?"

"Yes." Casey glanced at her watch. Almost ten. "Shouldn't you be in school?"

Nell's brow furrowed. "It's Saturday."

"Oh." Casey laughed. "I lost track of what day it was."

"That's okay." Nell chewed on a cracker. "You like it here?"

"I guess. I haven't been here very long. Do you?"

"It's all right. Want one?" She held out her crackers.

"Thanks." Casey eased onto the bench and accepted one of the orange squares. "You live in town?"

"No. My grandpa does. Over there." She indicated somewhere to the right. "I stay with him when my mom and dad are working."

The woman with the matching hair, perhaps?

"Your grandma, too?"

Nell shook her head. "She's dead."

"Oh. Sorry."

"It's okay. I never met her. I have another grandma, though. She lives in Boise."

"How far is that?"

She wrinkled her nose. "We have to drive there." She held out her crackers, and Casey took another one.

Casey couldn't see the title of Nell's book. "What are you reading?"

Nell laid it on the table, a battered paperback which had obviously been read many times.

"*Carrie*?" That was a surprise. Casey's mother hadn't let her read Stephen King until she was in high school.

"Have you read it?" Nell asked.

"A long time ago."

"It's my favorite. Here." She handed it to Casey. "You can borrow it."

Casey opened her mouth to refuse, but recognized desperation in the girl's eyes, reminding her of Vern. "Thank you. I'll enjoy reading it again."

A movement by the gas pumps caught Casey's eye. Death peered around the corner, gesturing wildly for Casey to come over. Casey shook her head, and Death waved harder. Casey got up. "See you around?"

"Yeah. I come here a lot." She leaned toward Casey, her bright hair falling around her face. "It gets boring at Grandpa's. He mostly wants to talk about football and what he did when he was young."

"I get it."

"But we play games, too. And he makes grilled cheese."

"The best."

"Yeah." She crumpled the empty cracker pack and swung her legs over the bench. "I guess I'll go, too."

"I can throw that away if you want." Casey held out her hand.

Nell placed the empty wrapper in Casey's palm. "Thank you."

"Anytime."

Nell waved and skipped away, disappearing down the sidewalk.

Maybe Casey would have better luck with the younger generation of the town's bright white blondes.

Death took the girl's place at the picnic table, wearing an old-fashioned Sherlock Holmes hat and suit, and holding a magnifying glass.

"You couldn't walk over and tell me whatever it is?" Casey said.

"I didn't want the girl to see me. I had the feeling she would have."

"You've let people see you before."

"I didn't think it was a good idea. At least not yet."

"Okay. What was so important?"

"Now's your chance to do some detecting. Vern's at the cash register and Dottie walked down to the pharmacy."

"Why are you so interested in that letter?"

"Aren't you?"

"Not especially."

"Oh, come on."

Casey sighed. "Fine. Let me tell Vern I'm going."

Death let out a sharp laugh. "You're going to tell him what you're doing?"

"Just that I'm running back to the house. It's the responsible thing to do."

"So you're responsible now?"

"Shut up."

Casey found Vern at the deli cutting meat, which proved he wasn't always where Death thought he would be. She told him she'd be right back.

The house was quiet. After calling Dottie's name, Casey made a quick search. The letter wasn't anywhere obvious in the living room or kitchen. She didn't dig into drawers or shelves, figuring Vern or Dottie would have tossed it on top of whatever was already there, rather than shove it underneath everything. They had no idea Casey would come looking for it.

Besides, Casey didn't have the time or inclination to do a deep snoop.

"Bedroom?" Death said.

Casey wrinkled her nose. "I feel so creepy."

"You look creepy, with all your skulking around. It's no big deal. You're doing what you have to."

"Don't you have a conscience?"

"Technically, no. Go check their bedroom."

"Again, not feeling good about this."

"I'll let you know if she comes home. You won't get caught."

"That's not why I'm feeling bad."

"I know."

Casey shook her head, irritated with herself for being so nosy and with Death for encouraging her to spy. The bedroom was plain, painted off-white, with a hardwood floor and a rag rug, which made the set of old, dark wood furniture stand out. The only decoration was a folk art piece with a Bible verse. The yellowed paper and faded frame made Casey think it had been up there for quite some time.

"Well, that could be telling," Death said.

"What?"

"The verse. Did you read it?"

She hadn't. She was more interested in getting out of the bedroom as quickly as possible.

For I am convinced that neither death, nor life, nor angels, nor principalities, nor things present, nor things to come, nor powers, nor height, nor depth, nor any other created thing, will be able to separate us from the love of God, which is in Christ Jesus our Lord.
—Romans 8: 38-39

"See?" Death said. "They're worried about something."

"Or proclaiming their faith in a dark world. People do that, you know. Especially people who have been shunned by the rest of society. Or at least a town. Now be quiet and let me look for the letter."

"You do realize most people speak to me with greater respect."

"You do realize most people don't have to deal with your smart aleck comments on a daily basis."

"Ouch. Harsh, but true."

Casey took a peek in every potential hiding place—the nightstand and dresser, under the mattress, closet shelves—and found nothing. She went quickly through their master bath, the other bedroom they used as an office, and another small bathroom off the kitchen. Zilch. Zero. Nada.

"Did you check this?" Death pointed to the trash can in the kitchen.

"I thought you were watching for Dottie."

"I am. Awesome multi-tasker, remember?"

Casey lifted the lid and gave a little laugh. The letter sat on top of a banana peel and the lid from a strawberry yogurt. "Found it."

"So what's it say?"

Casey picked the paper from the trash with two fingers, trying to avoid the worst of the slime. The note was still in the envelope, but torn in two. She slid the remnants from the envelope, which said only, DOROTHY, and held the pieces together. The writing was a messy scrawl in black ink. No greeting. No signature.

A cold breath tickled Casey's neck and she shivered. "I'll read it. Back off. Watch for Dottie."

Death swooped to the window.

"*Forty-five years,*" Casey read.

"*I'm sure you remember.*

"I know what happened.

"Come clean or you'll wish you had."

Casey checked the backs of the two pieces, but there was nothing else. Forty-five years. How old would Dottie have been? "Do you know how old Dottie is?"

"Seventy-three years, three months, twenty-eight days, nine hours, thirty-two—"

"—so she would have been, what? Twenty-eight when whatever it was happened. Do you know when she moved here with Vern?"

"No idea. From what she told you, he came to Portland right out of high school, and she soon moved here with him. So she was young. Nineteen, maybe?"

"I don't think the note-writer means Dottie's move to town. She wouldn't have to 'come clean' about that. Everybody knew when Vern brought her home. What we don't know is whether or not people hated her right from the start, or whether she had a few years when people treated her with friendliness before something happened, maybe this thing forty-five years ago?"

"Dottie alert! Not here, but coming."

Casey finagled the torn pieces into the envelope and tossed the note back in the trash, but Death held out a hand. "What if you need it again?"

"Why would I? And what if they notice it's gone?"

"Take a picture of it."

Casey felt dirty, but yanked the papers back out of the envelope, snapped a quick photo, and replaced it in the trash can. She needed another shower to rinse off her guilt, but instead she dodged out the back door and ran painfully toward the store, where Vern put her to work picking through his wilted produce section and replacing it with fresh.

Chapter Fourteen

As Casey ate supper, she wondered what illness was eating away at Dottie. The multitude of pill bottles on the counter could have told her what she wanted to know, but she bristled at the thought of anyone delving into her own private health matters… she wouldn't violate someone else by doing the same. Although she had dug into the Dailys' other private spaces earlier when looking for the note.

Ethics were complicated.

Casey spelled Vern when she was done so he could eat. She wondered what he did when she wasn't around. Did he even have supper? Or lunch? Did Dottie meet him in the deli so they could eat together?

What a depressing life.

Casey didn't mind the long day. She spent a good part of it watching Vern work, which involved a lot more than she expected from the owner of a general store. He dug up a tiny screwdriver to fix a woman's glasses. He called the Methodist church to see if they would pay for a man's gas so he could get to a doctor's appointment in Boise. He filled a teenager's car tires with air, helped a mother disinfect and bandage her son's scraped knee, and handed out free sandwiches and potato salad to scrawny kids who hadn't eaten yet that day and looked like they hadn't had a bath or clean clothes for longer than that. Flower Pants, the flirty old woman from the day before, batted her eyelashes like an anxious butterfly and asked him to check the oil in her car, which he graciously did, and he sewed a button onto a working man's coveralls.

He was a man of all trades, apparently.

Every person he helped thanked him, shook his hand, or—in the case of one of the scrawny kids—gave him a hug. The people liked Vern. Casey couldn't go so far as to say they loved him, or fully appreciated how he spent so much of his day on nonprofit activities, but they treated him with respect and at least a minimum of gratitude.

Not one of them inquired after Dottie, asked how things were at home, or offered to do something in return for the service he provided.

He was out back helping a kid fix his bicycle tire when a large pickup truck pulled into the lot. For a heart-stopping moment Casey feared it was the guys from Beltmore, but the kid who hopped down from the cab was younger and redder, as if he'd been working in the field all day without sunscreen. His passenger stepped down, too, and Casey inhaled a calming breath.

It was Lance Victor, the teenage vandal from the night before.

"Well, well, well, this ought to be interesting." Death leaned on the counter, again wearing the flannel shirt, jeans, and boots which matched the incoming boys. Death, however, was also covered with a fine black dust. "That is the spray paint kid, right?"

"It is." She glanced at Death's clothes. "Where have you been? Crawling through somebody's basement?"

"Mining accident in Guatemala. Nasty business."

"Sorry."

"They're in a better place now."

Death didn't mean it as the cliché humans used, which angered Casey whenever she heard it. Death actually knew firsthand where the miners went, so Casey was more forgiving of the phrase.

The bell on the door dinged as the boys came in. Lance stopped dead when he saw Casey, causing the other guy to tread on his heels.

"Keep moving, dude," the second kid said.

"Sorry, Coop." Lance stepped sideways, his eyes on Casey as his friend walked past him into the store. "So, you're working here?"

Casey held back a sarcastic rejoinder. "I am."

"He's a smart one, ain't he?" Death said.

Casey came through with her own obvious statement. "They let you go last night, I see."

"No thanks to you."

Casey laughed. "I'd say it's no thanks to yourself, seeing how you were the one breaking the law."

"It wasn't…I only did it because of a dare."

"So you said." She remembered what the officer had told her, that Lance was a kid who unthinkingly followed his friends. Not a great quality in anyone, let alone a teen whose peers had questionable ideas of a fun night.

The door clanged and a man hurried in, checking his wallet. He glanced at Lance and held back, but Casey waved him forward. He paid for his gas and left.

Lance stayed where he was. "I don't do that kind of stuff, usually."

How should Casey respond to that? Congratulations? Good for you? Here's a gold star? She settled for, "Okay."

"One time is enough." Death looked the boy up and down. "And his boots aren't nearly as cool as mine."

"I don't even…" Lance huffed a breath out through his nose. "I don't have anything against her, Vern's wife, I mean, not like… like some people."

"And why is that?"

"She's never done anything to me."

"No. I mean, why do other people have something against

her?"

His lip curled. "How should I know?"

"Because people talk."

They stared at each other a little longer.

"You hurt my arm," he finally said.

"You hurt my ribs. And you flipped me off."

A smile flashed on his face, and Casey almost smiled back. What was wrong with her? Was she so desperate for friends she was willing to identify with a delinquent teen? Or were they actually sharing a genuinely funny moment?

Lance's friend Coop returned and dumped chips, beef jerky, and several cans of Red Bull on the counter.

Death eyed the stash. "Maybe I'll be seeing these kids sooner than I anticipated."

Lance's friend smirked. "And two packs of Camels."

"Sure." Casey smiled sweetly. "If you show me your ID."

Coop thrust out his jaw. "Vern doesn't make me."

"Oh, I doubt that. He seems like a stickler to me." She had no idea, actually, but it was the thing to say to a smart-alecky, annoying wiseass.

"Fine. Forget the smokes."

Casey rang him up. He paid with several crumpled bills that smelled like smoke. So somebody else was supplying him. At least she wouldn't have to feel guilty about it. Casey bagged his junk food and he stormed away, bumping Lance's shoulder as he passed.

"See ya around," Casey called.

Lance held the door for a moment, looking back-and-forth between Casey and his friend's truck. "Oh, I'm sure you will."

The bell dinged as the door closed behind him.

"What did he mean by that, I wonder?" Death said.

Casey wasn't sure she wanted to know.

Chapter Fifteen

When Vern came back from supper, Casey said, "So, I'm assuming you make teenagers show their IDs when they ask for cigarettes."

Vern gave a startled laugh. "Sure. I get caught selling to underage kids, I run into trouble. If not with the law, then with their parents. Well, some of them."

"That's what I thought."

"Some kids give you a hard time?"

"Nothing I couldn't handle."

"Good. Now, come with me." Vern took her out back and had her use an old-time theater popcorn popper to fill bags for the Saturday Movie Night he was hosting. The flat white side of his building, adjacent to his and Dottie's backyard and freshly painted by Casey the night before, served as the screen. Casey set up a table along the side of the yard for snacks, and people brought their lawn chairs and blankets to set up all over the grass, leaving only a zigzagging path for walking around. Casey served popcorn for fifty cents and candy bars for a dollar, while Vern sold drinks people dug out of large coolers of ice.

Flower Pants, the flirty woman Casey had seen twice now, showed up with her friend Wilma, who instead of orange was now wearing a flattering navy blue. Casey figured if the flirty chick continued popping up on this regular basis, she'd learn her actual name. But for now…

Flower Pants joined the drink line, moving up a step at a time until she stopped in front of Vern.

"Get you something to drink, ladies?"

Flower Pants did her whole blinking like there was no tomorrow thing, and smiled. She had lipstick on her front teeth, making Casey look away.

"How are you, Vernie?"

Vernie? Casey gagged, coughing to cover it.

"Doing fine," Vern said. "And you?"

"I'm feeling good. Ready for anything." She paused, but Vern just looked at her. She kept smiling. "And how's Dorothy?"

Casey snapped her head around to stare at the woman. Not because she was the first person to show interest in Vern's wife, but because it was directly after making a point about how well she herself was.

Vern's face shut down, and he worked his jaw.

Casey stepped beside him. "So, what was it you said you'd like to drink? Ma'am?"

The smile on Flower Pants' face faltered, and her friend tugged on her elbow.

"Iced tea," her friend said. "Two of them."

Casey grabbed two cans from the cooler and collected the money while Vern stood silently, his eyes on his knuckles.

"Who's next?" Casey said.

The man behind the old women cleared his throat, and Flower Pants and her friend finally shuffled away. By the time the next customer had his drink, Vern was back in working order and Casey returned to her own station.

She served a mass of giggling girls, several kindergartners who paid with pennies, and a very nice woman named Tara, who introduced herself as the Dailys' next-door neighbor and wore huge, dangly earrings. She indicated the single-story brick house on the other side of a now-barren flowerbed, and said Casey should let her know if she needed any help getting to know the town.

Hey, what do you know? A nice person.

When the rush died down and the movie started—some Disney family film—Vern sent Casey to find a place to sit. She meandered away and took a seat on Vern and Dottie's back steps, where she could see the movie but also study the crowd.

Casey counted sixty or so people—maybe seventy?—in the flickering light. It was hard to get an accurate count because people kept coming and going to get snacks or use the store's restrooms or simply change seats to join a different group. Casey recognized a handful of customers who had come into the store, but most were complete strangers. They ranged from toddlers to old folks, men, women, teenagers, kids of all ages. Some had brought dogs, in most cases better behaved than some of the children. Apparently Vern and Dottie's backyard was the place to be that night.

She thought, with a shock, that most likely one of them put that anonymous note on Vern and Dottie's doorstep.

Casey watched for anyone who looked guilty or suspicious, but seeing how she didn't know them, it was an impossible task. Flower Pants and her friend took seats close to the drinks table, directly in Vern's line of vision, although he did his best to ignore them. Casey wouldn't put it past those two to do something hurtful to Dottie, but would they do something that would also hurt Vern?

Surprisingly, the crabby cappuccino woman was there, sitting with a man Casey hadn't seen before but who could be her husband, except for the way she rolled her eyes at him. But then, maybe that meant they were married. Did the woman's irritability extend to everyone, or focus on the Dailys and anyone associated with them? And the poor guy sitting beside her.

Even Lance Victor and his angry buddy Coop were there, huddled in the far corner with several other teenagers. They weren't smoking, most likely because they'd get yelled at. She didn't trust them not to do something else stupid, though, seeing how they'd already done something dumb the night before. Besides, why would a bunch of teenagers be hanging around a family movie with all of the town's old people and children? She'd keep an eye on them.

"You're living here?" Nell, the white-haired girl from earlier in the day, stood in front of her.

Casey scooted to the side of the step and Nell plopped down beside her. She still wore the Beck's sweatshirt, jeans, and pink boots, but had added a long necklace with a bunch of charms including a knife, a book, and a unicorn.

"They have a room in their basement. I'm staying there for now."

Nell nodded, a Tootsie Pop pushing out her cheek.

"What flavor?" Casey asked.

"Root Beer. It's my favorite."

"I like sour apple."

Nell tipped her head, her bright white hair falling to the side. "Those make my mouth water."

Casey laughed, then stopped as people glared at her.

"Sorry," she breathed.

Nell giggled. "It's okay," She spoke in a stage whisper. "People get real serious about movies."

"You don't?"

"Not this kind."

"What kind do you like?"

"Scary ones."

"Right." Casey remembered the book Nell had lent her. "So who all do we have here tonight?"

"Nobody. I mean, the usual."

"But who's the usual? Is your grandpa here?"

She pointed to some older men in the back. "He's the one with suspenders. I keep telling him that's not cool, but he doesn't care."

"They usually don't. What about your folks?" Casey hadn't seen the woman with the white hair, but that didn't mean she hadn't slipped in. Assuming she actually was Nell's mother.

"Nah. They don't come. I'm staying overnight with Grandpa, so they probably went out to eat or something. Then Mom has to work tonight. She's a nurse."

Casey pointed toward the crabby woman. "Do you know who that is?"

Nell followed her finger. "That's Annie's mom."

"Annie's a friend of yours?"

"Not really. She's sitting over there." She indicated the group of giggling girls Casey had served earlier. They were Nell's age, maybe a year or two older, perched like a bunch of self-conscious cats on a blanket, where they pretended not to know a group of guys behind them watched everything they did. Casey didn't remember ever acting so silly, but she probably had. Nell, with her odd seriousness, probably hadn't.

"Do you know anything about her?" she asked.

"Annie?"

"Her mom."

"No. But Annie's grandpa died last month. She doesn't have a grandma, either. My mom says she left a really long time ago. I don't think Annie ever knew her."

"What do you mean, she left?"

Nell shrugged. "I don't know. She just…left."

Something in the movie *banged*, and the blanket girls all jumped and shrieked. The guys crossed their arms and swaggered, like they hadn't been startled by the noise or noticed the girls' reactions.

The screen door behind Casey squeaked open, and Dottie stepped out. Casey and Nell jumped up to let her down the steps. Casey offered her hand, which Dottie accepted. "Thank you. It's a little dark to be doing this." The sun had set completely now, and the sky was black. Vern had turned off the store's security lights to make it easier to view the movie, so the steps were lit only by the flickering light from the screen.

"We got you," Casey said.

But Nell had moved back, her eyes wide as Dottie moved painfully down the stairs. Casey stepped around to get a better grip on Dottie's arm, since Nell obviously didn't want to help.

Once Dottie had navigated the last step, Casey accompanied her to a sturdy lawn chair, which sat beside one other empty seat. Vern's, perhaps.

"You all right here?" Casey asked.

"Oh, yes." Dottie gave a ghost of a smile. "Go. People are watching."

Casey straightened. Sure enough, observing them were a number of people, including the group of old men, teenagers, Annie's crabby mom, and, of course, Flower Pants and her cohort, who in the movie light looked like they might belong in one of Nell's horror flicks. The only people uninterested in Casey and Dottie were parents with small children and the hormonal middle-schoolers.

Casey refrained from making a dramatic bow, and returned to sit by Nell, who had reclaimed her seat on the steps.

"Do you know her very well?" Casey asked.

"Mrs. Daily?" She leaned over to toss her empty Tootsie Pop stick into a trash can, then hugged her knees. "I see her sometimes when I come down for milk or bread for Grandpa, or get a snack. I see Mr. Daily more."

"Are your grandpa and Mr. Daily friends?"

"Everybody knows Mr. Daily."

That wasn't the same as being friends. Vern had lived most of his life in this town and probably knew the group of old guys, including Nell's grandpa, since they were kids. Did his marriage to Dottie void the friendships he should enjoy at this stage in his life? Or was Casey not seeing how things actually were, since she arrived in town a little over a day ago?

Vern ambled past and handed Casey a bag of popcorn. "Last one. Better take it while it's here."

Casey smiled up at him. "Thank you."

He handed Nell a sucker. "Root beer."

Nell took it somberly, not saying she'd just finished one. "Thank you. You always remember the kind I like."

"That's my job." He winked and walked to Dottie, where he sat in the chair beside her. No one joined them. No one walked over to say hello. Several people glanced their direction, and Flower Pants could have lit a campfire with the hatred flaring in her eyes, but Vern took Dottie's hand and ignored everyone else. How—and why—did the two of them stay in this town? There must be a reason, but Casey couldn't think of one strong enough to make up for the things she'd seen in one day.

Casey tilted the bag of popcorn toward Nell, who stuck Vern's Tootsie Pop in her pocket and took a handful. The two of them munched and watched the movie until the bag was empty, except for unpopped kernels. Nell fidgeted, obviously not riveted by what was happening on the screen.

"So what got you interested in horror?" Casey asked quietly.

Nell shrugged. "I hear stories, you know? Real life ones. I don't know if they're true or not, but I figure they could be. And horror is so much better than other stuff, like who likes who, or aliens, or whatever. Grandpa says some people enjoy being scared, because they like how it makes them feel."

"Do you?"

She rested her cheek on her knees, still pulled up to her chest. "I don't really get scared. I always know movies aren't for real, and I forget about books as soon as I stop reading. And what's there really to be scared of? We're all going to die someday."

Yeah, she definitely would be able to see Death. With Nell's interests, she and Death would be besties within moments.

Casey crinkled up the popcorn bag, earning her more glares from the people seated in front of her. "You seemed a little scared by Mrs. Daily a few minutes ago."

Nell looked at her boots and tapped the toes together. "She's got some disease or something. I know I shouldn't be weirded out by somebody being sick, but Grandpa won't tell me what's wrong with her, and she always looks so gray." She pulled out the new sucker, unwrapped it slowly, and slid it into her mouth. Once she had it wedged firmly in her cheek she pinched the wrapper into a tiny ball and threw it toward the trash can. She missed. She and Casey craned their necks to see where it landed, but it had disappeared in the grass. "If she was a vampire or serial killer or something, I could handle it because then I'd know. But this is…"

"Scary."

Nell's voice was low. "Yeah. Her hair's so thin you can see her scalp, and she walks all wobbly, like she's going to fall over if somebody touches her." She glanced at Casey. "She smells funny, too. Sort of…dead."

Casey rested her elbows on the top step. "I get it. Sickness is creepy. You don't know what it's going to do to someone."

"So you don't think I'm awful?"

"Of course not. And I'm sure Dottie—Mrs. Daily—doesn't, either."

"I think she does. She doesn't talk to me."

"She doesn't talk to many people, I don't think."

"Grandpa says she likes to keep to herself. That she always has."

"What about Vern? He talks to people all day long."

"I guess maybe when she's not around it's different."

"He's different?" Casey hadn't seen that yet.

Nell waggled her head. "I'm not sure. I think once Dottie dies it will be better. For him, I mean. People will be more comfortable."

"Because she's sick and they don't know what to say?"

"Or they just don't like her."

Casey was surprised and a little disturbed at Nell's insights, which were truer than Casey would like to admit. This nine-year-old saw things more clearly than most adults.

"Do you like Mr. Daily?" Casey asked.

Nell looked at her boots again. "He's nice to me."

Once more, she dodged the question.

"From what I can see he's nice to everybody. He's also terribly sad."

Nell blinked. "Why?"

"Wouldn't you be sad if nobody wanted to be your friend? If you helped them but they treated your wife like a stranger?"

Nell's eyes flicked toward the girls on the other side of the lawn. "Yeah, I would be sad if that happened."

Casey regarded the Dailys. Nobody paid them any attention. The nearest people were fifteen feet away. Vern and Dottie were alone, even as half the town occupied their lawn.

Nell went stiff beside Casey. "What are they doing?"

A bang rent the night. The movie screen went dark.

Chapter Sixteen

Screams rose from the crowd, some frightened, some thrilled. Children cried and laughed, and adults called for kids to "Come here!" or "Stop that!" Phone lights punctuated the darkness, making faces glow blue.

Nell didn't scream, didn't cry, didn't even seem scared. Interested, maybe, and a little excited.

"What did you see?" Casey asked.

"Those guys." She pointed toward the corner where Lance Victor's friends congregated. "One of them was pointing to something up there."

It was too dark for Casey to follow Nell's finger, but "up there" could only mean a few things, and one was a power box on a utility pole.

Casey jumped up. "Will you be okay if I check things out?"

"Sure. I'll stay here. Unless you need me to come."

Casey admired the girl's bravery, but wasn't surprised by the offer. "Thank you. Give me a few minutes first."

Using her phone as a flashlight, she made her way to Vern and Dottie.

"What happened? What's going on?" Dottie clutched Vern's arm.

"It's all right, Dot." Vern's voice was gentle. "I'll find out."

"You stay." They jumped at the sound of Casey's voice. "I'll see what I can do."

Vern's brow furrowed. "You sure?"

"Sit here with Dottie. Or maybe…why don't you take her inside?"

He rubbed his face. "Okay. Thanks. I'll stay with her. Want to go in, Dot?"

Casey skirted the back of the crowd behind the old men, making her way to the corner with the teenagers. Casey found them sitting in a tight circle, laughing and whispering. Staying on the outer rim of their phone lights, Casey listened, hoping to find out exactly why a group of teens would spend Saturday night at a family movie.

"Is he doing it?" someone said. A girl, Casey thought.

A guy answered. "He better be, since he crapped out last night."

"Can you hear it?" another asked.

They went quiet, but the rest of the crowd talked and laughed and whooped, so whatever they were listening for was either too quiet to be heard, or hadn't started yet.

Someone rushed by Casey and dropped into the group. "Did he do it?"

"Can't tell. Nice job with the lights."

"Easy reach from the roof."

One of the girls giggled. "And you didn't get electrocuted."

"Yeah." One of the guys elbowed him. "Good job not dying, Coop."

Coop. Lance Victor's lovely friend who tried to scam cigarettes that afternoon. Which meant…crap.

Casey left the teens and jogged the perimeter of the crowd, her light pointed at the ground so she could dodge toddlers and dogs. She stumbled over a picnic basket but kept going toward the front of the yard, hoping to be in time, listening hard for the sound she was expecting. She avoided a collision with two men picking their way around, and caught a few words about the electrical box, and how they might replace the fuses.

Then she heard it. The hiss of spray paint.

Casey was in the clear now, at the front of the crowd in the empty swath of grass beside the store, but she still couldn't see anything. She could smell, however. The sharp, tangy smell of paint. Should she shine her light on the vandal, or would that bring attention to what was happening? If she could stop him while it was still dark and use his can to paint over the message before those men reached the power box…

The security lights on the outside of Vern's store flicked on, and Casey hissed through her teeth. Fortunately, the lights were aimed several feet from the wall, rather than right on it, so the damage could still be handled. A shadow moved within striking distance, an arm swiping up and down. Casey breathed deeply and eased behind the kid, as she'd done the night before. This time he spun around as she arrived. Swinging his arm, he caught her on the side of the head with the paint jar. It stung, but a container of spray paint didn't hold much heft. Casey ducked a second swing and grabbed his arm. Using his momentum, she yanked him toward the ground and he landed on all fours. Casey placed a foot between his shoulder blades and shoved. He fell onto his face with a grunt. Casey wrenched the paint can from his hand and held it like a weapon, dropping her knee onto his back. "Don't move, Lance, or I will empty this can on you."

He struggled, as if to turn over. Casey grabbed his wrist, bending his hand backward toward his arm. "Don't. Move."

His head fell, forehead to the ground, and his body relaxed. Casey's didn't.

"I got it!" someone called. "Here comes the light!"

"No." Casey waved her arm. "Wait!"

The projector burst on, shooting a bright square of light against the wall, where the movie had played. The crowd, which had cheered at the return of the light, fell into a stunned silence.

The light now illuminated a different drama—Casey, a stranger to most of them, with her knee on the back of a local teenager. As background, the kid's message, which he had been able to complete this time, was displayed plainly, if not artfully.

DIE BITCH

Under the surprised scrutiny of the neighborhood, Casey relaxed her hold on Victor's wrist, but left her knee where it was, keeping him trapped. He pulled his hand under his chest and turned his face from the electrified crowd, which grew louder and louder as the moments passed.

Casey squinted through the people toward Vern and Dottie's chairs, but the light, shining full-force in her face, was blinding. She hoped, prayed, that Vern had taken Dottie inside, where she wouldn't see this most cruel of taunts.

Flower Pants sat close enough that Casey could see the smirk on her face. The old lady wasn't appalled by the disrespect shown to Dottie. She was pleased. Casey wanted to smack the expression from her face, but unfortunately she was a little busy.

Footsteps rustled in the grass, and Casey looked up at Officer Whistler. The officer propped her fists on her hips. "Looks like the three of us need to have a chat."

It wasn't a secret who had painted the words. Lance wasn't talking, and his friends had scattered, but his fingers were tipped with black, and he had a smudge on his face. Casey couldn't see how there was anything to discuss.

Whistler motioned for Casey to move. "I got him. I promise. Plus, I have backup." She indicated another cop who had arrived, huffing and puffing. His freckled, pale face, a bit haunting underneath scarecrow red hair, washed out in the bright light, but his eyes sparkled, intelligent and alert.

"So this is the woman I was telling you about." Whistler jerked her thumb toward Casey. "The one who called when genius kid here did this last night."

The new cop's eyes lingered on Casey's colorful cheek, which Casey had to assume glowed nicely in the bright lights. "Nice to meet you."

Casey nodded. "I'd shake your hand, but..."

He smiled, suddenly looking as young as the kid under Casey's knee. Casey grinned back.

Whistler nudged her partner and pointed at the wall. "Get a picture of that."

When he was done documenting the crude painting, Whistler turned toward the crowd, hand over her eyes like a salute. She squinted toward the projector. "Turn that thing off, will you? Hey!" She waved and pointed to someone in the back. "Turn it off!"

The light blinked off. Casey was left in relative blindness. She knelt a little harder into Lance's back so he wouldn't get any ideas.

"Any time now," Whistler said to Casey.

Oh. Right. Casey eased off Lance's spine and stepped away so he wouldn't try to kick her.

Casey's eyes adjusted, and she could soon make out Lance and the cops. People milled around, using their phones to light up the wall. The beams cut across Lance, still lying on the ground holding his wrist. Whistler and the other officer took one arm each and dragged him to his feet.

"Come down to the station?" she said to Casey.

"Can I check on Vern and Dottie first?"

"Sure. You know where we're located?"

Casey remembered seeing the city building on her way into town. "Brick building on the corner."

"Right." Whistler contemplated the defaced wall. "I wish we could nab the whole lot of these punks, but they've disappeared. It's just Austin and me on duty, and we've got to take care of this little creep."

Lance frowned. "Hey."

"Shut up," Austin said.

Whistler turned to Casey. "Think you can find somebody to clean this up? Nobody needs to keep it around. We have plenty of witnesses." She gazed out at the people who hung around, watching the drama unfold. "A whole community of witnesses, in fact." She raised her voice. "Go on home, everybody! Movie night's over!"

Complaints of, "But it wasn't finished!" and "It's early!" pierced the air.

"You can thank Lance here for messing up your night."

"Hey," he said again.

This time Whistler told him to shut up, although she might have added something stronger, like, "Shut the hell up, you freaking idiot."

She and Austin led the boy away, their expressions hard. Lance scowled over his shoulder at Casey, and she shook her head. *Do not test me*. The cops yanked him back around, and he was gone.

Casey relaxed her neck, swooping her chin to her chest. Who would paint over the words? She had yet to see anyone step up for this couple. She'd do it herself, using the paint left over from the night before.

A pair of black, old man shoes appeared on the ground under Casey's gaze. She lifted her head.

"I found this in the back of the store." Roger held up her can of white paint. "Should I cover up the words?"

Relief rushed through Casey, and she summoned up a smile. So at least one person had Vern and Dottie's backs. "That would be great. Thank you, Roger." When he stared blankly at her, she raised the volume and said it again.

He nodded and set the can on the grass in front of the graffiti.

"Does he need help?"

Casey looked down at a mop of bright white hair.

"You are awesome to ask, Nell. Thank you."

Nell didn't move.

"You okay?" Casey leaned over to see the girl's face.

"I feel bad."

"About what?"

"What he wrote. Because Mrs. Daily gives me the creeps."

She was honest, at least. Casey understood how the girl felt. "Sometimes we do nice things for people even if they give us the creeps."

"You do sometimes? Do nice things for creepy people?"

"Oh, yes."

Nell's lips thinned. She took a breath, then joined Roger at the wall.

Casey watched as Nell helped the old man open the can. "Your grandpa still here?"

Nell pointed toward the back, where the old guys had been. "But if he's not, he lives close."

"I'm going in the house for a minute. If you need somebody to walk you home, come knock."

"I'll be fine."

Nell had lived there long before Casey showed up, so she most likely would be fine. But she also hadn't had a night like this one. At least, Casey hoped she hadn't.

Casey wove her way through the departing crowd. The tables were still set up, but Vern had put away the candy and chips during the movie, before Lance and his friends ruined everything. The popcorn-maker still sat on a rolling cart, so Casey pulled it into the store. By the time she got back out, someone had folded up the tables and carried them inside. They'd done this before, it seemed. Just not at this high level of drama.

Casey hesitated, her hand on the screen door. Nearly everyone had left, except for a few small groups talking, and some children squealing and chasing each other in circles. Casey wasn't sure what to do. Should she wait until everyone was gone? Ask them to leave? She didn't recognize anyone except Nell's grandpa, and she only knew him because of the suspenders.

"I think you can go in. Tonight's damage has been done." Death stood beside her in a red-and-white striped Wiener Hut outfit, which would be right at home in a movie theater. The nametag read, Alfie. Casey had no idea who that was, but was sure Death could give her a whole lecture.

"You have no sense of pop culture." Death read her mind, as usual. "Supernatural? The Winchester brothers? Angels?"

Casey shook her head.

"You're hopeless."

"No, I have bigger things to think about. Did you see what happened here?"

"I did. Nasty business."

"Stupid business. Stupid kid."

"He's not alone."

"Yeah, he has stupid friends, too." Casey thought with fondness of a group of Kansas teens she'd met earlier that summer. For the most part they were kind and smart and nice. Did these Armstrong kids have those aspects, too, or were they somehow lacking?

"You checking on the Dailys?"

"Thought I should. Then I'll head to the police station."

"Want company?"

"I've been in police stations before."

"But police stations are so interesting. And I could wear a uniform."

Casey gave a big sigh and Death evaporated, this time smelling like buttered popcorn.

It was dark in the house, except for a light coming from the kitchen. Vern stared at the tabletop, his hands around a mug of what smelled like chamomile tea.

He glanced up.

"You okay? Dottie?"

He was quiet for a moment. "She didn't see it."

"Good."

"She's in bed. Rough day."

The anonymous letter, then an aborted movie night. That was hard. Vern, already a mess, didn't know it had also happened the night before.

"I'm headed to the police station. You need anything before I go?"

His head jerked up. "Why are you going there?"

"I stopped the kid. Caught him."

"But they know who did it. What will you have to add?"

"I don't know. But I said I'd come."

"You ready?" Death hovered by the front door, still in the Wiener Hut uniform.

Vern stared at the tabletop again, and Casey didn't want to interrupt his thoughts. She opened the front door and stepped outside.

"It's about time."

Casey shot her arm back into the house and flipped on the porch light.

Lance Victor's friends stood in an angry, ragged line, every one of them glaring up at her.

Chapter Seventeen

"Well, this is a fine pickle." Death proved once more that modern lingo wasn't the only language afforded immortals.

Coop stood at the center of the posse, fists clenched. Casey wished the kids had stuck around at the movie when the cops were there, so law enforcement could do the questioning.

"Who are you?" Coop barked, beating her to the whole questioning thing.

Casey sized up the group. She definitely did not want to engage. But she couldn't go back inside. The cops were expecting her. And she didn't want the kids banging on the door if she were to go through the house and out the back door. She stepped down the stairs and stood face-to-face with Coop. Three guys stood behind him, along with two girls hanging back and twisting their hair, eyeing each other. The boys were twitchy, the girls afraid, and Casey sniffed the air for the telltale scent of alcohol. She caught it.

"Whoo-eee." Death waved a hand. "That's more than beer, I'm afraid."

"My name's Casey." She ignored Death's theatrics. "What's yours?"

"What do you care? And your name doesn't answer anything. Why are you here?"

Casey held her hands at her sides, palms forward, making

herself as nonthreatening as possible. She was not going to punch the kid in the face, no matter how much she wanted to. "I'm just traveling through."

"Then why are you staying with them?" He jerked his chin toward the house.

"Why shouldn't I?"

His jaw worked. "Are you related?"

"No."

"You're sure?"

Casey laughed. "Of course I'm sure. I never saw them before yesterday. Never saw anyone from this town. Never even knew of this town."

"You don't like our town?"

Casey held her hands up by her shoulders now, palms still out, as in surrender. "I like your town fine."

"Then what do you have against Lance?"

"You mean besides him vandalizing the store twice in one day and writing horrible things about a very sick woman?"

"Sick? Yeah, she's sick." He gave a mean laugh, and the others followed suit.

"These kids have no respect for their elders," Death said. "Of which you are one, I'm afraid. Show them who's boss."

Casey took another step forward. "I need to go."

"No!" Death said.

Coop poked a finger toward her face. "You do. Away from this town."

Casey pushed down a desire to snap at his finger with her teeth. "I need to go to the police station. They're waiting for me."

"Because you attacked Lance?"

"I didn't attack Lance." She sort of did, but he deserved it. And she wasn't officially attacking. She was defending.

He looked sideways toward his buddies, who shifted, forming a tighter line.

Death drifted closer. "Watch it, sis."

Coop's lip curled. "I don't think you're going to make it to the police station."

Casey tensed. This was not looking good. For them.

"Maybe you need to be chased away." Coop leaned forward. "Or given a reason to leave." He sneered at her black eye. "Looks like someone else wanted you to take off, too."

"Yeah, but you should see the other guys."

Coop blinked. "What?"

Casey liked the idea of both being chased away and given a reason to leave, but on her terms, in a more immediate manner. She was not going to beat up these kids—even if she really wanted to and had no doubt she could. So she did what she should have done when she first saw the drunk guys in Beltmore.

She ran.

A quick step to the right took her beyond the steps and around a bush. Before the guys could react she was past them, sprinting down the sidewalk. The streetlights gave enough illumination as she dodged between some parked cars to run down the middle of the street, where she could be sure not to trip over broken concrete, forgotten toys, or the last stragglers headed home from the half-seen movie.

Yells rose up behind her, and the sound of pounding feet. She smiled. This felt good. Her aching ribs didn't even temper the joy.

The police station, being only a couple of blocks away, came into her sights within moments, and she let out a triumphant laugh. She would deliver the kids to the cops, after all.

Casey ran directly to the police station and yanked open the door. Officer Austin sat at a counter behind bulletproof glass, typing something into a computer.

"I've got a group of the kids coming," Casey yelled.

Austin jumped up and buzzed the locked door open, joining Casey outside. Coop and one of the others ran up, puffing.

"Hey, guys," Austin said, all friendly. "Come on in."

"No, we're not…we didn't…" Austin circled behind them

and held out his arms, herding them inside. Casey propped the door open, smiling sweetly. As soon as they were through and she ascertained none of the others were coming, she shut the door and allowed herself a few deep breaths.

"Now that was fun." As expected, Death dressed as a cop, but not in a uniform. More like Columbo, with the trench coat and loosened tie.

Casey pressed her side. "It was fun at the time. Now, not so much."

Death placed a hand over Casey's and the chill seeped into her ribs. She groaned with relief. "Why didn't we try this before?"

"Because you wanted to be all normal and everything."

Casey closed her eyes. Death really was better than ice, which poked, stung, and ultimately melted. At least her face had stopped hurting, and was now simply holding a fiesta on her cheek.

Death moved away. "Time to go in."

"Do I have to?"

"You're the one who agreed to it."

She entered the waiting area. Austin had disappeared behind the locked door with both boys.

Casey craned her neck, peering into the back hallway. "Shouldn't their parents be here?"

"Could be Lance and his buddies are eighteen. And Lance's parents have to be annoyed, seeing how they were here last night. Or early this morning."

The door opened, and Whistler stuck her head out. "Ready?"

Death followed as they walked past a room with raised voices.

Death chuckled. "What did I tell you? I do believe I hear annoyed parents."

"Lance's folks?" Casey asked Whistler.

The officer snorted. "How'd you guess? They were none too happy to hear what he's been up to this evening." She shook her head. "Stupid kid. Here. Have a seat." She led Casey into a small interview room with a desk and computer. Death floated along and hovered in the corner, taking in everything with manic glee.

"You good with computers?" Whistler asked.

"No. I mean, I can e-mail and Google and stuff, but that's it."

"Not a crack typist?"

Casey laughed. "Hardly."

"No problem. You talk and I'll type."

It didn't take long for Casey to make a statement which included both graffiti incidents. She gave her full name and home address, since her ID wouldn't have matched otherwise. Whistler didn't bat an eye, probably already figuring Brown wasn't the real deal.

She eyed Casey over the computer. "I don't suppose you want to say any more about why you're here?"

"Nothing really to say. I'm traveling, didn't know where I was going to go. Ended up here."

"But how? I mean, this really isn't someplace people, you know, end up."

Except for Dottie. She kind of *ended up* there.

"I took the train up from Colorado, got off when it felt right, and started walking."

"And when did that happen?" Her face, Whistler meant.

"Last night. No, two nights ago. Thursday. I stopped to sleep in a little town and some guys found me."

Whistler waited.

"I should have run, but the window of opportunity vanished pretty quickly."

"And they beat you up? No. Let me guess. They planned on assaulting you, but you took things into your own hands. They were drunk, you were not. You got the best of them and took off."

Casey went still. "What do you know?"

Whistler leaned forward, elbows on the desk, fingertips touching. "One of the Beltmore cops came by earlier asking if we'd seen you. Seems he has some questions."

Casey stayed quiet.

"I didn't give you up." Whistler smiled. "And since Austin

hadn't actually seen you yet, he could truthfully say he hadn't, either, since he's a Boy Scout and would have a hard time lying to another cop. I, on the other hand, could lie to that particular craphole every day and never feel guilty."

"You know him?"

"Oh, yes. All the cops around here do."

"What will Austin do now he's seen me?"

Whistler hit a key and the printer hummed. "Look, all us cops know what the other cops are like in surrounding towns. Most of them are good people. The force in Beltmore? Not so much. I called Wendy Justus, the only decent officer there, and asked what Craphole was going on about. She told me the story. Sounds like they've hired a new chief she's got hopes for, but so far he's reluctant to take sides without proper documentation of past bad behavior."

Exactly what Pastor Sheila had said back in the Harvest Church of Saints.

"Justus said if I saw you not to tell her anything. You know, so I don't have to lie. Now that would bring on guilt." She pulled the papers from the printer and slid them across the desk. "Take a look. If it's right, sign your name at the bottom."

"And Austin?"

Whistler shrugged. "If Officer Craphole calls or comes by asking again, Austin will send him to me. I'll do what I can to send him away unsatisfied. I can't promise anything, though. These guys may be corrupt, but they're also persistent."

Death's trench coat drooped. "Not exactly the confidence I was hoping for."

Casey pushed down her unease, and signed her name.

Chapter Eighteen

"Casey. Hey. Wake up." Death swooped low over the bed, curled in a misty, dreamlike wisp.

Casey pulled the quilt up to her chin. "Whaddo youwann?" She rolled onto her side. It had been late when she returned from the police station, and she had finally fallen into a deep slumber.

"Casey. Sleeping Beauty. I want to show you something."

A cold breeze blew over Casey, forming icicles on her eyelashes. "Stoppit."

"Then wake up."

Casey groaned, flopping onto her back and raising herself onto her elbows. Her ribs ached. She took a deep breath through her nose and blinked open her icy eyelids. "What? What couldn't wait till morning?"

"It's important. Get dressed."

Casey forced herself out from the covers. She sleepwalked through a dressing ritual, pulling a sweatshirt over her head and warm-ups over her shorts. She jammed her feet into her running shoes, then climbed out the fire escape.

Death waited in the shadows, eyes bright, clothes dark. "Ready?"

The cool night air woke Casey, and she stretched her arms toward the sky, then down to her toes. She dipped her chin to her chest, tipped her ears to her shoulders, took several deep breaths, and straightened her back. "Where are we going?"

Death didn't answer.

They set off down the sidewalk at a brisk pace, past the police department, the bank, the houses leading toward the edge of town. They kept going.

The clouds surrounding the moon shone with a silvery glow, the moon itself peeking out every few minutes, casting stark shadows. Death floated in front, leading Casey past the sleeping town. Casey shuddered, remembering the atmosphere of Beltmore only a few days earlier. Armstrong had its issues, but at least it didn't feel like a town forgotten.

"Where are we going?" Casey asked again.

Again, Death remained silent.

They continued into the country, passing a mint field, partially harvested. The sharp smell stung Casey's nose, and she marveled at how that crop became the scent and herb so many people loved. Lights pinpointed farmsteads spread across the land. Casey wondered if those families had been at the movie night fiasco, or whether they kept to themselves and let the town folks hang with their own.

After a few minutes of walking Death took a left into a beet field, leading Casey onto a well-worn track, used by machinery with wide tires. Lights from the central farm, which Casey assumed went with the field, glowed in the distance, and Casey hoped the owners weren't watching with shotguns as she trespassed. She needed her phone's flashlight now that she was off the road, but kept it pointed at the ground with her hand cupped around it.

The dry earth sent up puffs of dust, and Casey sneezed.

"Almost there," Death said.

Casey stumbled over a rock and righted herself. Death had stopped.

Casey placed her phone against her leg, shutting out the light. "What am I supposed to do? Stargaze?"

Death gestured to her feet and Casey looked down, leaking

some light from her screen. She hadn't tripped over a rock. She'd tripped over a gravestone.

Casey jerked the flashlight up to see that Death had reverted to the traditional Grim Reaper garb, a dark hooded robe and a scythe, held in skeletal fingers. No face was visible, just a dark void within the hood. Rather than being freaked out by this appearance, Casey felt mollified, like things had returned to their origins.

"We're in a graveyard? Out here?"

"From many years past." Death's voice echoed, as if spoken through a tunnel. "A generation has passed since the last soul was here laid to rest."

Casey rolled her eyes at the dramatics. "And why are we out here in the middle of the night instead of during the day?"

"This is the hour at which all secrets will be revealed."

"Seriously?"

The scythe dipped as some of the starch went out of Death's posture. "I thought it would be eerier this way." Death sounded like a disappointed child.

"Save it for Halloween."

"Which is coming up!" Death clapped, now like an excited child, ready for sugar.

"So…" Casey rolled her hand to move things along.

Death suddenly wore denim overalls and a John Deere cap. "Take a look at the gravestones. You may see a familiar name."

"Can't you just tell me?"

"It's not that big a graveyard."

"Listen, Father Time. It's late. It's dark. I've already tripped over a stone."

Death stepped back, arms crossed.

"Fine. But if I get shot, it's your fault." Casey swung her light in front of her. A small plot lay spread out before her, maybe a dozen graves across, with as many deep. She ignored the sleep itching at her eyelids, and began with the stone at her feet. Beverly

Adams, 1901-1954. She walked up and down the rows, skipping the stones with illegible markings, and ones which had fallen on their faces. A breeze started and she glared at Death, who hummed "Memory" from Cats. Casey zipped up her sweatshirt and kept on. Lots of local names, or at least, groupings of names. Gifford and Dryden. Ochoa and Barrios.

Finally, in the second to last row, she halted in surprise. "Daily? As in Vern and Dottie Daily?"

"As in."

Casey squatted by the stone, which sat to the side of a larger family one. Angels had been carved into the granite, and there was only one date. June 2, 1964. Above it loomed the name, Anne Marie Daily. Underneath, in cursive script, *Beloved daughter of Vernon and Dorothy Daily. Born into Heaven.*

Casey groaned. The epitaph was a phrase meant for stillborn children. How awful. She knew what it felt like to lose a child. But the Dailys had never gotten to know their daughter. Would that be harder than losing one in later years? Or easier? Or was it unfair to compare two unthinkable scenarios?

She placed her hand on the child's name. "Do you know what happened?"

"Dorothy contracted the German measles while Anne Marie was *in utero*, which caused complications. She died a week before her due date. I came and got her myself. I don't like the young ones to be afraid."

Casey swallowed. Death came personally to retrieve Omar, as well. That's how they first got acquainted. "And the Dailys—they never tried to have more children?"

"I'm not privy to everyone's thoughts. But you can see they don't have any."

This explained the haze of sorrow Casey felt the first time she entered the Dailys' house. It wasn't just Dottie's illness, but a black emotional void. How do you get over the loss of a child? If anyone anywhere knew the answer, Casey certainly hadn't heard it.

Casey stood, her heart heavy. "No wonder Dottie's bitter. No wonder they don't have any family photos." She stared blankly at the house across the field, the lights shining. "Wait. Their baby died in 1964? How old would Dorothy have been?"

"Nineteen."

"Wow. So young. Wait. She met Vern in Portland the summer right after high school, right? If she was only nineteen when the baby died, it was conceived that summer. Before they were married."

"That happens."

"I'm not judging. But back then was different. People weren't so forgiving of teens making mistakes. She did say she and her sister don't speak. Think it was because of this?"

Death swirled suddenly in a circle, back in Reaper gear, robes billowing. The displaced air smelled hot, like singed hair.

"What's wrong?"

Death didn't answer, and the circle grew larger, larger, until Casey was in the midst of it, lost in the churning darkness, growing colder. She wrapped her arms around herself. "Ankou? What are you doing?"

The circle of Death encompassed the entire cemetery now in a suffocating whirlwind. Casey's hair blew around her face, whipping her eyes and cheeks, blowing into her mouth.

And then the storm grew an eye, like a hurricane, expanding from the middle, blowing past Casey to the edge of the cemetery, until it exploded, silently, into nothingness.

Casey's breath came fast and loud, and she collapsed onto the ground. "Ankou? Azrael?"

Death appeared where the storm had begun, hunched in the Reaper robes, face a black hole, voice echoing. "Something is not right here."

"Something with the graves? The names? Dates?"

"I do not know."

The night lay still around them, even the insects silent.

"I do not know," Death said again.

Casey shivered, chilled from Death's disturbance. "What do we need to do?"

Death's tension dissipated, until the robes ceased their whirling and hung in suspended tension.

"You're okay now?"

But Death's aura had become even darker than usual. Deep… and dark…and ageless.

"Santa Muerte?" Casey's voice dropped to a whisper.

Something cold and ancient seeped from the place where Death's face should be. "I am not okay. But I'm not sure why."

"What can I do?"

Death's robes swished and straightened one more time.

"Simply come. Come, my love. It's time to go home now."

"No," Casey said. "Armstrong is not home."

"I didn't say it was."

Casey peered up at Death. Had Death become home? Was that why she was here, in the bone-numbing darkness, shivering under the onslaught of fear and uncertainty and doubt? She considered the setting, where once more she found herself among the dead, her only companion the one who literally was at home among graves and tombstones and corpses.

She tipped onto her back and gazed at the moon, hidden now behind the clouds. Why couldn't she find her way among the living? Why was this world, whether here in the cemetery or at home in Colorado, so full of pain and regret, why was it the only place she could discover? All it did was hold her back, hold her hostage, hold her down.

"Casey?" Death's robes fluttered over her. "It's time to move on."

Casey closed her eyes and took a deep breath. She held it until she began to feel dizzy, then let it out. When she thought she could stand, she rose to her feet and made her way down the track toward the road.

Chapter Nineteen

She was halfway to town when she heard the car. Death left without explanation several minutes before, so she had no advance warning of upcoming traffic. She was immediately taken back to the night in Beltmore and scanned the landscape for a hiding place, but there was nothing. No trees. No deep ditches. Not even a crop high and thick enough to hide her. She prepared herself to run.

"Casey?"

A cop car pulled up beside her. Casey kept walking until she was even with the driver's door. "Hey, Officer."

Whistler looked behind Casey, as if expecting to see someone else. "What are you doing way out here?"

"Couldn't sleep."

"Again? Isn't that why you caught Lance that first night?"

Casey didn't tell her that this time it was Death's doing. "Adrenalin was a little out of whack after what happened at the movie."

"Yeah." Whistler tapped her thigh. "Want a ride?"

"Sure."

Whistler leaned across to open the passenger door, and Casey rounded the hood of the car and slid in. Whistler eased back onto the road, driving slowly toward town.

"What about you? What brought you out this way?"

"Nothing exciting." Whistler snorted. "Unless you like this sort of thing. Some cows got loose and I had to help round them up."

"That's in your job description?"

"Everything's in the job description of a country cop. Cats up trees, keys locked in cars, one woman even called when her microwave stopped working."

Casey laughed.

"Of course there's all the usual stuff. Underage drinking, strange noises people think are burglars, cars breaking down. You never know from one night to the next. Keeps it interesting."

"I bet." They rode in silence for a bit until Casey said, "You know anything about a cemetery out this way?"

The officer raised her eyebrows. "You mean the old Raglund plots?"

"Don't know what they're called."

"Out in the middle of the beet field?"

"Down a tractor trail."

Whistler studied her in the dim light of the dash. "Is that where you were? How did you find it?"

She couldn't exactly tell her that. "Research."

"You're interested in graveyards?"

With Death as her companion, it did make sense. "I guess. Kind of. I saw a name there that interested me, for sure."

"Barrios?"

"No, Daily." Who was Barrios?

"Ah." Whistler checked her mirror and settled into her seat. "Vern and Dottie's baby, right?"

"So sad."

"From what I hear they've never gotten over it. At least, she hasn't. Did they tell you about it?"

"No."

"One of those unusual things, the German measles, even then. Mrs. Daily was unlucky, I guess, and the baby died." She shook her head. "Can't imagine losing a child."

Casey looked at the passing fields, the moon out in more strength now, casting its otherworldly light over the earth.

It was quiet for a minute before Whistler said, "Lots of interesting stories in that graveyard."

"Yeah?"

"It's old, you know. Newest graves in there are from forty or fifty years ago, and it goes back way farther than that. 1800s. Maybe earlier."

Some of those stones Casey couldn't read.

"So there's a husband and wife killed in a flood, a man caught in an auger—pretty gruesome, an unnamed man traveling through a hundred years ago…" She glanced at Casey. "He didn't speak English and died of some unfamiliar disease. The Dailys' baby isn't the only infant. That used to be a lot more common.

"Vern's got other family in there, too, since he grew up here. Both his parents. His mom died when I was a kid, but his dad's been gone a long time. The same year as the baby. Maybe a couple months later."

Casey had seen the family grave, but hadn't thought about it once she saw the baby's marker. Thinking about Vern's dad made her angry, the way he decided for them the way their lives would play out.

They reached the edge of town and Whistler slowed even more, until they were barely crawling. "But the best story… well, the most mysterious and weird, was from right before that cemetery was closed. The last person to be buried there was a woman who died at a Halloween party. That's the Barrios I thought you were talking about earlier."

Where was Death? This was right up Death's alley.

"I wasn't born yet, but my aunt told me, and every once in a while it comes up. Especially with that generation, you know, the older ones." She turned a corner, the opposite direction of the Dailys', her hand draped over the steering wheel. "When you were at the graveyard, did you look around for lights? Homesteads?"

"Sure. Saw a few."

"The closest one, to the east, did you see that?"

"Yeah. I figured they were the ones who own the field."

"They do. They're the next generation. The woman there at the time, the wife, she hosted the Halloween party. Invited all the women from the town—well, the ones in her age range, which was young mothers—to come in costume. Two people crashed the party, tied the women up, and threatened to set the house on fire."

"Holy crap. Did they?"

"No, but it didn't matter. The Barrios woman was so freaked out she had an anxiety attack and died."

"Are you serious?"

"Crazy, right? Another woman pissed her pants, and legend has it she wished she would've been the one to die, instead, she was so embarrassed. Can you imagine?"

Wanting to be dead? Peeing her pants? Threatening a group of women with imminent death? Casey could imagine the first and second, but definitely not the third. "Who were the people who crashed the party?"

"They wore masks. From what my aunt says, people had their suspicions, but no one was ever charged for it."

Casey would have to ask Death for details. Unless one of Death's faithful yamadutas had taken care of it, then Death might not know. There would have been plenty of mischief and mayhem going on that night all over the country, seeing how it was Halloween. Death would have been busy.

Whistler rounded another corner, glancing at the dark houses. "The woman who hosted the party was going through a nasty divorce, trying to keep her husband from gaining custody of the children, wanting to keep the house. So people said maybe he was going to burn the house down so she couldn't have it. He was mortified people thought he would kill all those women. From what I hear, he never recovered from the accusations.

"Another woman's husband was known as a groundhog. Whenever land came up for sale he snatched it before anybody else had a chance. He couldn't even farm it all, he had so much. Some people thought it was in retaliation for that, since his wife was there and he adored her. He's dead now, so there's no interviewing him, even if they wanted to."

"What about the women? Or did people only blame the husbands?"

"One was having an affair with a married man from another town. People thought maybe his wife came after her, or he himself was trying to break it off." She shook her head. "You look at this town and think everybody's so normal, but it's like anywhere. Look too deep and you find something rotten."

"Has anyone tried to bring back the case?"

"Not for years. Like the groundhog, there were others who passed away. The farther we get from it, the fewer people can answer questions."

"And they never narrowed the investigation down to any of those suspects?"

"Nope. But that didn't mean people didn't cast blame. That kind of stuff takes root, you know? People suspect others, or make comments, and they can never really forget what so-and-so said, or what might have happened. It's sad. And annoying, too, that people are ready to believe whatever somebody says."

She slowed as they approached the intersection. "The couple getting divorced split, and the husband moved away because so many people suspected him. The woman having the affair got dumped by both her husband and her lover, and ended up moving to San Francisco with another woman." She sighed. "People in this town can make your life hell if you let them."

Whistler took Casey past a few blocks of nice, mid-range houses, then made a right, where they met up with Main Street. Whistler stopped at the Dailys. "Thanks again for catching the boys tonight."

"Glad to help." Casey hesitated. "So were your predictions right about what happened to Lance last night?"

"Of course. Nobody wants to make these kids face the music." She barked a laugh. "I'm barely out of being a kid myself, but come on. Even after tonight, Lance's parents yelled at him for a while, then asked if they could take him home. They were madder about having to come into town again than what he painted on the store." She sighed. "We'll see if Vern will press charges or not. If he doesn't..." She shrugged. "And the other kids, the ones who encouraged him to do it, what can I charge them with? Being a dick?"

"Isn't there an accomplice charge?"

"Sure, but first we've got to prove it, and how is that going to happen? We dusted the fusebox for fingerprints, but it's such a mess it was useless. Somebody's gotta make these kids treat other people with respect. If their parents don't do it, who will?"

"You're doing your best."

She rubbed her hands on the steering wheel. "Am I?"

Casey waited for more, but when none came she opened her door. "Thanks for the lift."

"Any time. Give me a call if you need me. You've got my number."

Casey shut the door, and the cruiser eased away.

"Well." Death spoke from behind her. "Have I got a story for you."

Casey waited until she was back in her room—by way of the fire escape—and under the covers before responding to Death's prompt. Her ribs ached and her face tingled, which she hoped meant the healing had begun in earnest. "Okay. What story do you want to tell me?"

Death jumped onto the bed, making no bounce, wearing girls' pink pajamas with a red scarf, and long, dark hair pulled back in a ponytail. Again, a reference Casey was sure she should get, but didn't. For some reason, Jennifer Garner came to mind.

Some movie about turning back into a child? Casey wasn't sure. And she didn't care.

"My story could fit in the timeframe of the anonymous note. Forty-five years ago this woman, Wilma Adams, had a Halloween party to which she invited all of the young married women in the town, and right in the middle of the party—

"—two people tied them up and threatened to burn the house down. One woman died, and one woman wet her pants, which, apparently, is a fate worse than death." She gave a muffled laugh. "Isn't it nice to know you rank higher than excrement?"

Death's mouth turned down. "You sure know how to spoil a person's fun. And wasn't that cop saying something about showing people respect?"

Casey rolled onto her side and plumped her pillow. "You're not a person. And you shouldn't be eavesdropping on conversations when I don't know you're there."

"Fine. Anyway, what if this party is the thing the note was talking about?"

"What part would you think Dottie played in it? Frightened party-goer? Masked intruder? Caterer?"

"I don't know. Maybe she's the one who told everyone the other woman peed her pants."

"Definitely something to blackball someone for, with consequences lasting half a century."

"You women keep grudges for the longest time. Ask me some of the things I've seen."

"What do you mean, 'you women'? Look at what you're wearing right now."

"You just said I'm not a person. And being a 'not person' means I can be whatever I want, so for now I can say 'you women.'"

"Fine. But just so you know, men don't keep grudges because they kill whatever offends them. That's how wars get started."

"You don't have to tell me that. I know how they start and how they end. It's never for a reason that makes any logical sense."

"Mmphf," Casey said into her pillow.

"Go on, ask me," Death said.

Casey didn't respond.

"Ask me some of the things I've seen."

Casey closed her eyes. "I'm tired. Go away."

"You sure?"

Casey snored. It was fake, but she made it sound real.

"Okay. I can take a hint."

"Can you?"

Death harumphfed and disappeared.

This time, Death let Casey sleep until morning.

Chapter Twenty

After the interrupted night, Casey slept until seven-thirty, when a headache woke her. She wasn't usually a late sleeper, but could have used more before getting up for her run. Despite her head, she enjoyed the quiet stillness of the morning. She suspected most people in the town took the day off, using it for church and rest and family activities. She breathed in the fresh air and marveled at how the crops had changed in two days. After the first mile, her headache dissipated, and she sped up to her usual pace.

Vern told her that "of course" he would have his store open on Sunday, because apparently he didn't believe in days off. He wouldn't open until noon, at least, when people would be heading home after services.

Casey got in her miles and was performing a *kata* in the Dailys' basement when the stairs creaked. She paused in a crouch, watching as Vern's feet, then legs, then the rest of him appeared.

"We'll be leaving for church in a few minutes." He ducked his head below the ceiling to look at her. "We'd love to have you join us."

"You should." Death hunkered beside her, wearing a matching *dobak*. "You can't ignore God forever."

"I'm not ready," Casey said.

Vern waved that aside. "Nothing really starts for a half hour yet. For now it's coffee and snacks. We usually go over at nine-thirty, to avoid the crowd."

Casey bet they did. "I'll finish here, and then I'll see."

"It would be really great if you came."

Casey wasn't so sure. "Which church is it?"

"White one on the corner, with the yellow mums. Methodist."

"You go on. Maybe I'll meet you there."

He hesitated, then went back upstairs.

Death straightened, ready to speak.

"I am not ignoring God," Casey said.

Death's lips pursed. "Glad you can fool yourself so easily."

Casey finished her routine, kicking, rolling, punching. By the time she was done perspiration dripped from her chin. Death lounged on the exercise bike, drinking from a bottle of Purely Angelic H2O. Casey stalked to the shower to rinse off her sweat and irritation. When she came out, Death was sitting in the chair in her bedroom, wearing a black suit and shiny shoes, reading a newspaper entitled *Heavenly Happenings*.

Casey stood in her underwear. "I don't have church clothes."

"Don't think Vern cares." Death didn't look up from the paper. "I know God doesn't."

Casey let her chin fall to her chest, and her shoulders slumped.

"It would be nice for the Dailys to be accompanied by a friendly face."

"Azrael, they've been doing this for years. It's not like they're heading into a new situation."

"Except someone sent them that bitter anonymous note."

"What is anybody going to do at church? It's not like they're going to attack them in front of a whole congregation."

"Maybe not physically." Death peered over the paper.

"You're right. You're right! Fine. Church can be a nest of gossip, and the note-writer did say the Dailys needed to come clean or they'll wish they had. But wouldn't they give them more than a day to fess up to whatever it is?"

"That's the problem with an anonymous note. You can't discuss it."

Casey shuffled through her clothes to find something presentable. She picked her darkest jeans and a plain blue T-shirt. Her running shoes would have to do.

"You don't think they'll use the service as a way to come clean, do you? Like during sharing time? I really don't want to be there for that."

"Vern sounded desperate for company. Maybe he needs moral support."

"From someone he's known two days?"

"Honey, look at this room. It's beautiful and perfect and completely clean. Why? Were they waiting for you?"

"It sounds so creepy when you say it like that."

"It is a creepy. But also sad. They lost a daughter. Maybe they're looking for someone to fill a part of that empty space." Death let the paper fall flat. "And you know something about that."

Casey placed her hand on her stomach, which suddenly felt hollow. "I don't want to go to church."

"Okay." Death lifted the paper. "Don't know what you're going to do, though. Play games on your phone? A little Mario? Some FIFA?"

"I don't—"

"What was that?"

Casey listened. A tone sounded.

"It's the doorbell," Death said. "I guess you'd better answer it."

Just as Casey didn't want to go to church, she also didn't want to answer the door in someone else's house. But Death wouldn't let her hear the end of it if she showed fear of a simple doorbell. Death also wouldn't accompany her upstairs, and that wasn't doing anything to discourage her hesitation.

She leaned over the kitchen sink to peek through the window, but couldn't see the steps from that angle. She could see a man on the sidewalk, however. An old man, with suspenders. Ah. No wonder Death wouldn't join her.

Casey opened the door. "Nell?"

The girl let out a *whoosh* of air, and her face relaxed. She glanced behind Casey, as if afraid of who else might show up. She wore a denim dress this time, with the same pink cowgirl boots. The charm necklace hung around her neck, and her white hair was freshly washed, still a bit damp.

Nell's grandpa stood out by the street, one hand holding a Bible, the other with a thumb hooked on a belt loop. Casey didn't know if he was letting Nell have her moment, or if he didn't want to get too close to the house.

"What's up?" Casey asked.

"Grandpa said we could invite you to church. I mean, if you want to go. Do you want to go?"

Casey couldn't tell the girl how she really felt about going to church, so she tried to get out of it another way. "Which one do you attend? Because I told Vern and Dottie I'd go with them." If Nell went to the brick church, Casey was free.

"The white one on the corner."

So much for that.

"Actually, I was getting ready to go." Casey tried not to sound disappointed. "If you'll give me a minute..."

"What about Mr. And Mrs. Daily?"

"I'm meeting them there."

Nell's eyes lit up. "We'll wait for you."

Casey ran back down to her room to grab her phone. Death now had a cup of coffee in addition to the newspaper. A hint of hazelnut wafted past Casey's nose.

"Thanks for the heads-up."

Death took a sip. "Didn't know you needed one to talk with a nine-year-old girl. You're turning into quite the Nervous Nellie." Death chuckled. "See what I did there? Nellie? Nell?"

"Yes. You're quite the wordsmith."

"Go on, then. I'll see you after church." Death gave Casey a parental look over the reading glasses. "Don't forget to talk to God while you're there."

Casey stepped to go out the fire escape before realizing Nell and her grandpa might find it a bit odd. Well, her grandpa would, at least. She went upstairs and met Nell on the stoop, like a normal person.

Nell grabbed her wrist. "Come on."

When they got to the sidewalk, Nell's grandpa held out his hand. "Name's Bill."

Casey shook his hand and introduced herself. "Nice to meet you."

"Let's go!" Nell said.

Her grandpa chuckled. "We're coming, Nellie."

The three of them headed toward the church, Nell skipping in front. Casey was left with her grandpa, and no clue what to say. She could imagine Death's frustration with her lack of social graces.

"So, Nell says you're on a walkabout." Nell's grandpa stepped into the breach.

Casey laughed. "Did she get that term from one of her books?"

"Walkabout?" He smiled. "No, that's all me. Spent some time in Australia back in my younger years. Peace Corps."

They walked on in silence, which wasn't quite so tense now he'd broken it. But something felt off. Not with him, though. Or with Nell. Casey glanced behind her, but the sidewalk was empty. Cars lined the street, some with passengers, some empty. Nothing moved outside of the vehicles, except for leaves rattling in the breeze.

"Everything okay?" Bill asked.

"I'm not sure."

He stopped. "What is it?"

"I don't know. I felt like somebody was watching."

"You saw someone?"

"No, I—" How to explain? She couldn't, not really.

They waited a few seconds, but no one appeared suspicious. People got out of their cars, hustling to make the service on time, some worried, some debating whose fault it was they were late, some acting like it was the weekly routine.

"I'm probably imagining things." But she doubted it.

Nell was way ahead, jumping from side to side over a crack in the sidewalk. When they reached her, she pointed at the ground. "You have to step over it."

Casey did. "Anything else?"

"No. That's it." Nell skipped ahead again.

Casey laughed, and they continued walking. "So, did you grow up here?"

"Born and raised. Except for that time with the Aussies I've been here, or close by, my whole life. Worked in Boise at an engineering firm, but the wife and I didn't like the city for living. We brought our kids here, where we'd both grown up. Had to flip a coin to decide which church to attend, since she went to one, and I went to the other."

"And who won the coin toss?"

"We ended up at her church. Which means we both won." He grinned. "My whole family was there. Still is, although I'm on the older end of it now. Her family's not as big as mine, so her church had a little more variety."

Casey didn't understand what it meant to be surrounded by family. She never had much contact with cousins or aunts and uncles, since her extended clan lived in another state altogether. Her grandparents would visit, or she and her family would travel to see them, but her parents had met on a mission trip to Haiti, and decided to split the difference between their families and settle on Colorado when they married. Casey wasn't sure if they regretted that, but it was the way things were.

"So, if you've been here most of your life, you must know Vern and Dottie pretty well. "

He didn't answer for a few seconds. When he did, his voice sounded strained. "Vern, yes. Dottie, not so much."

"Why is that? Hasn't she lived here for fifty years?"

"She has, but…she came from a very different place, and her marriage to Vern was quite sudden. She never quite fit in."

Was that her fault? Or had the town closed ranks?

"You're thinking we mustn't have been very hospitable. That could be part of it, but some of us tried."

"She wasn't receptive?"

He frowned. "It's hard to know. Vern, I've always gotten along with. We played football together back in the day. The women would have been the ones trying with his wife, after he brought her here. My own wife would have been the one to ask, not me."

"Nell says she's no longer living?"

He nodded.

Casey sensed his reluctance to talk about it, and was spared coming up with more to say, since they'd reached the church. They were the last people to arrive, if the cars parked along the curb and the empty front steps were any indication. Even the people she'd seen down the street were inside.

"There you are!" Vern waited in the foyer. His eyes flicked to Bill, but he smiled at Nell. "Good morning."

"Hi." Her eyes were wide as she looked behind him.

"Dot's waiting in the sanctuary. Not feeling the best. You ready?"

"Okay if I sit with them?" Casey asked Nell. "They did invite me first."

Nell looked up at her grandfather. "Can I sit with Casey, Poppy?"

Casey didn't think Nell was aware of the sudden tension. Vern stared at the floor, his jaw bunched.

Nell's grandpa gazed at her for a moment before saying, "So, Vern, is there room on your bench for two more?"

Vern met his eyes, his stance softening. "Sure. Sure there is."

Bill nodded, and the four of them moved toward the door to the sanctuary. Bill gestured for Casey to go ahead of him and Nell, and she took a bulletin from the usher, following Vern. He slipped into the very back bench, where Dottie sat in the center. She smiled up at him, and then Casey, but the smile froze when she saw the other two.

The eyes of the back half of the congregation were on them, too. Nell seemed not to notice—or care—but her grandpa moved stiffly. He sat ramrod straight, eyes forward, gazing over the top of the crowd toward the pulpit.

"What are they doing?" Dottie asked, loud enough Casey could hear. "It's a little late, isn't it?"

He patted her knee. "Casey brought them."

It was actually the other way around, but Casey wasn't going to argue with a conversation she wasn't part of.

Dottie's hands clenched, her fragile fingers reminiscent of a bird's wings, which could be broken with a single touch. Her emotions were probably just as delicate after fifty years of whatever this town had done to her.

Casey hoped she wasn't going to see a display of any of that while she sat there, trapped like a rat in a cage, in the middle of a church pew.

Chapter Twenty-one

Despite Casey's fears, the service ended up being your typical Christian hour. Hymns, prayers, scripture, a sermon. A few things caught her attention—in good ways and bad—but mostly she let her mind wander, as well as her eyes.

Flower Pants and her friend were there, far enough forward that FP couldn't flirt with Vern. The crabby cappuccino woman sat on the outside aisle halfway up, along with her daughter Annie and the man Casey supposed was—or wasn't—her husband. Officer Whistler filled out the row across the aisle from Nell's grandpa, beside Officer Austin, his hair slicked back and his cheeks rosy. Roger, freed from Vern's cash register, snuck in during the first hymn and sat beside Dottie, which pleased Casey. Other than those few Casey could name—or at least nickname—many of Vern's other customers were scattered throughout the room. Even Lance Victor was there, sandwiched by his parents. He spent most of the service with his eyes cast down and his neck and face red, as if assuming everyone in the church was judging him. Casey wasn't sure how many of the congregants even cared about what he had done, but she hoped the theme of the morning—loving your neighbor—made an impression on him. She doubted it would.

Nell sat close, her boot against Casey's sneaker, her shoulder brushing Casey's. Casey didn't mind. Having the trust—or admiration—of a child was something you couldn't force. It felt…nice.

Neither Vern nor Dottie stood up during sharing time to confess their sins from forty-five years ago. Casey watched the people seated around them for any sign they were waiting for some kind of reckoning, but no one turned around or made awkward eye contact, or even seemed to be thinking about the people in Casey's row.

Before she knew it the final hymn was being sung. Casey stood with the rest of the congregation, but as soon as the music began, Vern and Dottie gathered their things and made to leave.

"We're heading home," Vern whispered. "You coming?"

Casey had no desire to stick around. "Be right there." She leaned down to Nell. "I guess we're going. Thanks for inviting me, and sitting beside me."

Nell frowned. "But it's not over. And there's Sunday School."

"I think Mr. And Mrs. Daily need to get home so he can open the store in time for everyone who needs it. I should help him."

"But you're not supposed to work on Sunday."

"But what would somebody do who needs to get gas, or forgot to buy hamburger buns for lunch? I'll see you soon. I promise."

"All right. Bye." She shifted her boot away from Casey and turned toward her grandpa. Casey hoped she hadn't irreparably damaged their new friendship. Nell looked back over her shoulder and shot Casey a grin.

Casey grinned back and excused herself as she scooted past Roger. He blinked up at her and she hesitated for a moment, wondering if he was going to be all right on his own. But then, he had gotten there on his own, so he should be able to do the reverse. She blinked back at him and exited to the lobby, past the usher.

Vern and Dottie had already left. As soon as Casey was alone in the hallway, her skin prickled. Someone was there. Something in the air felt…still. She held her breath and listened. It was too silent, as if she weren't the only one trying to be invisible. She studied the hallway and saw it—a shadow around the corner by the front door. A big shadow.

"Beware." Death hissed. "A foe awaits." Death was dressed in Uma Thurman's shiny yellow body suit from *Kill Bill*, one of the few movie references Casey was likely to get.

"How do you know they're waiting for me? Maybe they're just waiting for the service to be over."

Death's eyes widened. "Spidey-senses."

Casey nodded. She had also gotten chills when she saw the shadow, and felt watched as she'd walked to church. She hadn't been imagining things.

"Who is it?"

"No one I've seen before, or noticed, anyway."

"A guy?"

"Yes. A large one."

The shadow moved, but remained on the other side of the wall.

Casey spied another door at the far end of the hallway and trotted toward it. When she looked back, there still wasn't anyone visible, so she hustled outside. The door spit her onto a side street. Cars were parked all along the curb, as they had been in the front.

"Back way?" Death said.

"No. I'd rather see who it is and have him in front of me when I choose, than when he chooses."

"How right you are. It's all about control."

Casey rounded the corner toward the front of the church and stopped, causing Death to pass through her. She shivered.

"That's a big-ass truck," Death said.

Casey frowned at the vernacular, but had to agree. A rash of goosebumps raced over her skin. "Is it the truck from Beltmore? Is the guy one of the three drunks?"

Death swooped to the truck, then blew back. "Not the same license plate. If it were one of those guys, I'd recognize him. This one is different. It might not even be his truck."

"It wasn't here when we arrived, and we were the last to get here, other than Roger, and I can't see him driving that."

"Okay. So it's probably the guy's. What are you going to do?"

Casey strode up the front sidewalk until she could see the man through the glass front doors. He saw her, gave a start, and came out onto the steps. He was big, but definitely not Crash. This guy was in his forties, freshly shaven, wearing a crisp suit. He also didn't reek of cheap beer.

Casey looked up at him, her arms relaxed, breath even. "You looking for me?"

He squinted toward her, the sun in his eyes. "Are you Casey Maldonado?"

"I am."

He came down the steps. Casey backed up to leave a good ten feet between them.

He held up his hands. "I didn't come to cause trouble."

"Who are you?"

"My name is Will Spears. I'm the Chief of Police in Beltmore."

"Ah," Death said. "The new guy who didn't want to think badly of his officers before having a chance to catch them himself. Maybe he's starting to see what douches they are, after all."

Casey had a hard time not glaring at Death. The Grim Reaper was not supposed to sound like a teenager. But Death was right.

Casey studied the cop. Pastor Sheila had wondered aloud what kind of chief would come to an armpit of a town like Beltmore, and had ventured a guess he was escaping some kind of scandal. Looking at him, Casey couldn't see it. At least not on the surface. He reeked of seriousness, his mouth firm and his movements measured. But his eyes were bookended by laugh lines, and his stance respectful and watchful, but not intimidating.

He still held his hands in a non-threatening pose. His eyes wandered over the blooming bruise on her face. "I was wondering if I might have a word with you about Thursday night."

"A word?" Death scoffed. "How about many words? I'd be glad to offer them."

Instead of answering Casey said, "Did you follow me to church?"

"No. Although I did see you arrive. I checked at the Dailys' home first, but you'd already gone."

So her own Spidey-senses hadn't deserted her. Someone had been watching. "Why didn't you talk to me then?"

"Didn't want to interrupt church. I figured I'd wait in the vestibule." He checked his watch. "Can we talk now?"

"What do you want to know?"

The door behind him slapped open, and a young family burst out, the father with a tight grip on a squirming, red-faced toddler, the mother holding the hands of preschool twins.

The chief stepped to the side to avoid a collision. "Looks like church let out. Is there somewhere we could go?"

The door opened again, and more people emerged, including Flower Pants and her buddy, who gave Casey and the chief an intense study as they passed. Casey and Death stepped into the grass, letting the stream of non-Sunday School attendees make their way home.

Just when Casey thought they'd seen the last of the crowd, Officers Whistler and Austin strode out the door, laughing. They trotted down the steps and their laughter faded. Their smiles didn't.

Whistler frowned, studying the chief's face. Casey saw a subtle change in her demeanor, as if she clicked into work mode. "Wait. Aren't you Chief Spears? From Beltmore?" Whistler looked from the chief to Casey and back again.

Casey raised her eyebrows, but Whistler shook her head, like *I didn't do it.*

"I am," Spears said. "And you are?"

"Officer Nance Whistler, Armstrong PD. Off-duty today."

"Nice to meet you, Officer."

Whistler gestured to her partner. "This is Officer Austin, our newest recruit."

The two men shook hands.

"Everything okay?" Whistler asked.

"Yes, fine," the chief said.

Whistler looked at Casey, who gave a little shrug.

After a few seconds of awkward silence, Whistler took a step forward. "Well, then, I guess we'll be going. My mom's cooking, and I invited Austin over since his folks are in Hawaii on some cruise."

"She warned me about her mom's cooking, though." Austin grinned.

Casey laughed. "Bad?"

Whistler shook her head. "Horrendous. We figured we can always order pizza once she's out of the kitchen. See you later, then? Nice to meet you, Chief."

"And you."

"Sir," Austin said.

The two young officers headed toward a silver pickup. Whistler scooted behind the wheel. She hesitated, meeting Casey's eyes, and Casey waved her on. Casey wasn't feeling an immediate threat from Spears, partly because he was sober and his eyes held an intelligent spark, and partly because they were standing in the open on a public street.

"So," Spears said, "about that talk we were going to have."

"Come this way," Casey said. "I'll get you a cup of coffee."

She led him to Vern's, where she offered him one of the fresh donuts delivered that morning. Casey chose a Boston cream. The chief declined and sipped black coffee.

"He's no fun," Death proclaimed.

"So I got a call from Armstrong's Chief," Spears said.

They sat at one of the tables in the deli. Casey took a bite, hoping the chief would continue. He did.

"Chief Navarro claims my Beltmore officers are looking for you. I asked them, but they deny having made inquiries."

Casey could see Officer Justus being firm with a denial. She didn't have to make inquiries into Casey's whereabouts. She had Casey's contact information, should she want it, along with Casey's real name. The other guys, however…

The chief took another sip, and Casey another custardy bite.

"I have the feeling," Spears said, "that something is going on I'm not a party to."

"Maybe he's smarter than the rest of them." Death sat in a third chair at the table, chin on fist, wearing a Dunkin' Donuts outfit.

Casey wiped her mouth. "You've seen the police report from Thursday night?"

"I have."

"And you realize that's me."

"I do. However, I also realize your contact information somehow isn't on the police report, and Officer Justus has been tight-lipped about the incident." His eyes again roamed over her black eye. "I was able to get her to speak with me after the call from Chief Navarro. I promised Justus I would not disclose your location to anyone else in the department until I spoke with you personally."

"I appreciate that."

"So, why don't you tell me what happened Thursday? I've read Officer Justus' report, but I would like to hear it from you."

Casey set down the last few bites of her donut and licked a splotch of chocolate from her index finger. "Are you recording this?"

"No. We already have documentation written up by Officer Justus. Her work and the word of Pastor Sheila have me thinking I need to research my department and the behavior of some of its members. I'd like to make things right."

"Believe him?" Death asked.

She did.

She carefully folded her napkin. "How are they doing?"

"The men from Thursday night?" Spears took another sip of

coffee, then rested his elbows on the table. "A little sore. One has a concussion."

"From whacking the firepit," Death guessed.

"But really, they're mostly mad. And frightened. Which worries me. When guys like this get scared, they do stupid things."

"As opposed to the smart things they did Thursday?"

"Yeah. They are pretty dumb, aren't they?"

Casey smiled. "Really dumb."

A smile flickered on Spears' lips, but he grew serious again. "So what happened? In your own words?"

Casey told him. She walked him through sleeping under the pavilion, the guys' arrival on the scene, and her fight to get away. She ended with her sanctuary in the Harvest Church of the Saints, Pastor Sheila's plea to charge the guys with assault, and Officer Justus' professional attitude.

Chief Spears was a good listener. He asked pertinent questions, and his focus never wavered. When Casey was done, he took another sip of coffee, but made a face. "Cold."

Casey dumped out the dregs and poured him a new cup.

"So, question," Spears said after thanking her.

Casey anticipated the usual inquiry. "I'm just traveling through."

"Yeah, I got that. What I want to know is how you could fight like that? Not many women—none in Beltmore, from what I know—could have defended themselves like you did."

"Blackbelt in Hapkido." She took a last bite of donut. "If those guys had left me alone, they wouldn't have gotten hurt. I might have taken their keys and called the cops, but I wouldn't have...you know."

"Kicked them in the balls?" Spears' eyes sparkled.

"Well, yeah." Casey let out a short laugh. "If I'd thought fast enough, I would have just run away. That's always the best option."

"So now things are making sense," Death said. "About your life, I mean."

The front door jangled. Vern strode through the deli and unlocked that door, too. "You two doing okay? Need anything?"

"You notice he didn't inquire after my well-being," Death grumbled. "Or even include me in the head count. But then, with Dottie's condition, he's terrified of me right now."

"We're good," Casey said, "unless..." She looked at Spears.

"I've got what I need." He held up his mug. "Thank you."

Vern stopped by the third chair, where Death was sitting, and rested his hand on its back. He shivered, then glanced at the ceiling vent, pulling his hand away and sticking it under his other arm. He gave Casey a meaningful look, and she smiled. "I'm fine. Really."

"All right. I'll be up front if you need me. I open in ten minutes, but people sometimes come early. I guess that's my own fault if I unlock the doors..." He ambled away, still talking.

Spears twisted his mug on the tablecloth, making little semicircles. "The Beltmore guys...there are all kinds of stories about their history of assaulting women. And driving drunk. And generally being assholes. We don't have actual documentation—"

"Because of favoritism from certain police officers."

He rubbed his eyes with a thumb and forefinger. "I'm working on that. If people like you are willing to get them in the system, we can make changes. Give them what they deserve."

Casey searched his face for signs of weakness. She didn't see any. She wondered what he'd done to end up in a place like Beltmore. Others had mentioned scandal, or the hint of one, anyway. She didn't want to think that, because she liked him.

"They were here looking for me on Saturday. One of your cops, I mean."

"He didn't see you?"

"No."

"Maddy—Officer Justus—told me the other cops have been asking about you, saying they need to know to finish up the report. But she and I know where you are, and that's enough." He finished his coffee and looked around. "Where do the cups go?"

"I'll get it."

"Thank you." He stood and brushed off the front of his suit, as if he'd been eating a donut.

Casey glanced at her own shirt and realized he'd been giving her a hint. She stood, too, swiping at crumbs.

"We'll be in touch," Spears said. "We may need you to come by, talk to a judge or lawyers or someone else official."

Great.

"Can't promise how long I'll be sticking around," she told him, "but you'll be able to get me on my phone."

He looked like he wanted to follow up on that, but he didn't. Instead, he stuck out his hand.

Casey shook it. "Thanks."

"I'll be the one thanking you when this is all over." He smiled suddenly, changing his face, making sense of the laugh lines.

"You're new in Beltmore," she said. "Where did you come from?"

His smiled vanished as quickly as it had appeared. "Hell," he said.

And then he turned around and walked out of the store.

Chapter Twenty-two

"I did some checking." Death left and was back in an instant, wearing a Sherlock Holmes outfit, complete with the deerstalker hat and an electronic pipe. Casey didn't even know such pipes existed. Fortunately, the smoke smelled of lavender instead of chemicals. Underneath Death's coat, as the one non-period article of clothing, was a T-shirt plastered with a life-size photo of Benedict Cumberbatch's face. Casey could appreciate that one.

"Chief Spears came to Beltmore from Boise. Some really bad drug stuff went down there, and he was right in the middle of taking care of it. The mayor asked him to stay, but he wanted somewhere quiet and uneventful. Too bad for him you made an event."

"Those jerks were already making events. They just weren't getting caught."

"True."

Casey wiped off the tablecloth and deposited the mugs in the dish tub. "It's good to know he's above-board. I was hoping Beltmore hadn't gotten saddled with another corrupt cop."

"Excuse me?" Vern stood in the doorway, his forehead furrowed.

Casey forced a smile. "Talking to myself."

Vern checked her black eye, as if wondering if she'd suffered a concussion along with it. "What did that guy want? Does he have anything to do with the cop who was here Friday?"

"He's the Beltmore chief."

"The chief? He's not in collusion with the other cop, is he? Do you need me to talk to him?"

"Boy, he's getting all dad-like, isn't he?" Death puffed on the pipe.

"Actually, I think he's okay. He wants to make things right and have those guys answer for it."

"Well, let me know if any of them bother you."

"Thank you." Casey wasn't sure how an old guy with a pot belly would do any better than she could herself, but she wasn't going to turn down a friendly offer.

The bell at the front dinged, and Vern glanced at his watch. "Why don't you get some lunch? We had plenty left."

She was hungry, even after the donut. Plus, she never got protein after her workout, having been rushed off to church, of all places. "Thanks. I won't be long."

Dottie was sleeping, or at least in her bedroom, so Casey had a quiet lunch of macaroni and cheese with ham before heading back to the store. She was reaching for the deli doorknob when someone pushed through backward from the other side. Casey grabbed the handle and held the door open for the woman, who had two gallons of milk in her hands. She wore a pair of blue scrubs, as if she had just gotten off a shift at a hospital, and a pair of Nike athletic shoes. Her hair was caught up in a messy bun, and her purse had slid down to the crook of her elbow.

The milk she held was as white as her hair.

Crap.

The woman turned around, saying, "Thank you," and froze. "You again."

"Me. Again."

The woman took a deep breath through her nose and let it out. "You've been talking to my daughter."

So Casey had been right about the woman's relationship to Nell. "I wondered if she was yours."

"Because of the hair, right?" The woman let the door swing shut behind her. "I feel bad about that. Along with this hair comes skin that burns in a minute, and eyelashes that blend right into your face." She smiled. "I'm Gracie Achabal. Sorry about the other time. Nell says she's gotten to know you and you don't seem crazy at all." She laughed.

Death's head wagged side to side. "She doesn't know what she's saying."

"You had every right to think I was strange. I had a bad morning on the train and wasn't handling it the best."

"I'd shake your hand, but…" She held up the milk jugs.

"No problem."

Gracie stepped toward a maroon Taurus. "So you're staying with the Dailys?"

"For now. Don't know how long I'll stay."

"You a relative?"

"No. I was passing through and they offered me a place." How many times had Casey given the same explanation in the past two days?

Gracie's gaze shot around the parking lot, as if she were looking for eavesdroppers. "So is it true?"

"Is what true?"

Nell's mom leaned a little closer. "That they have a bedroom in their basement set up for their daughter?"

A chill ran up Casey's spine. "But their daughter's dead. They don't have a living one, do they?" Casey hadn't studied the shrine-like corner of the room any further after the first day. She'd either been too tired, or hadn't thought to do it. She would have to rectify that after last night's excursion to the cemetery.

"Right. Stillborn baby, way back in the sixties, maybe? The story is they have a room for her, to keep her alive in their minds. Kinda crazy, right?"

"Like you thought I was?"

She tilted her head. "I think it's a little more than that."

"It's a nice guest room. I figured that's all it was."

"But they never have guests. You're the first in…I don't know, ages."

A niggle of unease crept into Casey's stomach. She wasn't sure if it was the idea of Vern's insistence that she stay with them, or standing in the parking lot discussing it with some woman she'd never really talked to before. "I wouldn't know why it's there or whether or not they have other guests. I've only been here since Friday." This woman didn't need to hear about the Noah's Ark mobile or the wallpaper border of calliope horses.

Gracie Achabal shrugged, unbothered by Casey's reluctance to gossip. "One of those small town things, you know. Everybody thinking they know everything about everyone. Gets a little much sometimes." She gazed across the street, but not like she was looking at anything in particular. "Well, nice to see you again. And thanks for being a friend to Nell."

"She's a good kid. Did she tell you she helped clean up last night?"

"After the movie? Doesn't surprise me. She's kind of a neat freak when it comes to other people's stuff." She smiled. "Her own room, not so much."

"No, I mean what that kid spray-painted."

Gracie frowned. "Not sure what you're talking about. I'm just now going to pick her up from Dad's, and I haven't talked to anybody. Is Nell okay?"

"She's fine." Casey explained what had happened, and how Nell had volunteered to help Roger eliminate the graffiti.

Gracie's expression remained serious. "Why would Lance do that?"

"Apparently he was dared by his friends. Why they wanted him to write that, I really don't know. Do you?"

Gracie stood for a moment, mouth open. "It's one of those things I was talking about. Small town stuff. You know, old resentments, rumors that have never been addressed." She held up the milk. "Well, gotta get Nell and head home to sleep. Nice to meet you for real."

"Yes, you, too."

Casey watched her get into her car and leave.

"So what was she talking about?" Death wore scrubs, too, although these were white with brightly colored cats.

"Don't know. Vern and Dotty could have explained the stuff in the basement room, just like they could have let me in on the anonymous note, but they obviously don't want to discuss either. And who's going to give me town gossip? Roger?"

Death snorted. "Not sure he can speak that many words in a row."

"I'm certainly not going to ask Nell. I approached her with it, but as far as I can tell she doesn't know anything, which is only appropriate. I'll wait and see if anything else comes of it."

"Make sure you don't get caught in the middle."

Casey swung the door open and headed into the store. Death could very well say she shouldn't find herself in the center of whatever controversy was brewing. But it was too late.

By becoming a part of Vern and Dottie's lives, she already was.

Chapter Twenty-three

The remainder of Sunday passed quietly at the store, without incident and without any visits from unwelcome cops or vandals or crabby women. Most customers wanted simple things—Cheez-Its, Coke, or bread to make grilled cheese for Sunday supper. Vern shooed Casey out before ten and she crashed, still catching up from the previous night's graveside visit.

The next morning, Vern left her alone in the store while he took Dottie to a doctor's appointment. Casey wasn't sure how she felt about being in charge of the whole place, but he didn't really give her a choice. Again, she wondered what he'd do if she wasn't around. He could call Roger, she supposed. After Roger's help Saturday night with painting over Lance Victor's handiwork, and his quiet willingness to sit beside Dottie in church, Casey felt more confident that Roger was actually more of a help than a hindrance.

In addition to her unease with the store responsibilities, Casey was surprised she was still in Armstrong at all. The events of the past few days straddled the whole interesting/too much trouble line, and she wasn't yet sure on which side she'd fall. She hadn't made any friends, unless you counted Vern and Dottie, or maybe Nell.

Perhaps the most telling thing of all? She missed Eric. Casey pulled out her phone to see where he was. Once the image stopped spinning she saw the tiny, reassuring dot, along with an image of his face. He was in Clyde, where he said he'd be. The address placed him at his mom's B and B. Maybe he was eating pancakes, or fixing something. Or sitting with his mother and her partner, wondering how he ended up back home. Casey missed his easy smile, his kindness, his sense of humor. The way his hair flopped over his forehead… Casey closed the app and slid the phone back into her pocket.

What was she doing in this little Idaho town when her family, and her house, and everything that had ever been steady in her life was back in Colorado? Could she really not face life without Reuben and Omar? Or was she afraid that moving forward meant leaving them behind? She wasn't sure anymore.

Her injuries were healing faster than she dared hope. Her ribs, evidently not broken, had dulled to a chronic ache rather than sharp stabs every time she moved. Aches, she could live with. Her face, while pain-free, now sported a lovely yellow blotch. She could also live with that, because, really, who cared?

Vern didn't bring up the threatening note he and Dottie received, and Casey didn't ask. For the time being she decided to forget it, and hope it didn't happen again. She and Vern also didn't speak about the graffiti, and she doubted they would. It better not happen again, though, or some teenagers in town were going to be hurting.

Vern and Dottie also neglected to tell Casey what illness Dottie suffered from. She assumed it was something major, given the gentle kindness with which Vern treated her. Customers discussed it from the other side of the register, but seeing how their "knowledge" of Dottie's disease ranged from a reprise of her German measles to lupus to chlamydia, they didn't know any more than she did.

Chlamydia? Really?

She was stocking shelves with cheap Halloween masks and accessories when the mail carrier crossed the front window. She heard the mailbox lid slap shut and watched the woman stride away, digging into her bag for the next house's letters—which Casey realized would be Vern and Dottie's personal residence. Casey set down the orange-handled scissors she was using to open the boxes and stepped over a pile of plastic pumpkins to retrieve the mail, but a customer came in. She went behind the counter to help him buy lottery tickets. By the time she figured out exactly which tickets he wanted and how to sell them, she'd forgotten the mail.

Not until a few hours later did she remember to grab what the letter carrier had brought. She took it to the office to sort, slitting the envelopes with the scissors, which she fetched from the Halloween aisle. The distribution wasn't hard—bills on one pile, circulars on another, political ads straight to recycling.

But what about plain white envelopes with no address?

Casey's stomach dropped. Could it be another anonymous letter? She turned it over. The envelope was not sealed.

"Go ahead, you know you want to." Death stood with an elbow on the customer side of the counter, dressed in a postal uniform. The name tag read, "Newman."

"It's not my mail."

"How do you know? There's no recipient listed."

"Because no one who would send me mail knows I'm here. Unless you told them."

Death's hands shot up in a surrender gesture. "Not a word has passed my lips concerning your whereabouts. Not even to poor, dear Eric pining away in Ohio."

"He's not really pining, is he?"

Death made a "zip my lips" gesture. "I'll never tell. Now come on. Open it."

Casey stared at the envelope. If it was another threatening letter, she wanted to save the Dailys. But if it wasn't…

"Then you pretend you didn't see it," Death said. "What harm could there be?"

"It's a felony to open someone else's mail."

"Not if they don't find out. Besides, the envelope isn't sealed, so you're not technically *opening* it."

"You're going to get me sent to hell," Casey said.

"Not gonna happen. Who am I going to have take you there? I'm certainly not going to do it. And my *yamadutas* refuse to venture that direction. Not that I would ask them to."

Casey set the base of the envelope on the counter and gently bent the top apart, peering inside.

"It's a photo."

"Let me see." Death swooped through the open part of the cashier's window to hover beside Casey.

Making sure no customers were approaching the store, Casey slid the photo out of the envelope.

The picture was old and faded, the colors dim. This copy had been made from an original, as if someone scanned in an old Polaroid and printed it out. All of the images in the picture blurred at the edges, but Casey could still make out the subjects of the shot.

The scene was a party. A Halloween party, specifically.

Death gasped. "Do you think that is *the* Halloween party? The photo looks old enough."

A thrill of excitement shot through Casey. "Could be."

Everyone in the picture was in costume, seated on and around a couch. From what Casey could see, it was all women. She picked out Princess Leia, Wonder Woman, Lucy Van Pelt from *Peanuts*, Dorothy from the *Wizard of Oz*, several witches, three rubber masks—Richard Nixon, wearing a suit and striped shirt; a clown, with a drooping trick carnation; and a devil, with a flowing red cape and horns—a nurse, not unlike Death's rendition of Nurse Ratched, and the Bride of Frankenstein, complete with beehive. The photo could have been taken in anyone's house, Casey supposed, although the orange-and-brown macramé artwork hanging to the left of the group was…original. It also placed the photo firmly in the sixties or seventies, because, macramé? Really?

In black Sharpie underneath the picture words had been printed in block lettering:

WHO ARE THE ONES WHO DON'T BELONG? I THINK YOU KNOW.

AND I THINK YOU KNOW WHERE THEY ARE NOW.

The bell dinged above the door and Casey smacked the photo facedown on the counter. After checking his ID she handed the young man a pack of cigarettes—much to her dismay—and sold three family-sized bags of chips, a bag of beef jerky, and an entire twenty-four-pack of extra-caffeinated Mountain Dew to the woman who came in after him. Casey felt just great about her role in degrading the health of Armstrong's citizens.

"So is one of them Dottie?" Death asked when the customers had gone.

Casey turned the photo back over. "It's hard to tell. She would be a lot younger here."

"Forty-five years younger, perhaps? Like in the anonymous note? Officer Whistler did say the party happened around that time."

Casey checked out the *Wizard of Oz* Dorothy because of the name, but that woman's facial structure didn't fit with Dottie's narrow face. She scanned the rest of the group, but between the picture's bad quality, the faded colors, and the obvious length of time since the photo was taken, she couldn't pick out who might be the female half of her new landlords.

"I do believe that's old Flower Pants." Death pointed at Princess Leia. "Since her hair is still that color, it makes it a little easier. Plus, she's got that arrogant glint in her eyes. I can imagine her being the only one bold enough to wear that gold bikini top."

Casey could see it. But she couldn't see anyone else she recognized. The sender, who had also scribbled "Who are they?" at the bottom of the page, could have been asking a few different questions. Names for all of the women. Those people whose faces were covered. Or maybe party-goers who were now unfamiliar, who moved away or had been visiting at the time. They could even be asking the identity of the party-crashers who threatened them and caused the woman to die, if the photo actually was from that fatal night. There was no way for Casey to know what was behind the question, but the sender obviously thought Dottie or Vern would be able to answer it.

And what about the second line, about where "they" are now? Where could they be? Boise? Brazil? Graveyard? Jail?

Death drifted up to sit on—or above—the counter. "If you found some old photos in Vern and Dottie's house you might be able to figure out who they are. Or at least who Dottie is. She's bound to have some pictures of herself from back then, even if they don't have them sitting out."

"More snooping?" Casey picked up the envelope to replace the photo, but Death waved a hand over it.

"Snap a picture first."

Casey frowned, but used her phone to do as Death suggested. If she was going to put names to faces she would need a copy, even as blurred as it was. "Remind me again why we're getting involved? Why I don't take off down the road?"

"Because that's what you do."

"Stick my nose in other people's business?"

"No, take care of people around you. Especially ones who have been kind and given you a place to stay when you were injured."

"Maybe they did that so they can kill me in my sleep." She slid the photo into the envelope and stuck it on the bottom of the bill pile. "I should leave and find someplace else."

Death took on the annoying know-it-all tone Casey hated. "Do Vern and Dottie look like serial killers to you?"

"What exactly do serial killers look like?"

"You know. Crazy."

Casey shook her head.

Death hopped off the counter, moving in a remarkably human-like fashion. "Wherever you end up there's weird stuff happening.

You know that. It's human nature. And it's your life. You're a drama magnet."

"But why is it always creepy drama? Because you can't tell me this isn't creepy. A threatening letter, an ancient photo from a fatal party, and the town treating Dottie like a pariah."

"The townspeople don't seem to care when it comes to what they can get from the store. Lunch, movies, that tiny little screwdriver to fix glasses. It's like Vern by himself is okay, but when you add Dottie into the mix…"

So Death had seen the same contradiction.

The back door slapped shut, and the sound of footsteps filtered into the office. Casey checked quickly to make sure the photo was out of sight under the other letters as Vern came around the corner. The look of devastation on his face told her all she needed to know about Dottie's appointment. She shoved papers off the chair behind the little desk, and he dropped onto it.

"Should I close the store? Vern?"

"What? Oh, no. You can't close."

But when the door dinged he spun to face the back of the room.

Casey rented the customer the latest *Fast and Furious* movie, sold him popcorn and candy, and saw him out the door.

"Vern? What's wrong? What happened?" The envelope with the Halloween photo lay unremarkably under the stack of bills, so he couldn't have seen that. Unless he and Dottie had gotten another one at their house.

But she knew it wasn't about that. This was worse.

Vern's expression was bleak. "It's Dottie. The doctor said she has only a few weeks to live."

Chapter Twenty-four

Casey's stomach dropped and Death shot away, maybe to check on Dottie.

"I'm sorry." Casey wasn't sure if Vern wanted to talk, or if she should leave him alone, so she waited.

"It's cancer," he said. "You probably guessed."

She had, even though the rest of the town had not. Or maybe they wanted her to be dying from something rare and exotic. And scandalous.

He swiped a hand down his face. "She was diagnosed last year when she started having back pain. The doctor ran tests and gave us the bad news. Would you believe it originated as lung cancer? Never smoked a cigarette in her life, hasn't lived with smokers. Docs say it could be from radon, or asbestos, or who-knows-what. I don't know why they even guess. I don't think they really have any idea." He let out a long breath. "She's been through it all. Radiation. Chemo. Surgery. All of it stopped working eventually. Now she's on an experimental hormone, takes it in pills. But we found out today…it's not working anymore." He stared at the wall.

A customer came in asking for a receipt from the gas pump, which had run out of paper. Casey printed it out and thanked him. He saw Vern, but either didn't have anything to say or didn't want to.

"So what's next?"

Vern shook his head. "There is no next. We've exhausted our options. Now next is..." He rested his head on his arms.

"Why don't you go home? I'll call if I need anything."

He sat quietly for so long Casey thought maybe he'd drifted off, but he soon sat up. "Dot's sleeping now. Nothing I can do, anyway, except house stuff, and she gets upset if I do too much because then she feels like she can't do anything." He slapped his knees and stood up. "So, how 'bout I show you how to change the paper in the gas pump?"

Casey didn't argue.

On the way out Casey slipped the blank envelope from the bottom of the bill pile and shoved it under her jeans at the small of her back, hidden by her T-shirt. Vern and Dottie had enough to deal with. They didn't need to try to decipher another cryptic message.

After a quick tutorial on changing the receipt roll, she and Vern were met by Roger, who came by in his usual unscheduled fashion to work. Vern and Casey used the time to clean out the deep freeze, which opened into the back hallway. They didn't talk much, but Casey felt it might be a good time to find out some things, while they were both busy doing stuff.

"So," Casey said after a trip to the Dumpster with some freezer-burned hamburger, "I re-stocked the shelves with those Halloween costumes today, and the new boxes of Halloween candy came in, too. Does Armstrong go all out for this holiday, or what?" She hoped a casual inquiry might lead to that tragic Halloween so long ago.

Vern sat back from where he crouched in the far corner. His lips were turning blue.

"We're almost done, right?" Casey asked.

He stood up, flexing his fingers. "Probably should take a break." They went into the main store and he blew on his hands. "Guess I ought to do this in shorter stints."

"So…" Casey tried not to sound too pushy. "Halloween?"

Vern wouldn't meet her eyes. "Just another excuse to get out and have a little fun. An hour of trick-or-treating, a costume contest down at the fire station. Nothing too big, but a little something for the kids. We don't get many people from out of town, like some of the wealthier places, but a few come to beg for candy down Main Street, mostly." His voice stayed level, not matching the enthusiasm of the actual words.

"Do you give out anything here at the store?"

"Sure, a little treat, and I grill hot dogs for the families who are out. It's a fun night."

Casey watched as he absent-mindedly straightened soup cans on a nearby shelf. "You don't seem to be a fan. Or…" Shame washed over her. "I'm sorry, I'm being insensitive after today. Of course you don't want to talk about Halloween."

"No, no, you're right. It isn't my favorite holiday. Not Dottie's, either."

Should she ask? He gave her an opening. "How come you don't like it?" She thought about the photo shoved in her jeans. Could the party have anything to do with the couple's feelings about the holiday? There was obviously something connecting the Dailys to the group of women in the picture, or the anonymous sender wouldn't have sent it, well, anonymously. Casey didn't know for certain Dottie was in the shot, or if it was even the deadly party. It could have been from a different year altogether.

But she doubted it.

"I told you before," Vern said.

"I don't remember you saying you don't like Halloween."

"No, about her moving here with me."

"That was at Halloween?"

"No." Vern moved down the row, straightening boxes, flicking dust with his fingers. "A long time ago, when Dottie moved here with me, she had a hard time fitting in. That's what I told you. You know, everybody had grown up here and had lots of family around. She felt like an outsider. This town didn't embrace her like I'd hoped. She was a city girl, coming to the country, and maybe she could have been more approachable. I'm not going to say she was perfect, but she was one woman, and they were…a clique."

"That's hard."

"It is. Was." He walked into the cafe and slumped onto a chair. "There was one person who took the time to get to know her. One. Out of a whole town. It was pathetic."

Casey sat at the next table. "Who was it?"

"Marianne Rush. She and Dottie hit it off like you wouldn't believe. It made all the difference. If it hadn't been for Marianne, I don't know, maybe we wouldn't have stayed. I sometimes wish we hadn't, and I kind of blame Marianne, maybe unfairly, but there's no point in dwelling on that, I guess."

"So where is Marianne now? I don't remember meeting her." Or maybe they weren't friends anymore. Casey winced. Maybe it was Flower Pants.

Vern scratched his nose. "She's gone."

So, not Flower Pants. "Gone as in dead?"

He jerked his head up. "No! I didn't mean that. Gone as in… somewhere else. Just up and went. A long time ago. Took off with some guy, left her husband and kids. Her children came home from trick-or-treating, divvied up their candy before bed, and didn't realize until the next morning that she was gone."

"Oh. Halloween."

"Right." He sat back. "Dottie and Marianne were going to hand out candy at the church that night. Marianne called to say something had come up and she couldn't do it, she was sick or something. Dottie was upset and said some things she regretted immediately, but when she tried to call Marianne back, there was no answer. Dottie was heartbroken. In fact, I don't think she's ever recovered. Sometimes I wonder if it didn't contribute to—" he waved his hand "—what's going on now. "

A broken heart certainly could mess with your health. Casey knew that for a fact. She herself may not have cancer, but if she didn't force herself to run and perform her *katas*, she would have a hard time getting out of bed in the morning.

"Did Dottie know the guy Marianne ran away with?"

Vern rubbed at something on the tablecloth. Dried ketchup, maybe? "If she did she's never told me, and that would be a big secret to keep when you're as close as we are."

"It was a total surprise? Dottie didn't have a clue?"

"Looking back she could see some changes. Canceled lunches, a new haircut, a diet. At the time she thought Marianne was trying to better herself, you know? She was a young mother, feeling trapped and like she'd lost part of herself."

That would have been tricky, since Dottie had been hoping to be a mother, too. How do you sympathize with your friend for feeling like a homebound mom when that life was stolen from you?

"But Marianne took it farther than we ever imagined she would." He shook his head. "Everybody blamed Dottie."

"Dottie? Why? She wasn't the one having an affair, and if she didn't know anything—"

"Who's going to believe that? Her best friend has a lover and she doesn't know? The whole town thinks she's been holding back all these years. That we have."

Could that really be the reason for all the bad feelings? That they didn't believe she didn't know about her friend's affair? That seemed like a stretch.

"Didn't Marianne tell her family it wasn't Dottie's fault? If Dottie told her how bad things had gotten—"

"Marianne never got in touch with her family after that night."

Casey stared at him. "What?"

"Never called them. Didn't want anything to do with them. She wrote to Dottie once—one time—to say she was all right and was sorry for leaving, but she hadn't been happy here. She had to go. Wasn't even a return address on the envelope. Dottie never…she never had another friend like that. It about killed her." He looked exhausted, and Casey felt a twinge of guilt for making him remember such a sad time, especially on a day when he'd already had enough bad news. But she still had one more question.

"How long ago was this?"

He glanced at her, then quickly away. "This Halloween it will be forty-five years."

Casey kept her face blank. Vern didn't know she'd read the anonymous note, and there would be no other way for her to realize that number was important, so she couldn't let on that it meant anything. But forty-five years ago Marianne left her family and a local Halloween party turned deadly.

"Forty-five years is a long time for a town to hold a grudge. Especially when Dottie wasn't the one who did the actual destructive thing."

"Tell me about it."

Casey considered the photo she was hiding. More than ever she wondered if it was connected to the other anonymous note, or maybe Marianne's disappearance. There was no way for Casey to know without finding out more. Should she show the photo to Vern? She wished Death were there to tell her what to do.

Vern pushed himself up from the table. "I'm going to check on Dottie. When I come back you can take a break."

"I can stay."

"I'll see how long Roger feels like working. If he wants to go, I'll take you up on it."

He left, and Casey checked for customers before pulling the photo from her jeans. Was this picture taken before Dottie's best friend left town? Or was she missing from this picture, having already disappeared? But no, Vern had said Dottie and Marianne were going to hand out candy at the church, and Marianne had begged off. Did that mean they weren't going to the party at all?

Or was the party later, after trick-or-treating? That would make sense. The women would get their sugar-laden children to bed before going out to have fun themselves.

Casey studied the faces of the women, searching for Marianne, for someone who looked like she desperately wanted out, and was about to make that happen.

Casey was surprised how many of the women fit that description.

Chapter Twenty-five

Since Roger seemed happy to be hanging out behind the counter for another hour or so, Casey set up lunch—sausage patties on the grill—so Vern could begin cooking when he returned from checking on Dottie. He was back within five minutes.

"Still sleeping. So you go on."

"But it's lunchtime. You'll be busy."

"I've done it a million times before, and the customers know the drill. Roger can take care of the money. If it makes you happy, you can help clean up when you get back."

"But—"

"I was doing it myself long before you got here, and I'm violating all kinds of rules by having you work so many hours. So go. And don't come back for a while."

"The amount of time you spend over here can't be within the rules."

He grinned. "But I'm the owner. I can work myself as hard as I want. Who am I going to complain to?"

Casey laughed.

"Make sure you take one of the subs you made this morning. Don't tell the lunch crowd, but they're better than these sausage patties."

She had to agree. The patties resembled flattened mud pies, and didn't smell much better. But the men who showed up for lunch seemed to like them.

She chose a sub and purchased it from Roger—Vern didn't have to know—along with a cold water and some baby carrots that didn't look too old. The day was nice, if a little cool, so she figured she'd eat outside.

She ran to the house to get her sweatshirt and ditch the envelope stuck in her jeans, careful not to wake Dottie. She tiptoed downstairs and opened her door, pulling the envelope from her waistband.

Dottie was sitting in the L of the room on the soft chair, her head resting on the back. In her arms was the stuffed pink puppy, held tightly against her chest. Her head rolled toward Casey, and Casey recognized the look in her eyes. Pain. Physical? Emotional? Casey wasn't sure.

Casey held the envelope behind her and backed up a step. "I'm sorry."

"No." Dottie struggled to sit up. "I shouldn't have come into your room."

"Please stay. It's okay."

Casey glanced at Dottie's surroundings. The baby picture, the Boise State diploma, the mobile. Who were those things for? And what baby was that, seeing how the Dailys' Anne Marie was both stillborn and a girl?

Casey eased the envelope onto a shelf in the outer room, thinking that would be less obvious than sticking it back in her jeans. She slipped into the bedroom, skimming the foot of the bed, as far from Dottie as she could get, and pulled her sweatshirt from her duffel bag. "I'm heading outside for lunch. Do you need anything?"

"Could you stay for a minute?"

Casey tried not to think about the Halloween photo as she sat on the edge of the bed.

Dottie didn't speak. Instead, she gazed out one of the high windows. Casey waited. Not patiently, maybe, but calmly. After several minutes, her stomach growled, and she checked her watch. "Was there something you wanted to talk about, Dottie?"

"What?" She blinked slowly.

"Did you want to tell me something?"

"No, I…" She searched Casey's face. "Where did you come from?"

"The store. Vern sent me home for lunch."

"No, not the store."

"You mean on Friday? I'm just traveling through."

Dottie frowned. "But from where? Where have you been?"

"Colorado."

"Colorado?" She looked stunned. Surprised. "Why were you in Colorado?"

"I live there. Or, at least, my family does. Did."

"Your family." Dottie's eyes went unfocused, and her head drooped to the side.

"Dottie?"

The old woman blinked. "I'm sorry, I was…I thought you were…" She struggled again to get out of the chair.

"Please. Stay. I came for my sweatshirt. I'm going back out."

Dottie closed her eyes, then sank back into the chair.

Casey stood by the door, regarding her landlady. What had just happened? She didn't know.

But whatever it was, it gave Casey a hollow, icy feeling in her gut. What were all of those things in the corner? Vern and Dottie had no other children. No extended family Casey could see. Who was the woman with the baby? Who had worn the Homecoming banner? And who was this Anne Marie Daily who had earned the diploma?

The diploma.

A chill raced through Casey. There wasn't an Anne Marie Daily who had walked across a stage to shake the university president's hand, was there? There hadn't been a girl who had worn that ribbon, or carried those flowers.

It was all made up.

Dottie and Vern were so enmeshed in the past, so filled with regret and sorrow and wishes, they had made up their daughter's history. Her childhood, her adolescence, even her adulthood.

Casey's stomach roiled and she tiptoed back toward Dottie. The old woman's eyes remained closed, and her breathing had evened out. Careful not to wake her, Casey took a closer look at the photo in the frame. Could she see Vern or Dottie in the woman's face? Or in the face of her baby?

No. But she could see something else.

A tiny, almost invisible, company logo in the bottom corner. The photo was a stock image, sold with the frame. The subjects in it had nothing to do with Dottie and Vern. They were models, paid to be photographed.

A rush of sadness swept over Casey. Was she herself going to become like them? Was she going to find herself this way someday, broken and ready to die?

Oh, God.

Casey set the frame back on the shelf and tiptoed from the room, her heart in her throat. Maybe Death was right. Maybe she needed to move on.

Or maybe she needed to run farther.

Casey grabbed the party photo, stuck it back in her jeans, and trotted up the stairs, wondering if it was okay to leave Dottie alone. She reminded herself that Vern had gone back to work, and Death wasn't in attendance. That was a good sign, right? Or at least a sign that Dottie wasn't about to die in that guest room chair.

Casey took her lunch to the park and sat on a bench under a maple tree that had lost most of its leaves. She had just gotten settled when she felt someone watching her. Looking up, she expected Death, perhaps there to tell her to hightail it back to the house, or even to discuss Casey's newest revelations about her life, but was surprised to find herself looking at Flower Pants.

Casey waited for the old woman to approach, or at least say something, but she just stood on the sidewalk and stared.

"Can I help you?" Casey asked when she became too annoyed not to.

"Who are you?"

"Just someone passing through."

"But you've been here since Friday. I saw you at Vern's."

"I remember." Casey stood, not wanting to look up at someone, even if that someone was a little old lady who was hardly a threat.

"So?" Flower Pants thrust out her jaw. "Who are you? Are you related to Vern?"

"No."

"To her?"

Her. She wouldn't even say Dottie's name.

"No. Why does it matter?"

Flower Pants' mouth worked. She had no ready answer to that. Because she was nosy? Because she hated Dottie and wanted to use Casey against her? Or did she have something of her own to hide?

"Where were you that Halloween?"

Flower Pants' eyes angled right. A flush bloomed on her neck. "What Halloween do you mean?"

Oh, she knew exactly what Casey meant. "The one where a woman died at a party. Were you there?" Of course she was. Dressed up as Princess Leia, in the gold bikini. Casey knew it was Flower Pants, just as she knew the photo she carried was from that night. She wondered if the old bat would fess up to it.

Flower Pants breathed hard, her chest rising and falling several times before she sagged. Casey jumped forward and caught her. She staggered under the dead weight, but was able to drag Flower Pants to the bench and set her down. More gently than she deserved, perhaps, but Casey didn't need a lawsuit.

Casey used her empty lunch bag as a fan to bring Flower Pants back to consciousness. Casey studied her bright lipstick, the dyed hair, the garish clothes—today a pair of yellow pants and a shirt with yellow, orange, and red leaves. Yikes. Casey wished Death were there to comment on the outfit, but then, Death's presence might mean there was yet another elderly woman on her way out. So maybe it was best Death was not present.

After a few scary moments, Flower Pants blinked and sat up. Her eyes were bright with fear until she recognized Casey and her expression went back to judgmental and angry. "What are you doing?"

"You fainted. I was trying to wake you."

"Fainted? I never faint."

Casey stopped fanning her. "Whatever happened, you look fine now. Maybe you could answer my question?"

She straightened her blouse, averting her eyes. "What question?"

"The one about where you were the Halloween night a woman died at a party? How long ago was it? Forty-five years?" Casey crossed her fingers Flower Pants wouldn't hyperventilate again. At least this time she could keel over on the bench.

"Why should I tell you anything?"

A good question. Casey wasn't sure what to tell her except, "I heard about the tragedy from Officer Whistler, and can't help but think it still affects the town, especially people who were a part of the evening. It must have been terrifying."

Flower Pants waited so long Casey was sure she wasn't going to answer. Finally, her voice small, she said, "I was there. It was…awful."

For that moment, Casey saw Flower Pants as a real person instead of a flirty, stuck-up, mean old lady. She looked tired and uncomfortable and weary.

"What's your name?" Casey figured it was time she became something other than Flower Pants. "Mine's Casey."

The woman sniffed. "Ethel." She straightened her shoulders. "Miss Bernard."

Miss. So, not a widow, despite her age. A woman from that

generation would keep the "Mrs." forever if she'd been married. And she definitely wouldn't stoop to the progressive "Ms."

"So, Miss Bernard, what do you think happened that night at the party? Who were those people who threatened you all?"

Miss Bernard shook her head, still not looking at Casey. "I don't know. Nobody does. The police could never figure out anything." She brushed something from her lap. "There were strangers at the party with us and no one knew. But then, we did go through a lot of wine…"

Who are the ones who don't belong? I think you know.

Casey itched to pull out the photo and show it to Flower Pants, but what if the old woman herself was the one who had sent it? She certainly had enough animosity toward Dottie to pull that kind of trick, and Casey didn't want to give her the satisfaction of seeing the photo again.

"Did you really think they were going to burn the house down?"

Miss Bernard kneaded her hands. "We didn't know. It was so frightening. So unexpected. It was hard to think anything."

Casey knew the feeling. She found it hard to make decisions in times of crisis, as Thursday night's fiasco proved, and she was trained for it. How could a group of drunk housewives be expected to react to such violence? With fear and chaos. "And the woman who died?"

Miss Bernard closed her eyes and took a deep breath. "Amelia. She was so terrified, her heart gave out. She was dead before the ambulance arrived."

"I'm sorry."

"She was weak. I guess now they call it depression, or anxiety, or whatever term they're using, when really she just couldn't handle it. She wasn't strong like the rest of us." She sniffed, then quickly added, "God rest her soul."

Casey stared at the woman, who she deemed no longer worthy

of an actual name. To think that for a moment Casey had felt sorry for her.

"Don't get me wrong," Flower Pants said. "We were friends. I liked her well enough. Not like some people." She angled her eyes toward Casey, then immediately away. "My friend Wilma, you saw her, the one who was with me at Vern's. She wasn't the strongest, either. She wet her pants." She giggled, and her eyes sparkled as she covered her mouth with a bony hand.

Casey stood abruptly. "I have to get back to work. Do you need me to take you anywhere? I mean, since you got *weak* and fainted?"

Flower Pants' face went hard, and the sparkle in her eyes disappeared. "I did not faint." She stood up, shakily, Casey thought, and stomped a few feet away before turning back. "And why don't you ask your new landlady where she was that night? You might be surprised by the answer."

She didn't have to ask. Casey knew where Dottie had been. Vern said she was home, despondent over the argument with her friend and her friend's subsequent departure. But maybe that wasn't the whole truth. Maybe she went to the party by herself when Marianne ditched her.

Flower Pants narrowed her eyes. "They didn't tell you, did they?"

"Who? Tell me what?"

"Vern and that woman. That she's a murderer."

"What?"

"She came to town, made Vern marry her because of...because of that baby. And then the baby died."

"She didn't kill her baby. It was German measles."

Flower Pants sniffed. "Vern's father died two months later. Heartbreak."

"He was that attached to the baby?"

"No. But his son was saddled to that awful woman because of the baby, and there wasn't even a baby to raise. It wasn't the way Vern's life was supposed to go."

Good grief. Did the whole town feel this resentful? No wonder Dottie was unhappy there.

"So," Casey asked again, "was Dottie at the Halloween party?"

Flower Pants hit Casey with a gaze both feral and arrogant. "I told you before. Ask her."

And she turned and walked away.

Chapter Twenty-six

Casey watched Flower Pants totter away, restraining herself from tackling the woman and punching her in the throat. Her stomach growled. She ate her sub without pleasure, wondering how people can get so twisted, and hold grudges for so long.

"Now that is a good-looking sandwich." Death sat beside her, wearing jeans, white Nikes, and a t-shirt declaring: *Vote for Pedro*.

"*Napoleon Dynamite*?"

Death's face lit up. "You knew one! So proud of you."

"Eric loves that movie. Not sure why, but we watched it a couple of weeks ago. He thought I needed to add it to my life experience."

"And?"

"I laughed some."

Death gazed at her. "You are a piece of work. You know that?"

"No. That woman is a piece of work." She pointed toward the retreating figure and recapped the Flower Pants conversation.

With a sigh, Death said, "You know what you need to do."

"Punch her in the throat?"

Death laughed. "No. Although I'm sure you would enjoy that. You need to ask Dottie about the party. And about her friend Marianne."

"Az, she just found out she's going to die."

"I realize that. Doesn't that up the stakes? What if she dies without answering the questions?"

"Why should she answer them? She doesn't know me."

Death looked into the tree above them. "Something is festering in this town. You can feel it. Don't you want to find out what that is?"

"Not really."

"Then why are you still here?"

Casey took another bite of her sub. It was a good question. Why was she still there? To stay close to Beltmore, in case they needed her? To recuperate from her injuries? To fill the hole in her soul by solving other people's problems?

Oh.

"I guess I need to ask Dottie some questions."

Death smiled gently. "It may not fix you. But it helps. And in the process you could fix them."

The bench was suddenly empty, but Casey could smell a hint of bleach. Another nod to Napoleon.

She finished her sandwich and pulled the photograph from her jeans. Why put it off? She threw her trash away and headed back to the house.

Entering through the kitchen, she went directly downstairs. Her ribs protested, perhaps from the strain of rescuing Flower Pants in the park, but not so badly to take one step at a time.

"Dottie?" Casey knocked lightly and opened the door to her room. Dottie wasn't there.

Casey went back upstairs, but the living room was unoccupied, and Dottie's bedroom door was closed.

So much for that.

The silence of the house descended on Casey like an overcast day. She didn't want to stay, but Vern made it clear she wasn't to come back to the store until later. She tapped her finger against the envelope. There was another way to research that awful night forty-five years ago.

The small library in the downtown business district was as tiny as they came. One big room with several short stacks of books, three public computers, a children's area, and the checkout counter. Casey approached the librarian, a woman her age, maybe a little older. She was bright-eyed and colorful in a red shirt, huge dangly earrings, and nail polish to match. The earrings sparked some recognition, and Casey remembered seeing her over the weekend, buying coffee or gas or something.

"Can I help you?" The woman shot up eagerly. "Casey, right? Staying with Vern and Dottie?"

"Um, yes."

"I'm Tara, we meet the other night at the movie. I live in the house behind Vern and Dottie."

Casey relaxed. Right. She could picture it now, the woman buying popcorn on Saturday night.

"What can I do for you?" Tara asked.

"Do you have newspapers from the seventies?"

"Not the actual papers, but our larger library system—the county, you know—they put some online several years ago, received a grant for historical purposes and high school interns scanned them all in. What papers are you interested in?"

"Anything that would have local news stories."

"Local as in Armstrong? Or local as in the area?"

"Armstrong." Searching any wider would send her down too many rabbit holes, and she doubted the drama of Armstrong reached very far.

"So you could check out the *Idaho Press-Tribune*, the bigger newspaper that covers our county, or the *Armstrong Arrow*, which comes out Wednesdays and Sundays. That's just our town and one or two neighboring communities."

"Let's go with that one."

The librarian led Casey to one of the public computers. "So you've been living with the Dailys a few days now, is that right? I saw you running the other morning."

"Yup, I try to get out most days."

"Good for you. I'm lucky if I get out once a month. Not exactly my thing, you know?" She laughed. "My husband and

I walk our dog around the neighborhood a couple times a day. At least I get exercise doing that."

"So have you always lived in that house?"

"Oh, no. I grew up over in Elmore County. Met my husband at a football game, wouldn't you know, and when we got married I figured it was time for a change. His hometown seemed as good as any." She pointed at an icon on the screen. "That will get you to the database, and you simply choose the paper you want and the date range. It's quite easy, actually."

"Thank you. Do you know the Dailys well?"

"As well as neighbors do, I guess. We see each other in our yards sometimes, and Dottie used to make pies and bring us one every once in a while. She was really good at that, before she got sick. Used to take them to the fair and win ribbons, from what I hear. Now I'm the one who takes stuff over to their place when I can. I feel so sorry for them. It must be awful."

"You mean how sick she is?"

Tara glanced at her. "Yeah. That." She looked like she wanted to say more, but she didn't.

It was odd. Someone actually giving Dottie a passing thought that wasn't poisonous. And Tara wouldn't even know about the horrible news from the doctor that morning.

"So you and Dottie are two of the transplants in town."

Tara laughed. "Yeah. There aren't a whole lot of us, so we've bonded a bit over that. I've only lived here ten years. Will and I got married after I was done with college, and we moved here then. He grew up on a farm a few miles out, but didn't want to go into the family business, so we bought this place. Close to the library for me, and he works at the bank."

No wonder she had a clearer view of the Dailys than the rest of the town. She and her husband didn't grow up hearing all the stories about how Dottie had betrayed Marianne's family. Which still seemed like an odd thing to blame her for, especially for so long. And the ridiculous accusation that she killed her father-in-law by marrying Vern. Had Dottie being an outsider really meant that much?

Tara waited to make sure Casey got into the system. "There you go. If you have any questions, give me a holler. I'll be right over there doing librarian stuff." She gave Casey a quick smile and left her alone.

Tara was right. The system really was easy. A lot simpler—and less dusty—than the ancient microfiche machines Casey used in the past. She decided to go right for the target and clicked on the *Armstrong Arrow* which would have come out the Sunday immediately following Halloween forty-five years ago. She didn't think there would be anything about Marianne leaving town—because who reported on that sort of thing?—but maybe there would be photos from the town's Halloween costume contest, or trick-or-treating, or even a social pages article detailing the party with all of the women.

"So, are we finding anything yet?" Death hovered over the chair at the next computer. From what Casey could see—and hear, from the accent—Death was attempting to be Giles, the librarian and Watcher from *Buffy the Vampire Slayer*. But then again, it could have been any tall British guy in a suit.

"Just starting," Casey mumbled, not wanting the very nice and normal librarian to think she was talking to herself. She brought up the front page of the paper, and the first thing she saw was a headline about the fatal Halloween party. As Casey predicted, the article didn't mention Marianne's disappearance, and covered only the facts of the get-together, the masked intruders, and the death of the woman, Amelia Barrios. She scrolled down to the obituary photo, which took up several inches.

Casey choked.

Death shot closer to the screen. "Could it be?"

"It has to," Casey whispered.

Even with the black-and-white image, there was no hiding it—the young, dead woman's hair was as white as newly driven snow.

Chapter Twenty-seven

"You okay?" Tara stood up behind the counter.

"Do you know anything about this?"

Tara came to peer over Casey's shoulder. "Oh, sure. That Halloween party is the big town mystery."

"But this woman, Amelia Barrios. Does she have relatives around?"

"Of course. Everybody here—well, except for me and Dottie, and now you—has relatives in town."

"And who are they? Her relatives?"

"Well, her husband lives down the street. Bill Barrios."

Casey glanced at Death. Nell's grandma hadn't simply died. She'd been murdered.

Tara was still talking. "Her daughter Gracie lives out of town a bit. What's her last name? Another Basque one. Achabal, that's it."

"And Nell?" Casey wanted the confirmation, even though she knew the answer.

"She's Amelia's granddaughter."

It made sense now. Nell said her grandmother died a long time ago. But did the girl know how she died? And why? Her grandmother's death was like one of those horror novels she liked to read. Or the movies she watched when she could choose.

"Is this all true? Everything they say in the article?"

Tara took the seat at the next computer, which unfortunately already had Death sitting in it.

Death shot out of the chair to hover on Casey's other side.

Tara shivered and rubbed her arms. "Who knows what's true and what isn't, after all this time? But I would tend to believe that, rather than what people say now. It's like that telephone game. The more people tell the story, the more it changes."

"Tell me what you've heard."

"Okay, but remember I've been told lots of stories, and they sometimes contradict themselves. Also, keep in mind I came here ten years ago. I wasn't around when it happened. I mean, as a kid or anything."

"Just tell me the basics."

"Okay, well, there was a Halloween party. Obviously. One of the women had it at her house, Wilma was her name, but it was co-hosted by her best friend. Ethel Merman, I call her, because she wears lots of dark lipstick and over-the-top clothes. I mean, I like a little bit of color, but she goes crazy."

Death chuckled. "I do believe she means old Flower Pants."

"Her real name is Ethel Bernard. Anyway, Wilma and Ethel had this party, and from what the cops found out, some of the people showed up wearing costumes that covered their faces, so no one could give an exact list of who actually was there. I guess they were going to have a costume contest later on, and they were waiting until then to reveal who they all were."

Casey considered the photo she had stuck in her jeans and pictured the clown, Richard Nixon, and the devil. She knew there was something creepy about those costumes, but knowing they were truly unknown was even worse. Could they have been the intruders who tied up the women? Or were they simply party-goers who hadn't given their identities to the police? Or had the costumes been taken off by that time and discarded, thought to be unimportant?

"So, anyway, these people, who they thought were their friends in disguise, said they'd come up with a fun game for the party, kind of a magic trick, and did the other women want to see it?

The women at the party had already been knocking some back and were halfway to sloshed, so they thought it sounded fun. These women, the disguised ones, gathered up the folding chairs Ethel had gotten from the Methodist church, and lined them up in Ethel's living room. They had the women sit and used ropes to tie them all up. Like I said, the women were kind of drunk, so they let them do it. Once they were all tied up, the disguised ones told them they had to get themselves untied—"

"—while they burned the house down."

"Right. So the people in the disguises, whoever they were, took off. The women at the party thought they were about to die and tried to get untied, but they couldn't. So Joyce Staples, this woman dressed as Wonder Woman completely flipped out, screaming and going crazy, so everybody was paying attention to her. Nobody realized Amelia Barrios—dressed as Lucy, of all people, you know, the crabby girl from Peanuts?—was having a heart attack. By the time they noticed, they couldn't help her. The Bride of Frankenstein, I think, was the first to get free, and she called the ambulance, but it was too late. By that time everybody forgot the house was supposed to be burning."

Casey met Death's eyes, stunned. Officer Whistler hadn't had this amount of detail. "That's horrible."

"Yeah, it really is," Tara said.

Casey thought about the photo. Had anyone in the public seen it before? It wasn't in the newspaper. But would film have been developed that quickly back in the seventies? She hesitated, then pulled out the envelope.

Tara gave a little laugh. "What's that?"

"Have you ever seen this?" Casey slid the photo onto the table.

Tara looked at the picture for a few seconds before her eyes widened. "Oh, my gosh. Is that—that's the women from the party! Where did you get this?"

So the photo was new to her. Where had it come from?

"Do you know who these people are?"

Tara's eyes roamed over it. "Most of them."

"Is one of them Dottie?"

"Oh, no. She didn't go. She was home with Vern, handing out candy, so she didn't experience any of it." She squirmed. "Some people say it was Dottie and Marianne in the costumes, but it doesn't seem possible since Dottie was home with Vern, and we all know now that Marianne had taken off with some guy."

"Which Marianne's family blames Dottie for."

"Isn't that crazy? I don't see how that's supposed to be Dottie's fault."

"They needed someone to blame, I guess."

"Stupid."

The door opened and a couple of older women came in. Neither one was Flower Pants or her friend, but Casey still took a good look. Were they in the Halloween picture?

"I've got to help these ladies," Tara said. "They come in every day to Skype with their grandkids. It's sweet, I guess, but since the grandkids are too young to actually talk, it seems kind of pointless."

Casey laughed. "They probably just like seeing them. Do you need me to move?"

"Nope. They can use the other two computers."

Tara went to get the women set up. Casey scanned the next few issues, but was able to find only a few more articles in the *Idaho Press-Tribune* before the stories faded away. Not once did the group photo show up, nor did the cops put forth a solid lead on the intruders. The rumors about the divorcing couple, the woman having the affair, and the greedy landowner, were simply that. Speculation that ruined lives.

There were no articles that mentioned Marianne or her flight from her family, but Casey wasn't surprised. What Marianne had done wasn't criminal. It was too bad the town and all of its judgmental citizens didn't realize the same thing would apply to Dottie.

Tara got the other women situated and came back to Casey. She plunked down some old books and Casey recognized the format. Yearbooks.

"Thought you might find these interesting." Tara sat in the same seat as before and opened the top one. "You'll recognize some faces. It's the class of 1963 you'll be most familiar with. This is their senior year."

"Who should I be looking for?"

The phone rang at the desk. "I'll be right back. Take a look while I'm gone."

Casey slid over the open book and turned to the pages filled with senior portraits. The first one to catch her eye was Ethel Bernard. Good old Flower Pants. Her expression was surprising. Softer. Happier. Without the pinched, angry countenance, she was actually pretty. The quote underneath her photo proclaimed, "Most beautiful girl in town."

Huh. Not something Casey would ever have suspected.

Casey didn't recognize anyone else on that page. She turned to the next and was confronted with a younger version of Vern. As with Flower Pants, his photo spoke of an easier time. His eyes sparkled, and he looked rather handsome in his suit coat and tie. His quote said simply, "Most likely to succeed."

Did running a convenience store for an unappreciative, unfriendly town count as succeeding? Casey didn't think so.

Casey paged through, recognizing Flower Pants' friend Wilma and finding other familiar people, such Nell's grandpa Bill Barrios and her late grandmother Amelia, and Stuart Rush, who, because of his last name, must have been Marianne's husband.

Casey went hot and cold, realizing she hadn't seen Marianne. What had her last name been before she got married? What did she look like? Casey didn't know.

She got through all the pages of seniors, then went back to the beginning. She scanned the first names until she found Marianne close to Flower Pants, where Casey had missed her the first time around. Marianne Cenarrusa. "Most likely to be mayor by the time she's twenty."

Interesting.

But not as interesting as her picture.

Marianne's photo was different from the other girls'. Sure, she wore a formal dress, and her hair was set in a flip of the times, but it was the look in her eyes that set her apart. Confident. Intelligent. Not going to take crap from anybody.

Casey could respect that.

But she couldn't respect abandoning her friends and family without a word.

"How's it going?" Tara was back.

"Just found Marianne."

"It's sad, isn't it? To think how she let everybody down." Tara held out her hand. "You haven't found it yet, have you? I can tell."

"Found what?"

She waggled her fingers and Casey gave her the book. Tara paged through. "I used to study these when I first arrived. All the years up to the day I got here. That's what comes from being a librarian. I want to know all about everybody." She grinned at Casey before going back to the book. She went quickly through the sections of sports and choir and clubs and scholar awards, stopping often to point out a picture of Vern, who was involved in every sport and served as class president, until she arrived at the one she'd been looking for. She turned the book toward Casey.

Prom king. Prom queen. The guy with the crown was none other than Vern, smiling, handsome, his arm around the queen.

Flower Pants.

Casey shook her head. "Really?"

"Really."

"But were they…They got elected as king and queen, right? There was nothing else?"

Tara took the book back and turned to the final pages, where people were chosen as Class Clowns, or Smartest, or Most Fashionable, as well as predictions for coming years. And there, under the banner of Class Couple, Most Likely to be Happily Married with Kids, was a photo of Vern. With Flower Pants.

Casey's breath left her in a rush. So Flower Pants' flirting did make sense. There was a history there. Flower Pants absolutely did have a crush on Vern—now and back half a century.

Tara leaned over to study the photo. "I know, right?"

"So…" Casey took a moment to let it settle. "What happened?"

Tara wrinkled her nose. "It's kind of a soap opera. Vern and Ethel got engaged right out of high school. They were supposed to be married the next July. But then Vern went to Portland for a summer business course so he could help his dad with the store. A couple months later Dottie came to town looking for him. She was pregnant. They got married in October."

Wow.

Casey pondered young Flower Pants and how she must have hated his new wife. Had those emotions ever faded, even a little? Or had that resentment held on full-force for fifty years?

"Did you hear about his dad?"

Casey looked up from the yearbook. "You mean how he died soon after the baby?"

"Yeah. A lot of people blamed Dottie. They say his heart attack was because of her. It's ridiculous, but what are you going to tell people who have believed something for so long?"

A group of kids entered the library, and Tara looked up and smiled. "Time for my daily baby-sitting. I don't mind, really. But it does require my attention." She stood. "Feel free to look at these, but they do have to stay here. Reference books, you know."

Casey transferred the stack to the other side of the room and leafed through them. She found lots of photos of both Vern and Flower Pants, starting with their middle school years, but it wasn't until their junior year they began showing up together. It was disconcerting. Vern looked…joyful. She'd never seen that on him in real life.

But then, she'd only known him for three days, during this time when his wife was dying.

Casey thanked Tara and left. She still had some time before Vern expected her back at the store, and she had lots of questions.

More now than ever.

Chapter Twenty-eight

Casey was surprised by the number of people on the street, most of them young. She shouldn't have been, seeing how Tara had just been inundated with the younger generation. School must have let out. She watched for Nell, but didn't see her among the children on the sidewalks.

A copper-skinned boy with dark hair ran past her laughing, with another boy racing after him, their backpacks banging against them, shoelaces untied, coats flapping from their hands, because of course they weren't wearing them. Casey watched until they disappeared, a knot forming in her stomach. Omar would never run laughing down a sidewalk, never have school friends, never learn how to speak Spanish, or understand geometry, or write a persuasive essay. He would always be her baby, cooing and giggling and making the first sounds of toddler-hood. Until he wasn't.

Dottie hadn't gotten to know her child for even a day. Had lost her before she'd taken her first breath. Now Dottie had been tethered to this town where she had neither friends nor family because her daughter was buried here, had lived in her mother's womb here. Had died here. Was it worth it? The years of disdain and suspicion and mistreatment? Was it all because she didn't want to leave her daughter's grave? This, in addition to her father-in-law's controlling hold on the store. Casey couldn't imagine the pain.

No, that wasn't true. Casey knew the pain. Nothing else could hurt so badly as to lose her baby. Her husband. But Casey couldn't stay where she had loved them. Couldn't live in that house, see the things they'd touched, the places they'd walked. She'd been running from those memories since the day they died, and couldn't see herself ever stopping. At least, not as long as she had to bear those reminders every day.

She stopped in the middle of the sidewalk. Was that the key to her discontent? Seeing those things? Being reminded of what she'd lost?

But no. Even on the road, she remembered. Even here, hundreds of miles from home, it gnawed at her soul. Could she ever run far enough?

A kid on a bike flew past and Casey began walking again.

Dottie and Vern had chosen to stay in Armstrong. Chosen to deal with the bad treatment so they could stay close to their daughter and fulfill his father's wishes. Had it really served them better than starting over somewhere new? It didn't seem so to Casey. From what she'd seen, the Dailys' lives were basically empty of everything that made life worth living. Wouldn't they be better off if they'd moved on?

Would she?

The sound of a vehicle broke into her thoughts and Casey glanced at the street to see a truck cruising slowly beside her. The driver was Coop, Lance Victor's stupid friend. One of the girls from Saturday night sat in the passenger seat. Her window lowered, and Casey prepared to run the other direction.

"Hey," the girl said.

Casey stopped, and the truck did, too.

Casey looked from one kid to the other. "What do you want?"

Coop grinned. "Nothing. Except this."

The girl held up her phone. Casey looked at it, but it was only the back.

"Thanks for the picture." Coop laughed. "Although you could

have smiled." Laughing, he screeched away, leaving tire marks on the road. Casey checked for children in the street, thankful they were all out of harm's way.

So, crap. What could he want her picture for? Was he in touch with people from Beltmore? Would he have any idea the cops were looking for her? Or was he just being a dick?

Thinking of cops, Casey made a detour and swung by the police station, hoping Whistler would be there. Fortunately, the young officer was sitting behind the desk, laughing at something with Austin. She stood with one hip against the counter, while he leaned backward in a straight wooden chair, the front legs off the ground. Whistler buzzed Casey into the back.

"Good lunch yesterday?" Casey asked Austin.

He grinned. "The burgers we snuck out to get afterward were great."

"I warned him." Whistler laughed. "He didn't believe me."

"Did so."

"Did not."

"I specifically said, 'My mom is a horrendous cook, we'll have to order pizza.' And you said, word for word, 'It can't be that bad.'"

"Well, sure, because everyone thinks their mother's cooking isn't that great."

"They do not!"

"Do so."

Casey cleared her throat.

"Sorry." Whistler's eyes sparkled. "Did you need something?"

"Well, yes. That's why I'm here."

"Right. That's usually why people come in."

Casey grinned back—because how could she not?—and sat in an empty chair. "Remember that Halloween party from a long time ago? The one where the woman died?"

"Sure. The town's big mystery." She spoke in an exaggerated whisper, as if the whole thing were kind of a joke. But that could have been that she and Austin were in a joking mood and she hadn't transitioned back to serious cop mode.

Casey could forgive the attitude. She would give anything to feel that lighthearted again, even for a moment. "What about Marianne Rush?"

Austin frowned. "Who's that?"

"The town's other big mystery, I thought."

Whistler tapped her pen on the counter. "Right. The woman who disappeared."

"When was that?" Austin dropped the front legs of his chair onto the tile.

Whistler shared a smile with Casey. "You have to forgive him. He's new."

"Not so new."

"You're a baby."

"Am not—"

"So what do you know?" Casey asked, before they could get into another lengthy back and forth.

"She took off the same night as the Halloween party, right? Marianne Rush up and left her family. Didn't tell anybody, except supposedly Dorothy Daily."

"Supposedly?"

"That's the rumor, you know? That Dottie—and Vern, of course—have known all along where Marianne went, but they've refused to tell. The family is still mad."

"But the Dailys say they don't know?"

"That's what I'm told. Not that people really talk about it much these days. I've never asked the Dailys. We're not investigating either of those cases anymore."

"Why not?"

"What evidence could there be now that wasn't around forty-five years ago? It's not like they would have known to keep DNA samples, or anything. And stuff was so crazy that night, it was impossible to categorize all of the forensic evidence. Not that people thought about forensic evidence very much back then."

Casey could believe it. If anything had been collected, there was a good chance in a small precinct such as this things wouldn't have been processed correctly, or even at all. Not that the cops were bad—they probably weren't trained to do it.

"Has anyone ever suggested the two things are connected?"

"What? The Halloween party and Marianne Rush taking off? Wouldn't know why."

"Because they happened the same night."

"Oh, well, sure. I guess they might have considered a connection, but there apparently wasn't any. Dottie was helping Vern hand stuff out at the store, and Marianne took off while her kids were out trick-or-treating with their dad. Neither one of them was seen at the party."

Which they wouldn't have been if they were hiding behind full-face masks. But why would they lie about that? And how would their presence not have been documented when the police and ambulance arrived?

"So how come you're asking about this?" Whistler asked.

"I don't know. It caught my interest."

Austin snorted. "Not a lot in this town to do that. It's no wonder it stuck out."

"This town's okay," Whistler said.

"If you like boring."

"It's not always boring."

Casey turned away and walked out while they bickered.

They didn't even notice she'd left.

Chapter Twenty-nine

The streets had cleared out, and Casey saw only a few kids as she headed back to the Dailys'. How odd was it, really, that Marianne disappeared the same night as the fatal Halloween party? Was it the nature of the holiday? A huge coincidence? Or was there more to it than that?

Unsettled, she arrived at the house and went in the side door. The TV murmured on low volume in the living room. Vern would be over at the store, so she was hopeful Dottie was awake.

Dottie sat on the love seat, facing the television but not really watching it. She was so still Casey would have thought she was dead if she hadn't blinked once, very slowly.

Casey sat on the chair catty-corner from her. "Hey. Are you all right?" It seemed like a stupid question, with the news Dottie had gotten earlier that day, but Casey meant it in a more immediate kind of way. Dottie didn't look so good.

Dottie scrutinized Casey's face, as if trying to figure out who she was, or where she had come from.

"Dottie? It's Casey. Remember? I'm staying in your basement."

"Of course." She nodded, and refocused on the TV.

"Dottie..." Casey considered what she was about to do and wondered if it was smart. Or kind. Maybe it was neither, but it seemed necessary if she was going to figure things out and help Dottie and Vern get out from under the accusations. She slid the Halloween photo out of her stack of copies and held it out. "Do you recognize this picture?"

Dottie went very still. "Where did you get that?"

"It came in the mail to the store. There was no return address."

Dottie stared at the photo, but didn't say anything.

"Do you know when this is from?"

Dottie looked away. "A long time ago. Another lifetime."

Casey set the photo back on her lap. "Do you remember that night?"

Dottie's face remained blank. Stony. Finally she said, "That was the night Marianne left me."

"Forty-five years ago?"

Dottie's eyes drifted up to Casey's face. "Yes." Casey heard the question Dottie wasn't asking, and wasn't sure how she was going to answer. Did she admit she dug through their trash to find the anonymous note?

"Did you and Marianne go to the party?"

Dottie turned away, toward the kitchen. "She was supposed to meet me to hand out candy at the church, but said she was sick." Her breath became labored. Loud.

"Dottie—"

"I helped Vern hand out candy at the store. And then we came back here." Her jaw worked, and her face grew red. "Marianne left me that night. She didn't come back."

Dottie put a hand over her chest and closed her eyes.

"What's happening?" Death sat on the opposite end of the love seat wearing workout clothes, as if interrupted during a training session. The jersey said, "Do It Anyway."

Casey grabbed Dottie's wrist. Her heartbeat was rapid. "I don't know. I didn't mean to upset her."

Dottie didn't seem to notice Casey talking to someone else. Her eyes were glassy, and sweat broke out on her forehead.

"Should I call 911?"

"No. Calm her down. It's not her time yet."

"Dottie. Dottie." Casey knelt in front of her and held her hands. "Look at me. It's okay. You're all right." Was Casey lying? She kind of felt like she was.

Casey let go of Dottie's hands and placed her own on the woman's cheeks. "Look at me, Dottie. I'm here."

Dottie met Casey's eyes with her panicked ones. Casey smiled. "Deep breath." Casey took one, hoping Dottie would mimic her. "Deep, slow breath."

Dottie followed Casey's lead and breathed in, held it a few moments, and let it out. After several more of these shared inhales and exhales, Dottie's pulse slowed, and the red in her cheeks faded to pink.

Casey reached for a tissue and blotted the sweat on Dottie's face. "It's all right. You're better now."

Dottie patted Casey's hand. "Thank you, sweetheart. I can always count on you."

Casey hesitated, then kept dabbing Dottie's face with the tissue.

"My sweet Anne Marie. I knew you'd always be here for me."

Death's brow furrowed. "Oh, my. She thinks you're her dead daughter."

Dottie wiggled around on the love seat, looking for something. A pillow. "If I could...lie down for a bit."

Casey jumped to grab the throw pillow from her chair and set it on the end of the love seat, shooing Death away. Dottie lay down and Casey ran to Dottie's bedroom to grab an afghan. She draped it over Dottie and tucked her in. Dottie closed her eyes and gave a huge sigh, a smile on her face.

So much for getting any worthwhile information from her.

"Crisis averted," Death said. "Now I can get back to my work-out. The Olympics is coming up, you know. I need to be ready."

Casey sat on her heels and wiped her face. She hadn't been prepared for such an intense few minutes.

Death flexed. "Looks like you could use a workout, too."

"I have to get back to the store. I've already been gone too long." She picked up the photo. "I still think there has to be something about this party that's important to Dottie. Why would someone send this photo to her otherwise?"

"Someone thinks she knows something."

"Or believes she was there."

Dottie's eyes shot open. "I couldn't have gone there."

Casey suppressed a gasp. "Right. Because you were home with Vern."

"No. Not because of that." Her lips trembled. Her eyes watered. Casey grabbed another tissue and wiped the old woman's eyes.

"Why then? Why couldn't you be there?"

"All the young mothers were invited. I wasn't…a mother."

Casey's breath left her in a whoosh. The other women wouldn't have been that cruel, would they? "Wait. Wasn't Flower P—Ethel there? She didn't have kids, did she?"

"No, but then, she was Wilma's best friend, and Wilma was the one hosting the party."

And not too many years earlier, Dottie had married the man Flower Pants had been engaged to. Casey couldn't imagine Flower Pants would want to socialize with the woman who stole her fiancé.

"I couldn't have gone because it would have been too hard, knowing what they all had that I didn't." Dottie closed her eyes. "But the real reason I wouldn't have been welcome wasn't about having children. It was the same with Marianne, and she already had two babies."

"I don't understand. What was the same?"

Dottie curled her fingers around the edge of the afghan, pulling it closer to her neck. "The two of us couldn't have gone to the party, even if we had wanted to."

"Why not?"

"Because when all the invitations went out, neither Marianne nor I received one." She let out a long, slow breath. "We couldn't go to the damn Halloween party, because we weren't invited."

Chapter Thirty

"Can you believe that?" Casey made her way to the store from the house. Death gave up on working out and tagged along like one of the children headed home from school. Death's shirt bore a sticker reading, "Save Ferris."

"I don't know why they stayed in this town," Death said. "I mean, I know why, with their baby and the store and everything, but I don't think it paid off."

"Exactly what I was thinking earlier."

Death grunted.

"What?"

"Does seeing their situation make you think about yours?"

"It is not at all the same." Casey heard the defensiveness in her voice, hanging there, she was certain, because Death had hit on the very thing she'd been considering only minutes before.

"Fine." Death's head cocked. "Gotta go."

Casey, alone again, was greeted by Roger as she stepped into Vern's. Well, not exactly greeted. He ducked his head, exited the cashier's area, and left the store. She wondered where Vern went. He wasn't at home, and she didn't hear him in the store.

Since Casey left, the lunch crowd had been and gone, leaving the front section a mess. As she cleaned, she studied the photos surrounding the cashier window. She'd noticed them her first day but hadn't stopped to look at them. They ranged from present-day athletic teams and the high school's show choir to decades-old photos. Forty-five years? Casey searched for Vern, since she might now recognize him after seeing the yearbook.

She finally found him toward the ceiling, holding the rack of a dead buck, which lay on its side by Vern's feet. His rifle rested on the ground, and his smile told a story of victory and pride.

Other than that, she couldn't find him anywhere, although she did see a photo of Flower Pants and Wilma, along with some of the other women from the Halloween photograph. Lucy and Wonder Woman and, she thought, the Bride of Frankenstein. They stood in front of the white corner church many years earlier, Frankenstein's Bride wearing her own, real-life wedding dress. Marianne and Dottie were, not surprisingly, absent.

Casey sold some Bugles and Gatorade to the under-twelve demographic, weeded through the DVDs Vern had asked her to sort, and was cutting orange and black ribbons for some Halloween decorations in the bread aisle when a beeping noise split the air. Casey dropped the scissors and searched the room—was it the smoke alarm? The gas pumps?

No.

It was her phone, in her pocket, actually ringing. When had anyone ever called her?

She dug it out. The number came up without a name. "Hello?"

"Casey? Officer Maddy Justus, from Beltmore."

"Oh. Hey. Everything okay?"

"I'm not sure. Are things all right in Armstrong?"

"Depends on how you define 'all right.'"

"Why? What's wrong?"

"It's a strange town with dark undertones. Lots of old grudges, unsolved mysteries, and layers of resentment."

"Hmm. Sounds like most small towns."

Casey laughed. "Yeah. I guess."

"So why I called…I think you might get some company."

"Company? As in… Oh, crap. The guys from the playground?"

"Or their friends."

"How did they find me?"

"That's the weird thing. You're online."

"I am? I really haven't been." Casey tried to think of the last time she'd used her phone, or even pulled it from her pocket.

"No, not you personally, I mean, you haven't been doing stuff. But there's a photo of you. It got sent here, put up by some kid named Brian Cooper? He's asking if anybody knows you."

Casey gripped the phone. "That little creep. I was walking home less than an hour ago. He pulled up beside me and the girl in his truck took my picture."

"Well, that takes care of that. You haven't seen anybody yet? From here, I mean?"

"No. Should I tell someone?"

"I'll call Whistler, see if there's anything she can do. Protection she can offer."

"Not necessary."

"But—"

"I can take care of myself. I promise." Let them come.

"Chief Spears is trying to get the guys in custody, but he can't find them. They're probably hiding out in their hunting cabin in the mountains, but there's no phone service up there, and it would take hours to get to them. The chief is talking to the cops up there to see if we can get some assistance."

"Thanks. Sorry to cause all this trouble."

"No apology necessary. If we can get these creeps it's worth it. But I'm concerned about you."

"I'll be fine. Is Sheila okay?"

"Pastor Sheila's fine, other than worrying about you. I don't think those guys are stupid enough to mess with a messenger of the Lord."

Casey wasn't sure if she was joking or not, so she didn't laugh.

"So..." Justus coughed. "I'll let you know if I hear anything, and you do the same."

"You got it. Thanks."

Casey hung up and peered out the front door. No strange cop cars yet. And no huge trucks.

"Everything okay?"

Casey jumped as Vern called from the grocery area. "Fine."

"I'll be in back if you need me."

Casey was furious with herself. She couldn't lose focus like that again. If the Beltmore guys came for her, she had to be ready. She took stock of her body. Her face was still colorful, but she didn't need her face to protect herself. Her ribs, while better than three days ago, still ached if she pressed on them or moved too quickly.

She stepped to the end of the carb aisle, between the donuts and the door to the parking lot, and tried a few defensive stances. Nothing had changed since her workout that morning. Achy, but serviceable.

The bell dinged, and Casey straightened. Vern's customers didn't need to see his new cashier readying for battle.

Lance Victor stood in front of the cashier's window, shifting nervously from foot to foot. "I need some gas."

Casey input the amount and watched as he pumped the gas, not trusting him out of her sight. The last she'd seen him he'd been sitting by his parents in church, a red flush on his neck from the stares of the other congregants. Casey hadn't felt sorry for him then, and didn't now. She wondered if there might be a chance for him. If he wasn't the one instigating the vandalism, could he be persuaded to think before acting? To say no to his friends when they wanted him to run around painting slurs on people's buildings?

He came back in for his change. Casey dropped it into his hand. "You know you don't have to do everything that Coop kid tells you to do."

He didn't look up. "Yeah, I know."

"So?"

"He's my friend."

"Why?"

More shifting from foot to foot. "I've known him since I was born. He's always been there."

"He's been there, or been there *for you*?"

"There's a difference?"

Oh, young Lance. "A huge difference."

"I don't know what that means."

"It means you have to decide. Are you going to let him bully you into hurting people and getting in trouble? Or are you going to look around and see what—or who—else is there?"

Her words hung in the air. Casey wasn't sure he was able to catch them.

He shoved his money into his pocket, and went back out to his truck.

Chapter Thirty-one

Casey worked the rest of the day under a cloud of low-level anxiety. Had the Beltmore guys seen her photo? Would they rumble up to Vern's, hoping to make her pay? If they were hiding out in the mountains several hours away, she at least had time to prepare.

Casey offered to take the last few hours behind the counter so Vern could be home with Dottie, and for once he took her up on it. It only seemed right they would be together after the morning's news. The deli door and back exit were locked, so the only way customers could come in was through the front, where Casey could see them.

"This is one sleepy town." Death lay sideways by the camping gear, hovering over a heavy blanket and wearing flannel, which made Casey think of *Deliverance*. Not a calming reference.

"Sleepy is better than a lot of other things." Casey locked the front door and waited for Vern to come count and store the money in the safe. She pulled out a lawn chair. Her eyes were beginning to droop when a knock came. She shot up, ready to defend herself, even though the door was locked. But the face pressed up close to the window was a friendly one.

Officer Whistler.

"Hey." Casey unlocked the door.

Whistler checked the front area. Her gaze passed through Death, who now occupied the lawn chair. "Why are you sitting in the dark?"

"Just waiting for Vern to come and close. Want to hang out? There are more chairs."

"Can't. Got to drive my rounds. You okay? Maddy told me about the photo. Stupid kids."

"It was bound to happen sooner or later."

"Too much sooner than it should have. But what can you do with dicks like Coop running the show?"

"He's not running it."

"Yeah, well, you tell him that." Her radio crackled. "You got my number. Call if something comes up."

"Will do. Thanks."

"You bet. Oh, hey, Vern."

"Officer." Vern stepped from the shadows of the parking lot. His face, gray during the day, appeared ashen in the night. Casey refrained from feeling his throat for a pulse.

Whistler gave Casey a salute and drove away.

"You need anything else?" Casey asked Vern.

He took his spot behind the counter. "No. Thanks. I enjoy these hours. No customers to bother me." He grinned.

"I hear you. I guess I'll go, then."

He waved without looking, already counting. Casey made sure the door clicked behind her.

"He seem all right to you?" Death swooped alongside her as they crossed the parking lot.

"All right as he could be, I guess, after a day like this."

Casey bypassed the front door of the house and climbed down the fire escape into her room. She crossed in the dark and flipped on the light. And froze.

"What?" Death stopped. Immediately the room went cold.

Casey's breath puffed from her mouth as she spoke. "Someone's been in here."

"How can you tell?"

"I don't know." It wasn't anything obvious. An indentation on the bed, the way the handle on her duffel bag drooped, what looked like a footprint on the carpet. Carefully, she pulled apart the sides of her bag. Everything looked a little out of order, as if someone had gone through, from top to bottom.

Death peered over her shoulder, making her shiver. "You think it was Vern? He knew you wouldn't come back if you were the only one minding the cash register."

"It could've been Dottie. I did find her down here earlier today. But my stuff wasn't gone through then. I'm sure of it." A sense of unease began in her stomach and spread to her fingertips and toes. Her scalp itched.

Death circled the room, searching for clues. "What do you want to do?"

Run screaming.

But realistically? It was nighttime. It was dark.

She was tired.

Casey locked the window and took a quick shower. When she was sure she was alone, she locked the bedroom door, too.

Death had to usher some unfortunate but heroic missionaries to the Other Side, so for now, Casey sat alone in her window well, back against the wall. The moon again hung out of frame, but its glow lit the sky. She was afraid to sleep in case the creeps from Beltmore found her. Or Lance and his delinquent friends. She let her fingers graze the crowbar she found on the workbench in the Dailys' garage. A little something to even the playing field, should she get caught on her own again.

Thinking of Lance, she wondered if he was the one who had been in her room. Nothing had been spray-painted on her wall, she thought—with what might have been humor if she hadn't been so tired—so it probably hadn't been him.

Casey pulled the quilt tighter around her shoulders and thought about Dottie asleep upstairs. She wondered when Vern slept, or ate, even. How he survived with his schedule. It was a wonder he wasn't as sick as his wife. But then, who would care for her?

That was how it was supposed to be. Growing old together, loving each other to the end. Casey had loved Reuben to the end, of course. She still loved him. But they had been stripped of the later chapters of married life. Those things had been stolen from them in that brief moment, in the flare of fire and wreckage.

Death had changed her life in ways she'd never imagined. Who ever thinks, when they get out of bed in the morning, that their life is going to be irreparably damaged before the sun goes down? But you can't think that. You can't live each day fearing the worst, waiting for your life to be destroyed. Because what, then, would be the point of living?

Casey pulled up the app on her phone where she could Find a Friend. Reuben and Omar, of course, couldn't be found. She closed her eyes. So many people had uttered those clichés when they'd died. *They're somewhere better now. God needed more angels. They aren't gone, just in a new place.*

Such utter crap to say to a freshly grieving widow and mother. But that didn't mean she was unbelieving. She'd always thought heaven was real. Where it was, exactly, she didn't know, but... somewhere.

Were Reuben and Omar watching her? Did they have their own Find a Friend in the afterlife, where they could keep track of her? She shifted uncomfortably. If they were watching, what did they see? Were they pleased she still thought of them? Or were they frustrated with her? Impatient for her to get her act together and move on?

Casey gazed at the corner of her room with the shrine that seemed half about the Dailys' stillborn baby and half what they had hoped for her to become. Casey didn't want to be like them. Shells of former people. Waiting to die.

Her phone had gone to sleep. The screen refreshed to show the little circle with Eric's photo. Eric is at Home, it said. Casey's heart leapt, but then realized that Home meant Ohio, where he'd grown up. Where his mother lived. Where he ran his nonprofit soup kitchen.

Home, for him, was not Colorado. Not with her.

She gazed at her phone. At what it said. What it meant.

She didn't like it.

Chapter Thirty-two

Casey awoke suddenly. She lay scrunched in the window well, a crick in her neck. What was that sound? A slap? A bang? She strained to hear another noise, but there was nothing.

A chilling breeze blew over her. Death floated by the door, half mist, half swirling black robes. The bedside clock glowed red, not yet midnight.

Death flowed away. "Come."

Casey hopped down from the window well, adrenaline taking over. Death rushed through the basement and up the stairs, leading Casey to Dorothy and Vern's bedroom.

Casey's heart leapt to her throat. "Is she dead?"

Death disappeared through the door. Casey knocked, but received no response. She turned the knob and eased the door open. "Dottie?"

Only silence.

Casey pushed the door wider and stepped into the room. One side of the bed was empty. She went to the other side, where Dottie lay.

"Still breathing." Death hovered close. "But barely."

"What happened?"

"I don't know. I've been keeping a close eye and felt the end coming. But I wasn't expecting it tonight. I thought she had a few more days."

Casey felt for a pulse. Very slow. Very faint. She reached for her phone, but of course she didn't have it, wearing her night t-shirt and shorts. She ran downstairs and dialed 911 as she threw on a sweatshirt. She spoke to the dispatcher while she hurried to the store.

She banged on the locked door. The light from behind the counter glowed, and Vern appeared in the rectangular opening. Casey gestured frantically and he pushed open the door.

"It's Dottie. I called the ambulance."

Vern ran from the store and Casey followed after hearing the click of the lock.

"Dottie!" He shook his wife when he arrived at her beside. "Dot!"

Casey put a hand on his shoulder. He flung it off. "Did she say anything? Was she talking?"

"She was like this when I found her."

He stroked her cheek. "I'm here, Dot. I'm here."

"I'll watch for the ambulance."

Casey ran downstairs to scoop up her shoes and pull on warm-up pants, then raced outside. The siren split the night before she saw the lights, and she stood by the side of the road to flag down the driver. The EMTs were efficient and professional, asking Casey questions as they worked. Within a minute they were in the bedroom sliding Dorothy onto the stretcher.

Casey searched for Vern's car keys and found them on the kitchen counter. "Let's follow them. Do you have your wallet?"

They climbed into the car, Casey behind the wheel, and were ready when the ambulance pulled away. Fifteen minutes later they arrived at a hospital in a neighboring town.

Casey helped Vern find his insurance cards and take care of those things you don't want to think about while your loved one is in the ER. She swallowed the anxiety attempting to clog both her breathing and her brain. Hospitals held only pain for her.

"I don't understand." Vern's pen drooped. "When I left to go to the store she was fine."

Well, as fine as she could be after being told she only had weeks to live. And after Casey had asked her really uncomfortable questions. And after Dottie thought Casey was their stillborn baby, all grown up.

Death wafted through the doors separating the ER from the waiting room, wearing a doctor's white coat. Casey excused herself and went to the water cooler on the other side of the room. Death met her there. Casey turned toward the wall, facing away from Vern.

"I don't think she's going to make it through the night." Death's nametag read, Douglas Ross, MD, and Casey was taken back momentarily to those days when her mother faithfully swooned over George Clooney in his scrubs. Casey, too young to care, went more for the gore factor of the show.

"What happened? Why would Dottie die so suddenly after being told she had a few weeks?"

"I don't know." Death glanced at her. "You were half awake when I came to get you. Why?"

"Something…a sound. I'm not sure. Did you see something? Someone?"

"No. I went directly to their bedroom and saw she was as near to death as possible without actually being ready to go."

"And now?"

"I think it will be only moments. Perhaps an hour."

"Shall I see if Vern can be with her?"

"They'll soon come get him."

The double doors to the back swished open and a real doctor in a white coat appeared. She searched the occupants of the waiting room and her eyes landed on Vern. Casey strode across to meet her at his chair.

"Mr. Daily?"

Vern stood up suddenly, the clipboard and pen clattering to the floor. "Is she…?"

The doctor shook her head, but Casey could see in her face

that it wouldn't be long. "There's nothing more we can do, Mr. Daily. Since she has the DNR, the Do Not Resuscitate clause you wrote up a few years ago, we can't use our more extreme lifesaving measures."

"No. She doesn't want that. I don't want that." He took a deep breath, held it, and let it out slowly. "May I be with her?"

"That would be good." She turned to Casey. "You, too?"

"Oh, no. But thanks."

Vern grabbed her wrist. "Please?"

Death shooed her toward the doors. "He needs you. Who else does he have?"

"All right."

The doctor led them into a circle of curtained-off rooms. A movement caught Casey's eye, and she stopped. A woman in green scrubs stood at the curve of the hallway. A woman with bright white hair. Nell's mother hovered like a rabbit ready to run, then straightened her shoulders and walked the opposite direction until she was out of sight.

So this was where she worked.

Had she checked on Dottie? Did she care, or was it to gather gossip, like when she wanted to talk about the basement room? Or was Casey being too hard on her?

"Miss?"

The doctor came back for Casey.

"Sorry. Saw someone I knew."

"A patient?"

"Nurse. Gracie Achabal."

"Oh, sure. She's a great nurse. Wonderful with patients. Are you from Armstrong, too?"

"This week I am."

The doctor either didn't hear her, or didn't know how to respond, for she led her without speaking to a curtained-off square of a room with a washing area, bed, and cabinet. There were two chairs, one beside the bed, one by the sink. Dottie's body was barely a lump under the white sheet. Her eyes were closed, and her age-spotted arms lay over the covers, connected to machines by a clip over her index finger. A screen showed her vital signs and beeped every few seconds.

Vern eased into the chair by the bed, his eyes on his wife's face. He stared at her silently, his breath rasping, his hands clutching the arms of the chair.

"What happened?" Casey asked the doctor. "They were told today she would have a few weeks."

The doctor held her clipboard against her chest. "It's hard to be exact about these things. Sometimes the body, no matter what the signs, decides it's just…done."

"But it could be something else?"

The doctor frowned. "What are you suggesting?"

Casey let the events of the past few days roll through her mind. The anonymous note. The Halloween party photo. The graffiti. And a few minutes ago whatever noise had awakened her. She could almost convince herself it had been the sound of a door slamming.

"I want to make sure no one helped her along."

The doctor's eyes angled toward Vern. "You mean…?"

"No! No, I don't mean that at all."

The doctor stepped beside Dottie's bed and visually examined Dottie's neck and face. She rolled Dottie's arm to view the crook of her elbow, and used her fingers to open Dottie's eyelids, then her mouth. She indicated that Casey should join her outside the curtains. She spoke quietly. "I can't see anything to indicate violence, although I can't rule out a drug. We can do a tox screen to make sure nothing is in her bloodstream that shouldn't be."

Casey rubbed her forehead. "I don't know that anything happened, but they got that news today that it would be a few weeks. It seems odd this should happen tonight."

"It's not unprecedented. A patient hears the end is near and subconsciously decides they are ready to die. Was she suffering?"

"She didn't seem to be in pain. She was confused earlier today, but I'm not sure if that's unusual."

Death's upper body appeared through the curtain. "I will be taking her soon. You might want to encourage Vern to tell her whatever is left to say."

Casey stepped toward the curtains. "Thank you, Doctor. I'm sorry if I'm making this something it isn't."

"I'm glad you told me your concerns. I'll pass them along."

"Thank you." Casey slipped back through the drapes and knelt beside Vern. "Talk to her. While you still can."

"I don't know what to say."

"Sure you do. Tell her you love her. That you'll miss her. That it's okay for her to go."

A tear rolled down his cheek and off his chin. "But it's not okay. I don't want her to leave me."

"She doesn't want to leave you, either. But you can't keep her here. Not anymore."

Not now that Death was literally waiting by her bedside.

Vern dropped his face into his hands. Casey rested her hand on his shoulder, which shook with sobs. He cried for a minute or two before wiping his face and scooting his chair closer to the bed. He took Dottie's right hand in both of his and was about to speak when the curtain swished open.

The crabby cappuccino woman from the store swept into the room. "Oh, no." Anger lit her eyes. "She doesn't get to die before telling me everything I want to know."

Chapter Thirty-three

Casey blocked the woman's path. "What do you want?"

"What do I want, Vern? Huh?" Her eyes narrowed. "What I want is what I always wanted, but Dottie wouldn't give me. I want my mother back."

Casey stared at her. "Your mother?"

"Yes." Realization hit her eyes. "Vern didn't tell you? How he and his lovely wife kept the secret that would give me what I've been missing?"

"Oh." Death stepped close to the woman, studying her face. "I hadn't seen enough photos to notice the resemblance."

Casey felt like she'd been hit in the stomach. The crabby woman's demeanor over the past few days suddenly made sense. "You're Marianne Rush's daughter?"

The woman's eyes cut to her. "At least you know who she was. They told you that much. Did they also tell you where she went? Who she's with? That they didn't think we should know? Her own family."

Casey glanced at Vern. It was a conundrum. Why wouldn't the Dailys tell what they knew? Especially after all these years, with the whole town blaming them for Marianne's indiscretion? But that led to another question.

"Why would you even want to find her? She left you without ever getting in touch again."

Casey thought for a moment the woman's anger might turn to tears. "What business is it of yours? You've been here what? Three days? You don't even know my name, do you?"

The woman was right. She didn't. None of this was any of Casey's business, except here she was in the hospital room of a dying woman, with the woman's husband clutching her wrist like she was his only lifeline.

"I'm sorry. I'm Casey—"

"I know your name. Everybody in town knows it."

"What? Why?"

"Are you kidding me? First new person in ages, first person these two invite into their home? What makes you so special? No one can think of anything."

"So, what is your name?" Casey said instead of bashing the woman through the curtain.

"Lisa. Lisa Rush. Yes, it's my maiden name. Somehow the whole mother leaving me thing didn't make for the best marriage. I've been divorced since Annie was little. It's impossible to keep a relationship going when you know your own mother couldn't. Especially when you don't have any idea why she couldn't. That's why Dottie has to tell me what happened that night."

Casey hadn't asked for a life history. Just the woman's name.

"Dottie's not going to be able to tell you anything anymore. No matter how much you want her to."

Lisa took a shuddering breath. "But Vern can."

Casey looked at Vern's profile as he gazed blankly toward the bed. "Maybe at some point. But not right now."

"Why not?"

"Oh, my Holy One." Death looked toward the ceiling. "She's blinded by her hatred."

Casey agreed. "You can see, Lisa. Dottie's…dying."

"No, she's not. She can't. Not yet."

"The doctor said…" Casey stopped and indicated the opening in the curtain. "Let's go into the hallway, at least."

"I'm not leaving until—"

Casey shot out her hand and grabbed Lisa's upper arm, digging her finger into the pressure point behind her elbow. Lisa gasped. Casey spun her around. "We're going. Now."

Propelling Lisa before her, Casey shoved through the parting of the drapes and dragged her captive down the hallway. She flung Lisa's arm away from her, and the woman clutched it to her chest. "What is wrong with you?

"With me? Do you not see what is going on in there? Dottie is dying. Today. Right now."

"But she can't! Not without…not with—" Lisa's eyes filled, and she turned away.

"What exactly do you think she knows?"

"Where my mother is. She's the only one. Well, other than Vern, who won't do anything that woman doesn't want him to do."

Casey believed it. Vern protected Dottie the best he could from the town. If it hadn't been for their baby buried on the outskirts of town, Casey believed the Dailys would have been gone years ago. No matter the consequences of leaving the store.

"Why wait until today? Why not confront her years ago, when it could have made a difference? Your mom's been gone for decades. Do you really want her around Annie after she deserted you so long ago?"

Lisa stabbed a finger toward Casey. "Leave my daughter out of this. This has nothing to do with her."

"Wasn't Marianne her grandmother?"

"She never knew her. I was only a kid when she left."

Right. "So why now? Why not let it go? Let her go?"

Lisa stared at the wall, her jaw working. "You want to know? Really?" She thrust her hand into her purse and yanked out a piece of paper. A group photo. Of women at the Halloween party.

Casey gasped. "It was you! You sent that picture to Vern's."

"So what if I did?"

"Why?"

"What do you mean, why? Because it changes everything."

Casey studied the photo. There was nothing she hadn't seen before. But then, she didn't know who most of the women were, let alone what might be different. "How does it change things?"

"Why do you want to know?"

"Because I've been wondering what happened, too. The Halloween party, your mom leaving. That night still haunts this town. Isn't it time people moved on?" It would be too late for Dottie to benefit, but Vern still had a chance, besides Lisa and Annie and Nell and everyone else affected. She waved her hand at the photo. "So what is it?"

Lisa lips trembled. "See this person? The one in the Richard Nixon mask?"

"Sure. No one knows who it is, except that it was maybe one of the people who tied them up."

Lisa took a quick breath and blew it out. "See the shirt underneath the suit coat? Those broad stripes?"

"Yeah, sure." Casey had noticed it the first time she saw the picture. Not many people were wearing that kind of shirt in the seventies.

"There was only one person in Armstrong who would wear that shirt. My dad."

"But I thought the intruders were women."

Lisa's eyes rolled. "Are you stupid? Who else would have access to that shirt?"

"Wait? Are you saying..." She stared at Richard Nixon. "Is that—"

"Yes. The person who threatened all those women and killed Amelia Barrios? It was my mom."

"But your mom wasn't at the party. And neither was Dottie." At least, that's what she and Vern had proclaimed all these years.

"Apparently, she was. And so was the woman in that hospital bed."

Casey dropped onto a bench. "But why would they terrorize the other women that way?"

Lisa sat on the other end of the bench, tossing the photo onto the plastic cushion between them. "I wish I was able to ask."

"You never did answer me. Why did you wait this long? Why not confront Dottie earlier?"

"Because I just found the photo." Lisa sagged against the wall. "My dad died last month and I've been going through his things, getting the house ready to sell. I found a box in the basement that must have been my mom's. Letters and diaries and pictures, stuck way in the back, where Dad would never go. It was like she was hiding it in plain sight. You know, the stuff you keep from your life before you get married, but you're never quite sure what to do with."

Casey knew. She had her own box sitting in her garage. Would she want to hide it from Eric? There wasn't anything she wouldn't want him to know—he knew the worst by now, anyway—but there were private things from Reuben. She didn't really have anything from before him.

"My dad must never have looked in the box. Even if he would have found it, he's not—he wasn't sentimental. But I discovered it, and this picture was there."

"And the letters? The diaries?"

"From when she was younger. Once she had me and my brother, she stopped writing. Didn't have time, probably."

"But no letters from a man?"

Lisa rolled her head to look at Casey. "Not one. And I searched the whole place once I found that photo."

Casey leaned forward, elbows on her knees, and stared at the tile floor. Would Marianne have taken the letters with her? But why leave the photo, which could incriminate her? Why keep it in the first place?

"So you think one of the other perpetrators was Dottie?"

"Sure. The clown or the devil."

There was no way of telling which, with the flowing costume of the devil, and the puffy one of the clown. No way to see their body shapes.

"I would guess the clown," Lisa said. "Because she's standing next to my mom."

"But Vern said, everyone said, Dottie was at the store handing out candy. That she was supposed to meet your mom at the church, but when your mom called it off, she stayed home."

"Vern would say whatever Dottie wanted him to say. Who's going to argue?"

"Wouldn't people remember she wasn't actually at the store handing out candy?"

"Why would they? If it even crossed their minds, Dottie could say she was in the bathroom, or getting a refill of candy. It's not like people were watching. They didn't know they would need to." She stretched her legs and crossed her ankles, looking at her sneakers. "Besides, the party was after trick-or-treating, because everybody wanted to be out with their kids." Her face darkened. "Except for my mom. She said she wasn't feeling well. Which obviously was a lie, whether she went to the party or left with some guy."

"Casey." Death's voice floated across the air. "It's time."

Casey listened as the beeps on Dottie's machine slowed to a steady tone. A nurse and the doctor swept into Dottie's cubicle. Since she had a non-resuscitation directive, they wouldn't be taking heroic efforts to bring her back, but were still reacting to the alarms.

"You going in there?" Lisa asked.

"I guess." Casey winced. "Eventually."

Lisa stood, grabbing the photo. "You probably should. You may be a complete stranger to everybody in Armstrong, including Vern, but as far as I know, you're all he has. And no matter how much I hated Dottie, I can't make myself hate Vern quite as much. He was being loyal to her, no matter how much it hurt the rest of us." Her nostrils flared. "Dottie ruined everything by coming here, by marrying Vern, and stealing him from his old life. You're going to be hard-pressed to find anybody other than him who will be sad she's gone."

Chapter Thirty-four

Lisa strode down the hall and pushed through the waiting room doors. Casey watched them swing, shocked at the vitriol she'd just heard.

"Excuse me." The nurse stuck her head out of the curtains. "You're here with Mr. Daily, right? He could use you." Her voice was kind.

When Casey entered she could see immediately that Death was gone, as was the essence that made Dottie herself. Her body was there, but it was empty.

Vern sat, stunned, still clasping his wife's hand.

The nurse edged close to Casey. "Is there a pastor to call?"

Of course. Casey should have called him before, but it didn't even cross her mind. Thinking back, it might have been good for him to be there, instead of her, but how would he have known? Which made her wonder…how did Lisa know to find them there? Casey definitely hadn't called her.

The ambulance, maybe. Everybody in town would have heard the sirens. Most likely there were the usual suspects listening to the police scanner. Did one of them call Lisa, knowing she would be interested? Or had she figured it out herself?

No. Of course. Gracie Achabal, Nell's mother. She knew Dottie was there. If she and Lisa were friends, or even acquaintances, and Lisa had shared the Halloween photo with her, she would know how much Lisa wanted answers before Dottie died. She would want answers herself, seeing how her mother had died at the party. The two women had grown up in the same town, with the same tragic Halloween in their pasts. It would make sense if they shared new details.

"Miss?" The nurse was still waiting.

"Oh. Sorry. Yes. The pastor at…" Oh, what was that church called? "The white one on the corner. In Armstrong."

The nurse shook her head.

"I'll figure it out."

The nurse and doctor left to give Vern a few minutes, and Casey pulled out her phone to Google Armstrong's churches, figuring this was a time the "no cell phone use" signs could be ignored. Once she figured out which church was Vern's she stepped out of the cubicle and called the number. She listened to the message, which gave the pastor's number for emergencies. She woke him up, and he said he would be over as soon as he could.

Back in the room Casey studied Vern. Had he really chosen Dottie over the townspeople all these years? Or, as he claimed, was there nothing to tell? He said Marianne contacted Dottie once after that night to let her know all was well, but that there was no return address. There would have at least been a postal mark, right? To say what region the letter was mailed from?

Casey waited in silence for the pastor to arrive. Vern stared at his wife's body, not speaking. Not moving. Not even crying anymore.

After a while the curtain parted. Casey recognized the pastor from Sunday morning. She stood. "Thank you for coming."

"Of course. You are?"

"Casey. I've been staying with Vern and Dottie the past few days."

"I believe I saw you sitting with them in church. And with Nell and Bill, which was a nice change." He smiled gently. "Will you be staying?"

"No, I'll head back and see about the store. Can you give him a ride when he needs it?"

"Sure. At some point we'll need to make funeral arrangements."

Casey held up her hands. "I've been here three days. That wouldn't be any of my business."

"But—"

"Thank you for coming." She placed a hand on Vern's shoulder. "I'm heading back. Pastor…" Dang it, she couldn't remember his name. "Your pastor is here. He'll take you home when you're ready."

Vern didn't respond, but she hoped he'd heard her. If not, the pastor, whatever his name was, could relay the message.

The drive back to Armstrong was a blur as Casey mulled over the night. Lisa Rush, Marianne's daughter, blamed Dottie for her mother's disappearance, or at least for keeping her whereabouts a secret. But why would Dottie do that? What would she have to gain if Marianne left town, never to be heard from again? She'd lost her best—only?—friend, and gained the suspicion and disdain of everyone in Armstrong.

If, as Lisa suspected, her mother and Dottie attended the party and subjected the women to an evening of terror, why would Marianne take off and leave Dottie holding the bag? Although she really didn't, seeing how no one ever officially accused her. Did Dottie know something she hadn't told anyone? Was she really a part of that horrible night? She claimed to be ignorant of Marianne's whereabouts, and to be far from that party the night it all went down.

"You know what you have to do."

Casey jumped at Death's sudden appearance in the passenger seat, wearing the traditional Grim Reaper outfit, with the hood thrown back. Casey was thankful a head and face were along for the ride.

"Why are you back already?"

"Doesn't take long when they're ready."

"She was?"

"Yes. I know Vern said a few weeks, but she knew her time was up. Although…"

"Although what? Did she tell you something? Did someone kill her?"

"My, we are impatient."

Casey slammed a fist through Death, hitting the passenger seat. "Tell me!"

Death's body morphed, and reshaped. "Goodness, you are in a mood."

"I just spent hours in the hospital, where someone died. It's also the middle of the night and I haven't had more than an hour of sleep. What do you expect?"

"Knowing you, I should expect exactly this." Death held up a hand, stopping Casey from throwing another punch. "She said she's uncertain what happened."

"Oh, my gosh, are you serious? How can she not know?"

"Watch the road. Do you realize you almost sent a raccoon to its maker?"

"What did she say?"

"I guess you don't respect wildlife—Hey!"

Casey banged the seat again and again, turning Death into amorphous mist. When a shape returned, it was as Jessica Tandy, from *Driving Miss Daisy*. "Go ahead. Hit me now."

Casey cocked her arm.

"Fine!" Death's arms came up in an X for protection. "She wasn't sure, but she thought there was someone in her bedroom."

"She didn't see them?"

"It was dark. She was asleep, then gradually awoke with the feeling of someone bending over her."

"And?"

"And this person said she was going to pay for what she did."

"Man? Woman?"

"She doesn't know."

"How did she die?"

"She doesn't know."

"For heaven's sake. How convenient."

"It's not convenient. She's dead! And not a medical professional."

"I think you'd remember being strangled!"

"She wasn't strangled. At least, the ER doc didn't notice anything."

"So, smothered?"

"No sign of that, either."

"Poison?"

"Didn't the doctor say natural causes?"

Casey glowered at Death. "What good are you if you can't even tell how people died?"

Death gazed at her calmly. "I know you're feeling a lot of angst right now—"

"Shut up."

They drove in silence until Casey had a realization. "Lisa Rush."

"What about her?"

"She was the person in the room. Everybody knows Vern spends half the night in the store, and she could have seen him through the window. She confronted Dottie, terrifying her into cardiac arrest. I almost did it myself earlier in the day but was able to calm her down, remember? Someone waking her up, whispering accusations...that's enough to terrify even a healthy person."

"That makes sense. Will you ask her?"

"I'll have to. I basically told the ER doc someone murdered her. If all Marianne did was talk to her—"

"What you really mean is she broke into Dottie's home and threatened her."

"Right. Of course you're right. There's no excuse for that. At least not one that carries any weight."

Relieved to have that solved—at least in theory—Casey concentrated on the road until she said, "So what is it?"

"I thought you figured it out."

"Not how Dottie died. When you first appeared in the car you said something about what I need to do now."

"Oh, that. You've got to search for proof."

"Of someone killing her? I told the doctor what I suspected. Do I need to call the cops, too?"

"No, not that, although the cops probably would be a good idea. You need to search for proof of what Lisa was saying."

"The party."

"Of course the party. What if Dottie had something to do with it? What could that mean?"

Casey's vision blurred for a few moments before she blinked and focused again. "I don't think she could do that."

"Because she's a frail old lady?" Death's voice came out flat with irony. "She wasn't always frail and old."

Casey glanced at Miss Daisy. "I know that. I just don't want to think she could do that ever, even before I knew her. Because that also means…"

"That Vern did it?"

"That Vern lied. That he's been lying all this time." His voice rang in her head, a memory from Friday, when she ran to hide from the Beltmore police Officer. *Oh, I'm a good liar, all right.* Casey's insides went cold.

"What would I be looking for, exactly? What would tell us she basically killed Nell's grandmother? Or maybe I could find something proving she's known all along where Marianne went? What?"

"You answered your own question. Does she still have the letter she received from Marianne? Part of a Halloween costume? An incriminating photograph? Anything to shed light on this mess."

Casey let out a big sigh. All she really wanted was to go back to bed.

"If you put it off until tomorrow, Vern will be home. You can't go through his stuff with him there."

"But it's almost morning. I'll need to open the store."

"I think the people of Armstrong will survive one day without their morning coffee. And it will be good for them to realize how much they rely on him."

The street in Armstrong was quiet and dark. No curious gawkers. No caring neighbors. But then, why was she surprised? She suddenly realized—she was so ready to get out of this town. She pulled into the garage and shut the door. "Where should I start? The basement? That's where Marianne's box was hiding in her house."

"Use your brain, sister."

"My brain isn't working on all cylinders, remember? One hour of sleep, and it's the middle of the night."

"I forget about the whole sleep thing. So I'll help. You should start in their bedroom. You can search the rest of the place while he's sleeping, if you don't get through it all tonight."

Casey prepared herself to move. "Fine. Let's get this over with."

Chapter Thirty-five

Death was waiting in the bedroom when she arrived, still an old woman, but this time…Miss Marple? Or Jessica Fletcher? Casey was confused—did the same actor portray both characters? "There aren't a lot of hiding places in here. Shouldn't take long."

Casey tried not to feel like a horrible person. Going through a dead woman's belongings mere hours after her passing…how messed up was that?

A quick, but much more thorough, search than she'd made when looking for the anonymous note took her through the closet, the dresser, and the nightstands, proving only that the Dailys—or at least one of them—liked things neat. Even the floor under the bed was free of dust bunnies. Casey didn't find anything other than normal old people stuff. Clothes and shoes and books and Kleenex. Hand lotion. Baby aspirin. Denture cleaner.

The master bath was more of the same, and smelled strongly of lavender. She found the usual over-the-counter pills and creams you find in anyone's medicine cabinet, plus a few more. A linen closet with towels and washcloths and first aid items. A shower chair and handrails by the toilet. Nothing exciting.

"I've hit all the possible hiding places in here." Casey returned to the bedroom.

"So let's move on. I would suggest going through this level, because it will be easier to check the basement surreptitiously, if he should be around."

Casey followed Death's advice and was on her knees checking out kitchen cabinets when there was a knock on the door. She pulled her head out of the shelf containing pots and pans. "Did I hear something?"

Death swooshed away. "Back door. It's that youngish librarian. You know, the one from the library."

"As befits a librarian," Casey said dryly.

Casey opened the door. "Tara?"

"Hey." Tara wore a thick tie-around sweater but still shivered, hugging herself. "Everything okay?"

Casey gestured her inside.

"I saw the ambulance earlier, but couldn't get over here before they left. When I saw the lights now I wanted to see if I could do anything." She peered around Casey. "Are they back? What happened?"

Casey pulled out a chair at the table and sat in the one across from it. Tara eased down slowly.

"Dottie died a couple hours ago."

Tara gasped. "But didn't you say it would be a few weeks?"

"That's what the doctor said this morning." Casey shook her head. "Yesterday morning."

"Time." Death yawned. "So unpredictable."

Tara sat for a few moments, shaken. "So where's Vern?"

"At the hospital. Taking care of things."

"By himself?"

"The pastor's there."

"Pastor Echebarria? Good. He's great with that sort of thing." Her eyes filled. "Poor Vern."

Casey turned away, not wanting tears. Too tired to fight them.

Tara noticed the open cupboard doors. "So what are you doing?"

Casey went hot. How crass was it to be going through the

Dailys' house while Dottie's body lay cooling in the hospital? She should be ashamed. But then…

"Remember what we were discussing at the library?"

"You mean the Halloween party?"

"That, and Marianne Rush disappearing."

"Sure. What about it?"

Casey took a deep breath, not sure if she should disclose her secrets.

"You've got to trust somebody," Death said.

Did she? She supposed so. And Tara was the only person to make the effort to find out if everything was okay with Dottie.

So Casey took the plunge. She shared who had sent the photo, and how Lisa Rush thought the Richard Nixon mask was her mom's, which also meant Dorothy was there, which in turn meant Dottie and Vern had been lying all these years. She wondered aloud what this change of theories meant for Marianne's disappearance and the town's treatment of Dottie, and if the police knew about any of it.

"That's why I have the lights on and I'm going through the house while Vern is still at the hospital trying to figure out life without his wife. If there is no evidence of a crime, or even of deception, I don't feel I can tell anyone or go to the police or…" She threw her hands up. "I'm ashamed to be thinking this when they've been so kind to me and Dottie just passed away."

"Well." Death sounded a bit stunned. "That should cover it. I think that's the most words I've heard you put together in, oh, years."

Unlike Death, Tara sat silently. She swallowed. She chewed her lip. Did she think Casey was a horrible person? Was she going to go running to the police on her own? Would she tattle to Vern about Casey's middle-of-the-night search?

Tara shifted in her chair. "So, do you need some help?"

Casey let out a sigh of relief. "I've done the master bedroom, the guest room slash office, the living room, and the half bath. When you got here I was partway through the kitchen."

"Then let's finish it up." She strode to the middle of the linoleum. "Point me where you want me to go."

Twenty minutes later they had gone through every cupboard, the drawer under the stove, canisters of baking staples, and the refrigerator. Nothing out of place or secretive.

"Freezer," Death said.

Casey checked the small pullout at the bottom of the fridge. Nothing.

Tara stood with her hands on her hips. "Now where?"

Casey let her head fall back and tried to relax her shoulders. "We're assuming it was Dottie who hid these things, right? Not Vern?"

"Vern is a businessman. And, well, you know, a guy. Lots less likely to be sentimental and keep something incriminating. He'd be more likely to burn it, or throw it out."

"So we leave the garage for last?"

"Freezer," Death said again.

Casey pointed. "Except for the deep freeze."

They trooped out to the garage and dug quickly through the freezer, which held mostly packaged frozen dinners and three containers of frosted-over orange sherbet at various levels of use.

"I can't see Dorothy hiding anything in here." Tara surveyed the garage. "Not where Vern would spend a lot more time than she would. I can't see her doing anything with the cars. The cars are much more Vern's thing."

"So that leaves the basement, unless we think she would have hidden it outside."

"Can't search in the dark. Besides, where would we look? They don't have a shed, and unless we're going to dig up the yard, I wouldn't know where to start, unless it would be in the flowerbed between our properties."

Casey dreaded more searching. "What about a crawl space above this ceiling?"

"Could be. Not sure Dorothy could get up there."

"Remember this was forty-five years ago. If she wanted to hide something up there, she would have been able to."

"True. Let's check."

The trap door was right above the car, with a string hanging down. Casey backed the car out, leaving the lights off, and closed the door again so if any neighbors were watching they wouldn't know what was going on.

By the time she got back inside, Tara had opened the trap door and pulled down the built-in ladder. "I'm sort of afraid to look up there. Do you mind?"

Death flowed down the rungs. "It's clear. Not even a mouse. Spiders, maybe."

Casey climbed until her head and shoulders cleared the ceiling. Her phone's flashlight showed her what she'd expected to see. "Nothing but an extra pack of shingles, some two-by-fours, and an old can of paint."

"Well, it was worth a look."

Casey and Tara reversed their earlier actions, and soon the car was back in the garage. They stood in the kitchen.

"Let's go to the basement," Tara said. "If we get started, we'll soon be done."

Death groaned. "This is getting boring. I'll be back to see if you find anything worth all this dust." Death disappeared in a cloud of which Casey could only describe as asbestos. Casey coughed, waving her hand in front of her face.

"Okay?" Tara asked.

Casey nodded and headed downstairs.

They began in the furnace area, but quickly moved on to the main room. Tara started on the shelves of canned goods, and Casey dug under the pile of sleeping bags, which rested on some boxes. After going through three she'd found only canning supplies, a stash of stocking caps and scarves, and old paperback Westerns.

Casey sat on her heels. Lisa was positive it was her mom in

that picture, and therefore Dottie alongside her. Other than the shirt Lisa believed to be her father's, Casey could see no evidence a cop could use. And would that shirt even be evidence? The possibility of it still being in existence, and proving it was the same one, was so minimal it was hardly worth thinking about.

No matter how unlikely Casey thought the whole accusation, she couldn't find anything to prove the opposite. She also couldn't find anything to argue against Lisa's other complaint—that Dottie had known, but refused to disclose, Marianne's location. No letters, photos, or computer in the house which could hold e-mails. Not that there were such things back in the seventies. From what Vern had told Casey, Dottie pretty much believed Marianne had dropped off the face of the Earth. But then, maybe that was how she needed to see it if she had any chance of getting over the heartbreak of being deserted by her only friend.

"Any luck?" Tara stood over her, wiping her hands on her pants. "I'm done with those shelves."

"I'm beginning to think we won't find anything. I mean, what if she threw out the letter so Marianne's family would never find it?"

"If we don't keep looking, we'll always wonder."

So they kept at it, pawing through boxes containing antique dishes, high school yearbooks from the seventies—both Armstrong and Portland, and LPs of such groups as Earth, Wind, and Fire, and Simon and Garfunkel.

"Where are all their photos?" Tara asked. "They've got to have some somewhere, don't they? I mean, who doesn't have pictures? Especially people their age. I don't have a lot of photos and stuff because they're all online, but my grandparents have tons of albums. Takes up half their house."

"I noticed that, too," Casey said. "No photos anywhere. None upstairs. None on the walls. None—" She stood so suddenly her head spun.

Tara jumped up. "What is it?"

"There's only one photo I've seen, and it's not even a real one." She strode to her room and flung open the door. The picture of the mother and the baby boy sat on its shelf.

Tara wrinkled her nose. "Who's that?"

"It's a stock photo, came with the frame."

Tara looked around the room, from the bed to the dresser, and finally back to the corner with its bizarre accumulation of objects. She stroked the head of the pink puppy and reached her hand toward the mobile before letting it drop. "So it's true."

"What is?"

"This room. I thought it was a rumor, made up because of this town's fascination with Vern and Dottie's lives. But it's actually here."

It was the same thing Nell's mom had implied. That this room existed as a shrine.

"What had you heard?"

"You know, that they couldn't let go of their daughter's death and had this kind of…creepy thing. But what I don't get is, why put up a fake photo of this woman and baby? Whose Homecoming court ribbon and diploma? Whose flowers? It's weird."

Casey had to agree. The Dailys didn't have any other children, and she hadn't seen any sign they were in touch with extended family. In this whole search she'd seen nothing incriminating, or even informative. How could people live in one place for so long and have so little to show for it except a collection of what they would have wanted for their daughter, had she survived?

Casey cast her eyes over the small accumulation of souvenirs. Was the Homecoming ribbon Dorothy's, from her high school years? Was the diploma simply a fake, or had one of them altered an actual diploma to look like their dead daughter had graduated? And where had they gotten the dried flowers? It looked more like a bouquet than a Homecoming corsage. Their wedding, maybe?

Casey took a closer look.

Her heart missed a beat.

She pulled a flower from the middle of the bunch.

It was a faded red carnation with a bent stem, made to squirt water at unsuspecting victims.

Chapter Thirty-six

Casey stared at the fake flower in the palm of her hand.

"Oh," Tara breathed.

"What's going on?" Death appeared, half-dressed in black stretchy pants, t-shirt, and socks, as if caught getting into Reaper gear after a shower. Fortunately, all the private parts were covered, although Casey wasn't sure what would actually show up there.

"You're stressing," Death said. "I can tell."

Casey kept her hand outstretched with its incriminating evidence.

Death put hand to heart. "Holy flora."

Casey set the flower on her bed and slid the party photo from underneath her mattress, where she'd hidden it the night before.

Tara pointed at the clown. "It's really the same flower, isn't it?"

Casey's head spun. This changed everything. If Dottie was the clown at the party but had lied about it ever since...She dropped onto the bed, careful not to crush the carnation.

"What does this mean?" Tara whispered.

"It means everything she and Vern have said is a lie. She was with Marianne the night of the party. The two of them were there."

"But..." Tara sat beside her and repeated, "What does this mean?"

"It means Dottie and Vern have been living a lie all these years, letting people think it was random strangers who broke into the party. Letting all those other people be suspected." She thought about the divorced couple, and the woman who moved to San Francisco because she felt she didn't have any other choice.

"And Marianne? Where did she go?"

"What if she ran because she was afraid of getting caught, instead of leaving her family for some man? Maybe no one suspected an affair because it wasn't true."

"So she's the one who tricked everyone into getting tied up? Dottie's been covering for her all this time?"

Casey looked at the broken carnation. "But why would people think it was her, and not Dottie? Did her mask get pulled off? Did they recognize her voice? Since she and Dottie were best friends, wouldn't people suspect Dottie, also?"

Death made a choking noise and looked upward, as if toward heaven. "Oh, God. I think I made a big mistake."

Casey tried not to react, so Tara wouldn't question it.

"I'll be back." Death, who was pale even for the Grim Reaper, left so quickly Casey could have sworn it created a black hole right there in her bedroom.

"That's why people treat Dottie so badly," Tara said. "Isn't it?"

"What?" Casey had lost their train of conversation.

"That's why they were so mean to her. Didn't accept her. Because they think she had something to do with what happened at the party. They just couldn't prove it."

Casey wasn't sure. Dottie had stolen Vern from Flower Pants, showed up in town pregnant with his child, and been seen to keep Marianne's family in the dark about Marianne's location. She had a long list of faults.

"But why would she keep it?" Tara said. "Doesn't the flower incriminate her?"

"Not necessarily. What if she and Marianne had nothing to do with the trick played on the women? What if she simply didn't want people to know she'd crashed the party? It would have made her seem desperate, since she hadn't been invited."

"So she kept it as a souvenir of one of the worst nights of her life?"

Casey walked to the corner and stared at the weird collection of items. Nothing could be hidden in the mobile, or the Homecoming ribbon. She took down the diploma and removed the backing from the frame. Nothing but the paper, which felt flimsier than a diploma should feel. Didn't schools use card stock for that? She picked up the photo of the woman and the baby boy. The back came off easily, as if removed frequently. Casey's heart pounded, and she slid the photo from the frame.

But it wasn't the photo of the woman and baby that came out first. It was a picture of a bunch of women in costume, tied together on chairs, eyes wide. The sofa from the group picture sat in the background, and the ugly macramé hanger hung beside it. This was the same event.

But there were a couple of costumes missing. The devil sat in the second row of chairs, tied to Lucy and Wonder Woman. But Richard Nixon and the clown were nowhere to be seen.

Tara breathed in Casey's ear. "Oh, my God. They really did it."

They must have. Because someone took that picture.

A door banged upstairs, and footsteps tapped from one side of the house to the other.

Tara shot to the middle of the room.

Casey held up her hands in a placating gesture. "It's okay. We didn't leave any sign we've been going through things."

"It's not that. It's what we found."

Casey put the carnation back in the dried bouquet. She did the same with the photo, in the frame of the woman and boy.

Tara wrung her hands. "What are we going to do?"

"We're going to go upstairs and tell Vern how sorry we are. And then we're going to see what we can do to help."

"And ignore this?"

"For the moment. I need to…I'll wait until I can ask him."

"But—"

"His wife just died, Tara."

Tara closed her eyes. "Right. Sorry. I'm a little freaked out."

"Yeah. Me, too."

Casey led the way upstairs. Vern was not in the kitchen or living room, and the door to his bedroom was closed. A car was pulling out of the drive, its lights flitting through the window and across the kitchen, then living room, before shooting out and pointing down the street.

Tara peered out the window. "The pastor just left him here?"

"Vern probably told him I'd be around. I don't get the feeling Vern's too up on wanting people in the house." Except for when she'd shown up. He was all too ready to invite her in.

An invitation she regretted accepting at this point.

"I guess I'll go," Tara said. "Unless you need me to stay." She obviously didn't want to.

"We'll be fine."

Tara made a move toward the door, halted, then took another step. "Tell him…no, don't tell him anything. Let me know…" She shook her head.

"I'll be in touch."

Tara closed the door softly.

Casey dreaded the next few minutes. But she knew they had to happen.

Casey went to the hallway and looked at the closed bedroom door. She could hear Vern moving around in there. Opening drawers, closing them. The bed springs creaking, as if he sat down and got up again.

Tonight was not the time to bring up the carnation or the Halloween party.

Casey went downstairs and sat on her bed, staring at the corner shrine to…whom? Or what? The baby they'd lost, or the horror they'd wreaked on this town? Did Dottie get to die in peace after what she'd done? Did Vern get to mourn, when others in Armstrong weren't allowed closure after the death of Amelia Barrios, or the disappearance of Marianne Rush?

She retrieved the carnation and the photo of the terrified women, at the last second grabbing the group picture as well. She slid the photos into her back pocket and curled one hand around the flower. She knocked lightly on Vern's bedroom door. "Vern? You okay?"

The bed creaked, and the door opened. Vern's eyes were red, and his whole body slumped, as if the life had gone out of him.

So to speak.

They looked at each other for a few moments before Casey said, "Can I get you anything?"

"No." He cleared his throat. "Thank you, though. I'll be… all right."

He would be. After a while. It's not like Dottie's death was a complete surprise. He'd known it was coming, just not that night.

"How about some coffee? Or tea?"

He looked at his bed, which remained torn apart on Dottie's half, the covers flung back. "All right."

He followed Casey and sat at the kitchen table while she found what she needed, tucking the flower behind Dottie's pill bottles. In a few minutes she sat down with him, two hot mugs of tea in front of them. Casey's eyes felt like sandpaper from lack of sleep, but her blood pumped through her veins like she'd been sprinting. Or running from something. Which she kind of was.

"Vern…What happened that night?"

His head shot up and he spoke through clenched teeth. "My wife died."

"No, not tonight. The other night. That Halloween."

She saw the moment he realized what she was asking. His lips pinched into a tight line and he gripped his mug so hard Casey was afraid it might break. Or he might clock her with it.

"Dottie didn't help you hand out candy at the store, did she? And Marianne didn't beg off volunteering at the church."

He didn't move.

"You've been lying all these years. Hiding what really happened."

When it appeared he wasn't going to respond, Casey scraped her chair back and got the flower. She threw it on the table.

Vern's eyes went wide, and the blood rushed from his face, making him almost as pale as Death had been before flying off. His voice shook. "Where did you get that?"

"In the basement, in the middle of the dried flower bouquet."

He breathed with his mouth open, rasping. "Why did you… why did she…?"

"And then I found this." Casey slid the photo of the tied-up women across the table.

He put a hand to his chest. Casey felt *deja vu* from when she'd talked with Dottie the day before. Was he having a heart attack? Was he going to die because of her, like Dottie had died because of Lisa? No matter how angry she was at him, she didn't want that.

"Take a deep breath, Vern."

He rasped, clutching his shirt.

Casey grabbed his wrist. "Vern! Stop. Breathe."

He took several gulping breaths before managing a deep, halting inhale. He pulled his arm from her grasp. Pointed at the flower. "That's…"

"From Dottie's clown costume. And this?" She jabbed a finger at the picture. "This photo of these terrified women? It's from the same night as this one." She slammed the original group photo, before the "prank," onto the table beside the new one.

He dropped his forehead to his hand and rolled it side to side.

"Dottie and Marianne were there. At the party."

He stopped with the head rolling. Tears leaked from behind his hand.

"No. You don't get to play the victim here. You have been lying to this town for forty-five years. You let suspicion hang over those other people, ruin their lives—"

"What people?"

"That couple getting a divorce, the woman having an affair,

the greedy landowner. They had to move away because of all the crazy theories."

Vern waved dismissively.

"You've kept Marianne from her children."

He looked up at her, eyes wet.

"Why did she leave, and not you? What would have incriminated her? Why should she and her family suffer, but not you and Dottie?"

His face changed from despair to surprise, and finally anger.

"You think we haven't suffered? You think we wanted to stay here in this town, where everybody treats us like scum? Where we might as well have been strangers? Where they..." He choked up. "Where they blamed us for the death of our baby?"

"But her death wasn't because of something you did."

"Tell that to the women in this town, that Anne Marie's death wasn't something we could have prevented. Something Dottie caused."

"They blamed her?"

"She got sick with German measles, and it killed the baby. The others always hated Dottie, so this was just another reason to treat her badly, to say it was her fault." He strode to the doorway and slammed the flat of his hand against the jamb. "Why didn't they invite her? All of this could have been avoided if they'd just treated her with kindness." His chin drooped and some of Casey's anger melted away.

"I know they resented Dottie because she was an outsider," Casey said. "And they had to show loyalty to Flower Pa— Ethel. Right?"

"So someone told you, huh? That I was engaged to Ethel? That I got Dottie pregnant?" He shook his head. "I never meant to hurt Ethel. But I met Dottie, and I couldn't imagine life without her. I thought Ethel would get over it."

But Casey knew how a teenage girl's heart worked. How it could hurt. Could break.

"Did the others feel badly toward Marianne because she was friends with Dottie?" Casey remembered Marianne's picture in the yearbook. That confidence. That smile. Those eyes.

"They never were huge Marianne fans. Too self-assured. Didn't care enough what everyone else thought. Didn't want to go along with the crowd. So when Dottie came home with me, it was like a gift for Marianne. Someone with a fresh view, who hadn't been poisoned by the town." He shook his head. "I should have told Dottie. I should have looked out for her enough to tell her. It would have saved her. Saved us."

"Told her what? That the women in this town are spiteful and mean? I think she figured that out herself."

"No. I mean, she did. But that's not what I should have said." He rubbed his eyes. "I should have told her that if she wanted to make a go of it in this town she should befriend the crowd, and leave Marianne Rush the hell alone."

Chapter Thirty-seven

Casey screeched her chair across the floor and followed Vern into the living room. He stood in front of the picture window, staring at the closed curtain as if he could see out onto the street.

"You would have had her be friends with those awful women? Ethel? Wilma? The ones who were petty enough to not invite her to a frigging Halloween party?"

He spun on her. "And why do you think they didn't invite her? Huh? Because she was friends with Marianne, who had no use for all of those people, as she made very clear. As soon as I brought Dottie home, Marianne descended on her, didn't give her a choice. Came in preaching about the other women's small minds and stupid decisions. Didn't let her even try to get to know them. As soon as the first one showed up with a casserole, it was like they were trying to poison us."

"So why didn't you say anything?"

"What was I going to say? She was as in love with Marianne as she was with me. Or even more, sometimes. Speaking against her would have put a knife in our marriage." He closed his eyes. "Instead, Marianne did it herself. Killed their friendship. Almost killed us. But she didn't. It made us stronger."

"Did it?"

He glanced at her, pain in his eyes. "What do you know?"

Quite a bit. But she wasn't going to say that. "So getting back to that night...why did Marianne have to go, while you stayed?"

Vern turned back to the window. "Dottie loved her like a sister. Listened to her, believed everything she said. So when Dottie was ready to let the stupid women host their party, Marianne wasn't having that. Oh, no. They couldn't just let it happen and move on. They had to fight against it. Had to show those women who was boss."

He walked slowly to the puffy chair and sank into it. "So Marianne got this grand idea. They would go to the party. They would play this trick on the women and have the last laugh." His voice drifted away and he stared at his shoes.

"But it all went wrong."

"It was fine, at first. No one recognized them, not behind those masks. The women thought they were part of their in group, and they'd see who it was after the costume judging. So when Marianne said they had a magic trick to show them all, they thought it was fun." He gave a sharp laugh. "They were all drunk at that point. They did love to party, and having a free night away from the kids, what more could they ask for? Dottie said the wine, the coolers...those women drank and drank. It was no wonder they didn't recognize Dottie or Marianne, and no wonder they went along with the whole trick.

"Dottie thought tying them up was going to be the end of it. They would put them in knots and take off, get home to establish their alibis. No big deal. A joke. But Marianne couldn't leave well enough alone. Had to raise the stakes. She told all those women they were going to set the house on fire. No cell phones, of course, and the landline was far enough away no one could reach it."

"Why didn't Dottie stop her?"

"No one stopped Marianne. Besides, poor Wilma had already wet herself, and the others showed they couldn't act bravely. If Dottie admitted what they were doing, it would have been worse in this town than before."

"But couldn't she have at least said they weren't going to burn the house down?"

"And make Marianne angry? Then she wouldn't have had any friends at all."

"So they left?"

Vern shook his head. "Marianne threatened them with the fire, and she and Dottie ran out. They thought it was funny, or at least, Marianne did. They stopped outside and watched through the window while the women tried to get untied. They were yelling and crying and screaming, and then poor Amelia, she couldn't take it." His eyes were watering again. "Every time I see Nell, I just…"

"Did Dottie see what was happening?"

"She wanted to call an ambulance, but Marianne wouldn't let her go back in to use the phone because it would have given them away."

So Marianne had taken away any chance Nell's grandmother had of surviving.

"But Dottie said by the time she noticed Amelia, one of the women had gotten herself free and was able to call."

"But the ambulance didn't get there soon enough."

He leaned forward, clasping his hands between his knees. "Dottie and Marianne didn't stay to find out. They took off through the field. They'd parked their car out by an old cemetery, a half mile from the house."

"I've been there. I saw your daughter's grave." Casey remembered the way Death had reacted to something there. Something so awful Death couldn't even name it.

"They argued the whole way to the car. Dottie said she wouldn't keep it a secret, they would have to tell the police what they'd done. Marianne refused. Said the women had it coming. Dottie said she was wrong, that no one deserved to be treated that way. To die because of a prank gone wrong." He breathed in. Breathed out. "Dottie told Marianne she was going to tell, no matter what Marianne thought of it. Because it was Marianne's idea. Her fault. All Dottie had wanted was to stay home and feel bad about not getting an invitation."

"Dottie could have said no."

"To her only friend? Not such an easy thing."

If you were a wimp with no moral foundation. "So what happened? Why did Marianne disappear?"

"They struck a deal there in the graveyard, before coming back to town. There, in view of the farmhouse where it had all happened. Where our daughter lay in her grave." His lips trembled, and his face crumpled before he regained control. "Marianne said she would leave if Dottie agreed to stay quiet about what happened. At least that way Dottie could live her life, even if Marianne couldn't live hers. That would be punishment for her. To be away from her family, to never be in touch with them again. Dottie didn't want to do it, but Marianne wouldn't hear any other way."

Was that what Death had felt that night at the cemetery? This dark conspiracy to pervert justice? Was the evil of their decision still hovering over that place?

"So instead of telling the truth and accepting their own disgrace, they punished Marianne's family." Casey couldn't stop the judgment from leaking into her voice. "Let them think Marianne had simply abandoned them. Kept Nell from knowing what happened to her grandmother."

Vern stood up, his eyes sparking. "Who are you to judge? Those women made Dottie's life a living—" He choked on the word. "—a living hell. They blamed Dottie for our daughter's death! Having to go through with the birth almost killed her, physically and emotionally, and all the others did was make it worse. Are those the people you're so worried about?"

How did she answer that? Of course it was horrible, how they'd treated her. But that didn't make it okay to be horrible back, and cause one of them to die. Where the hell was Death when she needed help? Death was always running off these days.

Casey looked at the sorrow and anger and fear in Vern's eyes. Fear? That she was going to tell someone? That she would go to the cops?

A valid fear.
Vern was waiting for her answer.
She didn't know what to say.
The doorbell rang.

Chapter Thirty-eight

Just as the last time Casey answered the door, Nell stood on the stoop. Tonight she wore a jacket over plaid pajamas tucked into her cowgirl boots.

"Nell? I thought you went home."

"I came back. Mom's working and Dad's gone on a business trip. I have to stay with Grandpa, and he takes me to school."

Casey looked out at the street, but Nell was alone. "Where is he? And why aren't you in bed?"

"Grandpa's sick. I thought maybe you could help."

So she came here, the place Death had visited that very night, where something evil hovered. The girl had no way of knowing that. She had simply come to find a friend.

Casey glanced at Vern, who had given up waiting for Casey's apology, or explanation, and dropped back onto the puffy chair, head in his hands.

Casey stepped outside and shut the door behind her. "What's wrong with your grandpa? Do I need to call an ambulance?"

"He's throwing up. Says his stomach hurts and..." She leaned closer. "It's coming out the other end, too."

Yuck. "Something he ate?"

"He thinks so. He's all dizzy and his stomach is making these weird rumbling sounds. And he's hot, too. All sweaty."

Yup. Sounded like food poisoning.

"How can I help? From what I know, you pretty much just have to get through it."

"Yeah. He said that, too, but he feels so bad." She wrapped her arms around her stomach. "Can we get him something from the store? My mom cleaned all the stuff out of his medicine cabinet because she said it was too old, and he doesn't have anything."

Could Casey leave Vern? Actually, it might be good. Give them some space. Let them both cool off. "Let me grab the keys."

The living room was empty, and there was no sign of Vern. Probably for the best.

The store's security lights cast an eerie glow over the parking lot, the grill and rusty car silhouetted against the front wall. Casey unlocked the door, disarmed the alarm, and turned on the lights.

"Come on. First aid, this way."

But she didn't have to tell the girl. Nell strode straight to the aisle where the medicines sat in paltry rows.

"How about this?" Casey held out a bottle of Pepto-Bismol. The expiration date was a couple months in the future. It should still be good.

"He says that stuff makes him throw up more."

"Yeah, I hear ya. Maybe this?" She offered a box of Imodium, which cost three times what you would pay at a big store, and had a fine layer of dust on the top.

"I guess. Does it work?"

"It's worth a try." But nothing much worked for food poisoning except getting it all out.

Gross.

Casey studied the rest of the meds. "I'm not sure what else to suggest, unless you want to go with Sprite and crackers and chicken soup."

"That's what Mom always gives me."

"Mine, too. Although sometimes she gave me Coke because—"

The overhead lights flickered off, and the security lights snapped on.

Nell jumped next to Casey and grabbed her arm. Casey stood very still. What was happening?

Death appeared at the end of the aisle, all wild hair and long coat, like the professor from *Back to the Future*. "Get out of here. Go!"

Nell blinked. "Who are you?"

No time for Death to say, "I told you so."

Casey grabbed Nell and ran toward the front, but Vern filled the doorway. In his hands he held a rifle. Casey recognized it from the hunting photo posted above the cashier's window. Instead of using it for animals, however, it was now pointed at her.

And Nell.

Casey shoved Nell behind her. "Vern, what are you doing?"

"He's got more of a story to tell," Death said. "But he thinks you already know it."

Casey held out her hands. "You don't want to do this."

Vern's eyes were glassy. "She did it for us. We did it for us."

He steadied the rifle. Casey tackled Nell and dove as the gun fired. Chips and pretzels went flying, salty shrapnel of crumbs.

"Get up!" Casey yelled. "Up! Up!" Casey pulled Nell to her feet and pushed her ahead toward the deli, aiming for the door opened to the parking lot.

The gun boomed and drinks on the shelves to their left exploded, showering them with pop and lemonade and plastic.

Casey shoved Nell to the right, down the carbs aisle, toward the back door.

Vern roared and shot again, sending flour and day-old donuts pelting against Casey's back as she crouched over Nell, protecting her. Clacking sounds echoed and, too late, Casey realized Vern had reloaded the gun.

"Nell!" Death gestured from the right. "Come with me."

A bullet whizzed past, embedding itself in the far wall, above the canned soup and chicken broth.

Casey shoved Nell toward Death, away from the last possible exit, trusting her to listen and go where Death led.

Nell hesitated, but a glance behind Casey sent her running. Casey ducked and rolled to the left, hoping to take Vern's attention from Nell. She jumped up and ran several aisles down, hiding behind the almost-expired cereal.

"We had to do it!" Vern called.

"You already said that. You sent Marianne away to save yourselves." Casey ran on her toes, circling behind Vern. She peered around a stack of newspapers and viewed Vern's back as he stalked toward the end of the aisle. When he reached the far side, he spun, catching a glimpse of her. He swung the rifle toward her.

"Don't!" Casey yelled.

Vern's hands trembled, and Casey was afraid he would shoot her by accident.

"I won't tell anyone." Casey figured God would forgive her for lying in this instance. Because she sure as hell was going to tell someone the moment she had a chance. She should have done it earlier, as soon as she left the house.

Tears ran down Vern's face. "Dottie didn't mean to do it. She couldn't have."

Wait. What? "I thought Marianne planned the whole thing."

"Change of subject." Death was back, hunkered beside Casey, hiding behind the shelving as if a bullet wouldn't go straight through those Reaper clothes, which, truth be told, were looking a bit ragged.

"Where's Nell?"

"Walk-in freezer. I figured bullets couldn't get to her there."

"Good." The girl would be cold, but not dead.

"Who are you talking to?" Vern demanded.

"No one." She held up her hands. "Vern, what are you telling me? What did Dottie do?"

He sobbed once. Again. "She got rid of Marianne. She made her disappear."

Casey stared. "What?"

"It's true." Death's countenance was grim. "Dottie told me."

"They were running away," Vern said. "From the party. They were scared, Dottie was angry." He swiped at his nose with his left sleeve. "They got to the cemetery. Dottie reached the car before she realized Marianne wasn't with her. She went back. Marianne..." He hiccupped. "She tripped in the dark and hit her head on a gravestone. Dottie tried to wake her up."

Casey realized with growing horror where this story was going. She looked at Death, who nodded. "Remember the bad feeling I got when we were out there? I knew something was wrong."

"What did she do?"

Tears dripped from Vern's chin. "She didn't mean to."

"She did," Death said.

"She killed her?"

"No!" Vern waved the rifle. "She got in the car and drove home. She told me Marianne hit her head. I wanted to call the ambulance, but she said no, we needed to go back. Get her. Take care of it."

"So, yes," Death said, "she killed her."

Casey spoke in a whisper. "How could you not know?"

"There's no grave for her out there," Death answered. "No marked one, I mean. And I hadn't come that particular Halloween night to gather her or the other woman. One of my *yamadutas* had taken care of it."

"Flimsy excuse."

"It was Halloween. Crazy things were happening all over the world. How was I to know some little Idaho town would be important someday? I can't remember every person who's ever died. There have been billions."

"How could I not know?" Vern brought himself back into the conversation, assuming Casey's question had been for him. He shifted his stance, and Casey warily watched his finger on the trigger. "I couldn't know. I didn't. She wouldn't do such a thing, not my Dottie." He sniffed, an ugly, nauseating snort. "She hid Marianne's camera in the garage, and got some other supplies.

We drove back to the cemetery. She was quiet the whole way, wouldn't tell me what had happened. Wouldn't say anything about the party."

"She told me they hadn't been invited," Casey said. "Did you know they were going anyway?"

"She told me they were going to the church, to hand out candy and popcorn."

Casey couldn't believe it. Dottie had lied to Vern?

"So you got to the graveyard…"

He squeezed the gun and Casey stepped left, behind the shelving where she could still see him. Her legs knocked something, tripping her, and she felt around to find the box of Halloween decorations she had been working on earlier that day. Her fingers fell on the cold metal of the scissors, and she gripped it, point out. Ready.

"Marianne wasn't breathing. I told Dottie we needed to take her to the hospital. Dottie said no, because we would have to tell everyone she and Marianne threatened all those women. Had killed Amelia. Bill's wife. Gracie's mother."

The barrel of the rifle dropped as Vern's shoulders sagged. His eyes closed.

"She was so tired of getting blamed for everything. My father's heart attack, our baby's death. Ruining this town by marrying me. She just...she couldn't take being blamed for the Halloween party, too."

Casey took three steps forward to disarm him, but his eyes snapped open and he swung the rifle up. Casey grabbed the barrel with her left hand and tried to wrench it from his hands. He was bigger and stronger—and crazed—and held on. Casey hooked her foot around his leg, but with the size difference, she couldn't get the balance she needed to have any effect. Casey let go of the barrel and swung herself onto his back, looping her arms around his neck and her legs around his waist, squeezing as tightly as she could. She clutched the scissors with her right hand but didn't want to stab him if she could cut off his air supply long enough…

He scrabbled at her arms, clawing with his fingernails, stumbling across the aisle, swinging her, trying to knock her off.

Casey squeezed harder. She wished she could go for his eyes, his nose, but needed both arms to have any effect on a man his size.

He lumbered sideways into the cookies, knocking the shelving so hard it fell over. Casey cried out at the impact, and her arms loosened. Vern swung her again, this time at the opposite side of the aisle. The impact sent rolls and day-old bread tumbling to the floor, along with Casey. Vern brought up the rifle, pointing it at her as she sprawled on the floor.

Casey held up her hands. "Please."

Instead of shooting, Vern grabbed the barrel of the gun and swung it. Casey held up her arm to block it, and heard her bone snap as it hit.

She screamed. Death swirled around Vern in a cold funnel cloud. Vern drew up, shivering, looking toward the ceiling as if the air conditioner had suddenly come on full blast.

Casey jumped up and staggered away, holding her arm to her chest. She contemplated the back exit, but couldn't leave Nell in the freezer. What if Vern came after Casey and got her? Who would save Nell? With her right arm, she reached for her phone to dial 911. Whistler or Austin could be there within minutes.

She rested her broken arm on a shelf along with the scissors, while she tried to pull her phone from her left back pocket. "Vern? *Vern*? What happened next?" If she could keep him talking she could distract him until she made the call and the cops got there.

He didn't speak. Casey strained to hear any sound that would tell her what he was doing. Footsteps. Sniffs. Both came toward her.

"I could see the lights at the farm. Red and blue, flashing. The cops and ambulance were there. It would have been so easy to call them…"

"But Dottie refused?" Ah, finally, the phone slid out. She dialed 911.

"She said we couldn't. The town already hated us. Well, her." His lips trembled.

"So what did you do?"

The dispatcher's voice came over the phone. "What is your emergency?"

"Vern's. Come quickly."

Vern let out a sob. "Dottie brought a shovel. There was a grave that was used a month or two earlier." His eyelids fluttered, like he was having a seizure. "We put Marianne in the hole. Covered her up. Left her there. We drove home with our lights off so no one from the farm would see us."

"I have your position," the dispatcher said. "What is your emergency?"

Casey heard his footsteps coming her way from the right. She got up to run, but a wave of nausea and dizziness hit her so hard she dropped back to the floor. She shifted to the left and hid in the shadow of a stack of baked beans. The shelving behind her tilted, knocked off its level stance by one of Vern's earlier shots. Vern came into view at the end of the aisle, a dark blotch lit from the back by a security light.

"Stay on the line," the dispatcher said.

"What is that?" Vern said. "Who's talking?"

Casey hung up on the dispatcher and slid her phone back in her pocket. She picked up the scissors and held it, point out. The cops had her location. She had to hope they got there quickly. Until then, she had to stop him from firing. She watched his hands. "So Marianne did disappear. But not with another man."

"They disappeared her." Death stood beside Vern in a police uniform. "Stuck her in the ground when—"

"—she wasn't even dead," Casey said.

Vern wailed. "I'm sorry. I'm sorry. I'm so, so sorry." The rifle fell alongside his leg.

What could Casey say to keep him from raising the gun again? *It's okay? It will be all right? You did what you had to do?*

No.

Watching the end of the rifle's barrel, she got to her knees, keeping out of its target zone. Nell was still in the freezer, getting colder by the second, but Casey couldn't let her out until the threat of a bullet was gone. All she had to do was wait it out until the cops got there.

But were these young cops trained for this? Would Vern turn the gun on them?

Casey crawled from the shadow and grabbed onto the opposite shelving with her good hand, pulling herself to her feet. She spoke as gently as she could. As quietly as possible for him to still hear her. "Vern, Give me the gun. Please."

He kept crying. "I can't let you tell anyone. She was a good person. If they'd just given her a chance."

"Marianne gave her a chance."

"No. Marianne took away any chance she had to survive in this town."

"By being her friend?"

"If it hadn't been for her, the others would have come around. They would have."

His ignorance, and his refusal to accept responsibility for all he'd done, all the pain he and Dottie had caused, almost made Casey forget her wrist. "Those others blamed Dottie for your daughter's death."

"They would have loved her. I know they would have."

"Okay. Okay, I get it." Where were the police?

A shrill beeping filled the air. This time Casey knew what it was.

"What is that?" Vern shrieked. "Is that your phone?"

"I'm not answering it. See?" She held up her good arm, showing him her empty hand.

"Stop the phone! Turn it off!"

He raised the gun. Casey leapt toward him, scissors out, burying them in the shoulder of his shooting arm. He screamed and threw her off, blood spurting across her face. She slammed into the shelving. He fired the rifle.

The racks of canned goods exploded, and Casey disappeared under a hail of baked beans and creamed corn. She grabbed at the broken shelving and it crashed down on her, pinning her to the floor. She cried out for Reuben, Omar, her mother, Eric… but not for Death. Not this time.

With great lament she waited for a bullet, for this raving lunatic she'd known as her friend, to finish her off.

Chapter Thirty-nine

Casey woke to Nell pounding on the freezer door, and Death hovering over her, sending ice through her veins. After a quick assessment of the situation, Death led her to the carb aisle, where Vern lay bleeding out on the ground, the bloodied scissors on the floor beside him. His rifle lay at his feet, and Casey snatched it up, her head spinning.

She needed to call the ambulance to come for Vern—hadn't she already done that?—and retrieve Nell from the freezer. Reaching as high as she could, she slid the rifle behind the top row of cereal along the far wall, not wanting to rescue Nell with a weapon in her one good hand. The girl was blue with cold when she rushed from the freezer, but alive, unmarked by bullets. Casey grabbed a blanket and some first aid equipment and took her outside. They sank onto the picnic table bench, where Nell helped Casey strap her arm to her side with an athletic band.

It was too late for Vern, because Death was gone, but Casey still had to call the cops to make sure they were coming. She was on the phone with the dispatcher when she heard it. Footsteps.

"Who's there? Don't come any closer." Casey pushed Nell flat on the bench and gave her a signal to stay down, out of the line of fire. She eased her leg over the bench and stood between this new threat and the girl, finding her balance, forcing the fuzziness of her head away. Her broken wrist throbbed, but her other arm could strike, and she could use her feet.

"Who's there?" she asked again.

"No need to worry, Casey. It's only me."

She recognized that voice. She'd heard it the day before, when the girl took Casey's photo from the cab of the truck.

Casey set her phone, still connected to the 911 operator, on the bench beside Nell. She took a deep breath and stepped away from the table, wishing she still had Vern's rifle.

"Coop? Is that you?"

"Oh, it's not just me." Another shadow emerged from the darkness. This one Casey had seen too many times. Had restrained too many times. At least this time he didn't have a can of spray-paint in his hands. He looked miserable, scared, and ready to freak out.

"Lance?" Casey heard the disappointment in her voice. "You don't want to do this."

"Oh, he does." Coop grabbed his buddy's arm, as if expecting him to flee. "We all do."

"There's more of you? You and your so-called friends from the other night?"

Coop smiled a shark's smile. "And some new friends, too. Come on out, guys."

They slid from the shadows. Faces she last saw in the dark of the Beltmore playground. Cruel. Drunk. Stupid.

Were they drunk this time? If not, she had no chance. She couldn't run. Not with a broken wrist and a nine-year old girl.

Dammit.

Coop crossed his arms. "These new friends of mine—well, Lance's, too, and you know how good of friends you've become with Lance—they were so glad when I told them you were here." He stepped closer, checking out the front of the store, which somehow showed no sign of the carnage inside. "We stopped over at the Dailys' house first, but nobody was home. Not even you, down in your cozy little room, with its comfy quilt and squishy chair."

"It was you. You were in my room yesterday."

"Of course. It's not like it was hard to break in. That fire escape is good for more than getting out of the basement."

Keep them talking. The cops had to be on the way. Right?

"Anyway, enough of this small talk. At least between us. My new friends have a few things to say."

The passenger from the Beltmore playground was the first to step forward. Casey wasn't surprised. He'd been the ringleader the other night.

"Don't," she said.

He laughed and looked back at his friends. "But that's not the magic word, is it? I thought it was 'no.' No means no?"

"He's wrong," Nell whispered. "Now it's 'Yes means yes.'"

Casey waved her hand to shush her. She didn't want these guys paying any attention to Nell. She didn't trust them to pass up any female, even if she was only nine.

Casey took another step away from the picnic table, drawing the men's eyes her way. "What do you want?"

"What do you think we want? You caused us some trouble at home. We don't like trouble. We like things the way they were before you showed up."

"You mean before I beat the crap out of you and left you for the cops?"

Lance let out a bark of laughter, but cut it off quickly when Coop turned on him. "You think this is a joke?"

Lance blinked rapidly, reminding Casey of the way Flower Pants flirted with Vern. She wouldn't be doing that anymore. First, he was dead. Second, he and his murderess wife had lied to the town for years after destroying multiple lives. Casey wondered how old FP would feel about that.

Maybe not as surprised as one might expect.

"Sorry, dude." Lance scuffed the ground with his boot. For a moment, Casey felt sorry for him. But only a moment. She'd seen flashes of brains in him during the past few days, but unfortunately he failed to use them. That was on him.

The Beltmore passenger ignored the teenagers and stepped closer. Casey shifted on her feet, staying nimble.

"So Casey…it is Casey, right? Casey Maldonado." He spoke her last name with exaggerated vowels, stretching it out. If he thought it was sexy, or would scare her, he was wrong. He was simply an idiot who liked to intimidate women.

Not smart to make an angry woman even angrier.

Casey watched him. His eyes narrowed, and he cracked his knuckles, like he was readying for a fight. The guys behind him waited for a signal, a sign, permission from their leader. So Casey kept her attention on him. Even Coop, big man in this small town, stood a few feet behind the older man.

Older, but not smarter. Which was saying something.

If she could take down the big dog, she would be a long way to winning this fight. But Whistler and Austin would be here before that, surely?

One of the churches' bells chimed, a solemn, held-out ring in the night, and suddenly Death stood in the midst of Casey's attackers, again wearing a police uniform. "I'm back. Vern is not. I'm sorry. I know you kind of killed him and all, but you didn't mean it, and he's sort of glad, when it comes down to it. He was feeling pretty torn-up about how he'd lived his life. If it's any consolation, he and Dottie are together, and they realize how much they let everyone down. Including themselves."

Casey was relieved, and a little taken aback, that the Dailys had made it to the good part of the afterlife. She hadn't been sure what would happen following all they'd done.

"It's complicated." Death read her thoughts correctly. "They weren't all bad, which is pretty much what you have to be to go—" Death pointed to the ground. "They're still in shock, and I don't think they'll be hunting down Marianne for a while. They're a little afraid of how she'll react. Which is to be expected."

Casey gave Death an exasperated widening of her eyes.

Death regarded the angry group of men, as if just noticing

them. "But we have lots of time in the future to discuss this. Right now you need to concentrate."

Duh.

Death gave her a double thumbs-up and a manic, wide-mouthed smile. "You got this."

She shook her head. Where had she been when Death arrived? Right. Taking out the leader. "I'm surprised you're here without your baby-sitter."

The passenger frowned. "My what?"

"Your brother, the cop. Doesn't he keep you out of trouble when you've done something stupid? Keeps him busy, I guess."

"No one complained about anything I did. Until you."

"And until the new police chief came to town."

He blinked. "He's not going to change anything."

"I think you're in for a surprise."

"Watch out!" Death called.

But a sudden shift in the passenger's feet already alerted her. She was prepared when he ran forward, swinging.

An easy swivel sent his fist past her face, throwing him off-balance. Casey grabbed his arm and pulled, giving his momentum a boost. His head hit the Coke machine with a satisfying thwack, and he collapsed onto the pavement.

His audience of morons watched open-mouthed as their spokesman lay, apparently spineless, on the cold asphalt. None of them moved as they waited for him to get up. Because he would. He was too dumb to stay down.

Eventually, he groaned and used the pop machine as leverage to climb woozily to his feet. He turned and glared at Casey, swaying on his feet. If he hadn't been drunk before, this would have put him in the same brain space. "You bitch."

Casey sighed. "Can't you be more original than that?"

His face tightened. He charged.

The machine's whack on his head had disoriented him, so he was off-center as he came at her. Casey balanced on her left foot and side-kicked him with her right, the sole of her shoe hitting him square in the face. His head snapped back. Casey hopped onto her right foot, swung her left, and sent him careening onto the hood of the rusty Chevy. He hung there for a moment before sliding, slowly, to the ground.

This time he didn't get up.

Casey heard gravel crackling. She swung around as Coop ran at her. At the last moment Casey bent over double, pain cutting through her from her wrist, and curved underneath him. His arms, meant to grab her, encircled only air. Casey straightened, using her legs to push him up and over her back. He fell with a thud, his limbs jerking, eyes widening in surprise. He gasped for breath, and went to push himself up.

Casey crammed her foot on his throat. "Don't." She forced her lips to smile. "What do you know? There's that word again."

A sound behind Casey raised the hair on her neck. She prepared to swing around punching, but a *shhh* noise from Nell stopped her. Nell gave a little nod, and the okay sign with her fingers.

Thank God. Casey didn't know how much longer she could hold out on her own.

Crash, not seeing behind Casey in the dark, made fists and leaned forward. "Who do you think you are?"

"You really want to be asking that right now?"

"No." His nostrils flared. "I want to do this." He took two large, thumping steps forward.

Something clicked behind Casey. A gun swung into her peripheral vision.

"I don't think you want to do that." Whistler stood straight and still, her gun an extension of her arm. "And the rest of you? Stay where you are if you don't want a bullet."

But the driver, no smarter than he'd been the week before, turned to run. He stopped abruptly when faced with the barrel of another service gun.

"Hey, there," Austin said lightly. "Thanks for coming to Armstrong. We're always glad for visitors."

Sirens sounded across town, and within minutes the parking lot was filled with cops and ambulances and even a fire truck, although Casey wasn't quite sure what fire they expected to put out. Maybe they wanted an excuse to hit the Beltmore idiots with their fire hoses.

Soon Casey and Nell sat in the back of an ambulance with blankets around their shoulders and a paramedic treating Casey's wrist. Nell's mother was coming from the hospital, since Nell's grandpa was home with a bucket, so until then, Casey would stand in as her adult.

Death, sitting on Nell's other side, would have liked to help with the girl, as well, but seeing how the paramedics were oblivious to Death's presence, it wasn't possible. Nell, as aware of Death as she was of Casey, placed a hand on Death's arm, but pulled back quickly when the contact felt like a return to the walk-in freezer.

"You were very brave," Casey told her.

"You did all the fighting."

"You did all your surviving. You kept your head and did the smart thing."

"All I did was listen to you and Death."

Death's chest puffed with pride.

Casey smiled. "Sometimes that is the smart thing."

"Yeah." Nell looked at her toes. Casey hoped this night wasn't going to scar her too badly.

Nell spoke quietly. "There wouldn't be horror movies if people listened and did the smart thing. Because then they would never go into the dark basement or out to the woods or maybe even to Halloween parties." A sad smile flickered on her face.

Casey put her good arm around the girl's shoulders and squeezed. She was going to be all right.

Chapter Forty

The sky was a mixture of navy and purple and pink, with a few clouds striated across the horizon. A perfect evening, after a not-so-perfect day.

Vern was dead.

Dottie was dead.

Marianne, Amelia Barrios, Anne Marie. All dead.

Casey, however, was alive. Nell's lips had regained their pink hue. The idiots from Beltmore, along with Brian Cooper, were spending time in lock-up, while their case was being investigated. Assault. Public drunkenness. Driving under the influence. A whole mess of charges for a whole mess of morons. Lance, being the only one to hang back from attacking anyone in Vern's parking lot, got off with a warning.

Idiot.

The cops kept Casey all day. Forensics, along with Nell's testimony, backed up her story of Vern's attack. The cops accepted her timeline and what she'd discovered during the past several days, including the fake carnation and the photo of the women tied up in chairs. Tara gave a statement also, recounting how they found both of those items. She was quite shattered. Casey felt both sorry and guilty she'd dragged the librarian into it all.

Casey was so weary. Could it really be only since Thursday all this had happened? Since she had left Eric? Left home?

The one good thing that came from Armstrong was her friendship with Nell. The girl made Casey promise to keep in touch, and even helped Casey create a social media page where they could connect. Plus, the girl insisted Casey keep her dog-eared copy of *Carrie*.

"I'm sorry." Death plodded beside her, wearing a sackcloth, like those from the Bible, or that movie *The Ten Commandments*. "I let you down."

Casey wasn't sure what to say, because it was true in some ways. In others, she knew it was her own fault. She trusted Vern and Dottie to tell the truth. She based her belief about Armstrong and its tragedies on rumors and conjectures. She hadn't considered the possibility that what seemed to be fact simply wasn't.

Death sighed heavily. "I should have known. I've given up too much control. Had my underlings shouldering too much of the work."

Casey kept walking, gazing at the expanse of the horizon. "It's a lot to be responsible for."

"Yes, but I am the Grim Reaper. I am not a human. No matter how much I fit in."

Casey didn't argue, although the statement was far from reality.

"I don't really help anybody anymore. I might as well quit. I'm a waste of space and time."

Death moved slower and slower, until Casey realized she was on her own. She stopped and turned around.

Death sagged on the berm in a wrinkled, gray heap, exuding such despair Casey felt it from ten feet away. She walked back to her nearly constant companion of the past two and half years. "You're not a waste."

Death moaned. "What have I done?"

"You haven't done anything."

Death's moan grew louder. "Exactly. I've done nothing. Nothing to make the daily life on this Earth even one iota better. I should give up my robe. Let my deputy Reaper take on my duties."

Casey let out a short laugh. "You have a deputy?"

"Of course. What responsible boss doesn't have a second-in-command?"

"I thought you were immortal. Why would you need a second?"

"Didn't this past week prove that?"

"Come on. Let's keep walking." She continued down the road. Death soon caught up, burlap flowing like a sheeted Halloween ghost. "Everyone makes mistakes."

"Not I. I'm not supposed to make mistakes."

"I didn't realize. Are you God now?"

Death's mouth opened. Closed.

"That's what I thought. So doesn't that mean you're fallible?"

Death didn't speak for a few moments. "I didn't used to let things go so far."

"The world is a different place now. Death isn't so cut and dried. Death with a small 'd,' I mean. Not you."

They went a quarter of a mile before Death said, "I may not be able to accompany you as much anymore. Not while I catch up, see what I've been missing." Death swirled in front of Casey. She stopped before accidentally stumbling through the chill. "I don't want to let you down again, but I don't know how else to fix things."

Casey looked at Death, that ever-changing form she had clung to these past years. Clung to and flung off. Loved and hated. Searched for and hid from.

Or tried to hide from.

"You haven't let me down. You saved me. More times than I can count, or even remember. You helped me through. Seen me through."

Death straightened. "Really?"

"Really. And now…maybe you need to help someone else."

Death studied her face. "You're really ready this time? Because a couple of months ago you thought you were—"

"—but I wasn't. It's different this time. I'll be okay. Reuben and Omar, they will always be a part of me. I will always love them. But they're not here now." She caught her breath. Held it. Let it out. "I need to let them go. So we can all move on. Including you."

Death gazed at Casey with such love and pride Casey thought her heart might break, or she might dissolve into millions of tiny molecules and merge with the night. "You're ready." A statement this time. Not a question.

"I believe I am."

A hesitation, and then Death shimmered. Shook. Rumbled. The sackcloth blurred, and Casey wasn't sure what form she was seeing anymore. After several moments, the imaged focused. Beginning at the hem, the sackcloth transformed to shining black silk, rushing upward until Death's Reaper robe glimmered with red highlights from the sunset. A new scythe, shining and straight, pointed toward the sky, and the space within the hood, where a face should be, loomed dark and deep and ageless.

"I am not abandoning you." The voice came from all around, full, like a chorus. "I am not leaving you alone."

"No," Casey agreed.

And then she was standing by herself on the side of the road.

The sound of a car approached. Casey got as far to the left as she could since the setting sun would make it hard to see. But the car didn't pass. It slowed, then stopped.

Casey peered into the lowering driver's window. "Pastor Sheila."

The woman smiled and got out of the car. She took in Casey's still-colorful face, her broken arm, the duffel bag slung over her shoulder. Then, without warning, she opened her arms and wrapped them around Casey.

Casey stiffened, but the pastor was careful of Casey's arm, and avoided squeezing the side where her ribs ached from the early morning violence. Casey awkwardly patted the pastor with her good hand.

Pastor Sheila let her arms drop. "Thank you." Her eyes shone with tears. But they were happy tears, Casey thought.

"You're welcome." No point pretending she didn't know what, and how much, she'd done. Because of Casey the town of Beltmore, and, if they were honest, surrounding areas, would be safer. No more would those three idiots terrorize women and endanger everybody else on the roads. There were other idiots, Casey was sure, because there were always others, but at least she'd done her small part.

Sheila looked down the road. "Can I give you a ride somewhere? The train station?"

"Actually, the walk is doing me good. But I appreciate it."

"I wish I could do something for you."

Casey wished it, too.

"I want to go home," Casey blurted.

Sheila blinked. "That's good. Right?"

"Yes. I guess so."

When Casey didn't say anything else, Sheila cocked her head. "There's something else you'd like to say."

Not really. She didn't want to say it.

"But I'm not…" Casey looked at the sky. "I'm not sure what that means anymore. Home."

"I think I know what you're saying. Is home the place you live? Or the people you live among?"

Casey took a deep breath. Let it out. "And what's the answer?"

Pastor Sheila smiled. "I think we each have to decide that for ourselves."

"Thanks a lot."

Sheila laughed. "It's not my job to give you answers. It's to help you find them on your own."

"You're a weird pastor."

"Yeah." Sheila still smiled. "Yeah, I guess I am."

Casey found a smile to return the woman's. "I like weird pastors."

"Good." She looked at Casey. Looked down the road. "Sure I can't give you a ride?"

Casey felt her aching arm. Her complaining ribs. Her tired, tired soul.

"You know what? I think you can."

Sheila held out her hand. "Why don't you give me that bag? Then you get in the car when you're ready."

Casey handed over the duffel. The pastor put it in the backseat and drove the car ahead to wait.

Casey looked around at the wide, open fields which led up to the majestic mountains. Mountains that reminded her of home.

No. Not home.

She slid her phone from her pocket. She pulled up the Find a Friend app, where Eric's profile picture indicated he was at his soup kitchen. Most likely cleaning up after dinner. Or preparing food for the next day.

Casey let her thumb hover over the screen.

She pushed the button that said, "Share location."

And then she texted,

Will you wait there for me, Eric? I'm coming home.

She sent the text.

She held her phone tightly in her hand.

And she walked forward.